HONEYBALL

Pete Liebengood

Library of Congress Control Number: 2015913594
ISBN: Hardcover   978-1-5035-9981-9
               Softcover   978-1-5035-9980-2
               eBook   978-1-5035-9979-6

Print information available on the last page.

Rev. date: 08/20/2015

To order additional copies of this book, contact:
Xlibris
1-888-795-4274
www.Xlibris.com
Orders@Xlibris.com
716946

CHAPTER ONE

If he'd had it to do over, Big Erv Haslett would have checked his temper for once in his life.

It was unusually cool for an August night in Santa Barbara. Fiesta week normally equated to temperatures in the high eighties—never lower than the midsixties at night. Coastal fog had unceremoniously descended on the Earl Warren Show Grounds funneling in from Arroyo Burro beach off to the west and producing a light mist. Big Erv Haslett wasn't concerned about the fickle weather conditions, however. He saw it as a welcome respite from the heat that he'd experienced in the afternoon while riding his borrowed horse with the always popular Carrillo Caballeros in the Fiesta parade—something he did every year. The only reason he annually put on his flashy charro outfit and saddled up with the group was for the good public relations it generated for his car business—a business he'd started on a $50,000 loan from his father and had grown to three dealerships in three different cities. He was allowed to carry a Haslett Motors' flag as the group's sponsor.

The horsemen's precision movements in patterns that seemed almost impossible to navigate annually won the Caballeros first prize in the equine category. Big Erv placed all his winning trophies on prominent display at his Santa Barbara location on Lower State

Street. He'd grown up in a horse environment. His parents had operated a high-end guest ranch and horse riding stable in Santa Ynez—over the San Marcos pass from Santa Barbara. He'd ridden horses since he was in the first grade.

Big Erv, standing an intimidating six-foot-five and tipping the Toledo at 270 pounds, was anxious and excited to attend the first night of the West Coast National Horse Show in the arena. His car company was, for the first time, the event's title sponsor. The year 1985 was a special year for the show. It marked its twenty-fifth anniversary at the same venue. He had long wanted to get back to his roots in the horse industry—riding with the Caballeros in a handful of parades was the extent of his participation—but now he finally had the money to do it.

A longtime photo buff, Big Erv took a dozen or more pictures of the arena's marquis that prominently featured the Haslett Motors logo. He was an extremely proud sponsor. Only a protractor could have produced more angles than what Big Erv had Kodachromed with his trusty Canon camera.

He wandered the show grounds well before the event's start, shaking hands with patrons and kissing babies. He was decked out in what some would have labeled nerd mode—a stylish Stetson hat, fake bull riding champion belt, and buckle and snakeskin Justin boots.

"Hi, I'm Erv," he'd say to strangers. "I want you to know how proud I am . . . Haslet Motors is . . . to be sponsoring this event. I hope you'll come on down to 2504 State Street and check out my new line of Chevys. I've got a steal of a deal with your name on it." His thunderous laugh always followed his signature sales line.

In addition to acting like a celebrity, Big Erv was also quite proud of himself for finally being in a position to soon surprise his and Katherine's two kids: Rachel, age five; and Troy, four, with ponies of their very own. They would soon be able to ride them on a Hope Ranch property he was planning to buy. Escrow was set to close in a week. Hope Ranch was the most exclusive community in all of Santa Barbara. The general consensus among local residents was that if you lived in Hope Ranch, you'd made it. Fess Parker, TV's Davey Crockett, had a home there. The house Big Erv had chosen was a spacious ranch-style home complete with horse stables and an exercise arena and just happened to face the tenth green at the prestigious La Cumbre Country Club. Ervin Haslett—to club members—carried a six handicap. His goal was to get it down to a three with increased access to the golf course, and he'd have the time to dedicate himself to that goal as his business had expanded more rapidly than he could have imagined. Haslett Motors was fast becoming an established brand on the central coast.

With a few minutes to spare before the start of the horse show and as a surprise treat for his kids, Big Erv announced he'd bought tickets for them to ride on the pony carousel located between the Ferris wheel and the mini roller coaster just inside the entrance to the arena. The ride, operated by a traveling band of small-time carnies, featured a dozen ponies all attached to a rotating mechanical arm. Ervin, as Katherine also addressed her husband, had another motivation for the special treat. He liked the idea of show goers recognizing him from his TV commercials and seeing him as a fun and loving father. He'd long held the belief that a solid family image was good for sales of any product.

Little Rachel was beyond excited about her first-ever pony ride. Her hair was in a ponytail underneath a bright red cowgirl hat; she wore a cute red, white, and blue cowgirl dress that depicted an American flag. She was so anxious that she prematurely burst through the ride turnstile and had quickly picked out a palomino pony and mounted it herself. As soon as she was set in the saddle, she shouted to her dad, "I've named him Trigger!"

Big Erv had taken a position just outside the ride's gate in order to capture the mini adventure on film for Katherine to see, as she was attending a Linda Ronstadt concert at the Santa Barbara Bowl at the other end of town. "I think that name is taken, Rachel!" he hollered back.

Troy, who was an especially quiet kid, considering his genes, wasn't happy about his dad's surprise or even being at the show in the first place. He hated the black-and-silver Cisco Kid sombrero he'd been made to wear. And he didn't take to his black-and-white "painted" pony. As soon as the ride operator lifted him onto his pony's saddle, Troy started to cry. As the carousel began to move, his crying accelerated to screeching. No more than ten seconds into the ride, Troy, still screaming at the top of his lungs, his sombrero now resting in the dirt, tried to get off his pony only to get his foot caught in the stirrup. "Help me!" he cried out. Within seconds, he was head over heels, dangling from his pony with his fingertips actually bouncing off the ground. There was a great commotion as the operator yelled for a helper to stop the carousel. "Emergencia! Emergencia! Pronto!"

No longer engaged in taking photos, Big Erv vaulted the restraining gate looking very much like the talented athlete that he once was even while approaching the age of forty. With the carousel still moving, he hollered in the direction of the stunned operator, "Stop it! Stop it, you idiot!"

When the carousel ponies finally stopped, Big Erv grabbed both of Troy's still flailing arms; and instead of pulling him to safety, he hoisted him back onto the saddle. That only served to send a horror-stricken Troy into more hysterics. His eyes rolled back in his head, his face turned ashen, and he screamed uncontrollably. His instincts were to get down from his pony, but he couldn't release from his father's strong grip.

Big Erv's response to his son's panic was immediate. "You stay on that pony, son." He put his face directly in front of Troy's nose, much like a drill sergeant would address a raw recruit. "No son of mine is ever going to be a sissy. Do you hear me?"

Troy's response was to shut his eyes, perhaps in the hope that his nightmare would end if he shut them tight enough.

Big Erv wasn't done. He grabbed the frightened boy by his shoulders and shook him vigorously. "You're a coward." Big Erv's eyes bulged out from under his bushy eyebrows. "Look at your sister. She's the little man of this family. You're just a scared little candy ass. You should be ashamed."

By this time, his tirade had attracted a dozen or more onlookers, all of them shocked by what they were witnessing. Someone among the bystanders could be heard to say, "The boy didn't do anything wrong."

That didn't calm Big Erv's rage, however. He grabbed a still-shrieking Troy by his waist and lifted him off his pony, exhibiting enough force to orbit the young boy had he released his grip. Big Erv was in such a combustible state that calling for a haz-mat team wouldn't have been a far-fetched idea. "I should spank you until you bleed, Troy."

While her brother was being punished, Rachel watched with a blank look on her face. She'd witnessed the scene numerous times at home. The most recent rage-producing incident happened when he accidentally crashed his tricycle into his dad's new car, badly scratching the passenger door. As she watched, Rachel stood perfectly still just outside the carousel's gate. A woman dressed in a Spanish costume befitting the Fiesta celebration moved next to her as if to protect her from her father turning on her. "Are you going to be okay?" the woman asked Rachel.

Rachel remained expressionless and gave no answer.

During the commotion, someone got to a nearby pay phone and called 911. Before Big Erv could drag Troy away from the pony ride, a stocky sheriff's deputy who had a thick mustache, and a pair of exposed biceps that were shaped like ski run moguls, was dispatched to the scene. He'd already been assigned to the show grounds, so not much time had elapsed between the 911 phone call and his arrival.

The deputy marched up to Big Erv, carrying himself with purpose. "Sir, I want you to release your grip on the boy. He spread his legs for balance in anticipation of the confrontation turning physical. I have a report that this is your child, and you are abusing him. A complaint against you was phoned in by somebody from that pay phone." The deputy pointed in the direction of the show grounds' lone pay phone.

Big Erv let go of Troy, and he folded onto the dirt like he was a sack of potatoes. "Do you know who I am?" Big Erv asked the deputy while pointing his finger toward his chest.

The deputy released an ever so slight smile. "This may come as a surprise to you, but I don't know who you are, and I don't care either. How many times do you think I've heard that before?"

That made Big Erv even angrier. "When do you get off telling me how to parent my own kid? Why in the hell aren't you busy walking the grounds arresting cotton candy thieves?"

The deputy ignored the remark and made an attempt to pick up Troy from the ground where he was curled up in the fetal position and sobbing uncontrollably.

"Don't touch my son." Big Erv's booming voice attracted more and more onlookers with each outburst. He placed his big hand on the deputy's shoulder and tried to push him away from Troy.

The deputy's face contorted the instant Big Erv laid his hand on him. He quickly reached for his nightstick and presented the point of it to Big Erv's chest with a resounding thud. "Sir, you are under arrest for assaulting an officer to start with." His speech was rapid, no doubt the result of an adrenaline rush. Before Big Erv could respond, the deputy reached for and located his handcuffs and demanded that Big Erv place his hands behind his back, which he did reluctantly.

Big Erv was incensed. "You'll fucking pay for this, Barney Fife. I'll have your job, and by next week, you'll be working security at Jordanos, standing guard over grocery carts." Before the deputy marched his man off to a temporary substation at the far western edge of the show grounds, he radioed for a backup to take custody of the kids. "Get them to safety."

CHAPTER TWO

Big Erv's arrest led the eleven-o-clock news on Santa Barbara's lone TV station, KEYT. Maria Gonzales, one of the station's coanchors, opened the newscast with a graphic tease. "Local business figure busted for child abuse. Details on how a harmless pony ride turned into a child's nightmare, next on the news at eleven." What Maria didn't anticipate was an audio engineer's slow-motion response to closing her microphone, which allowed for her off-camera remark to go public. "I hope they hang that guy by his balls," she'd said, presumably to her coanchor, and then laughed at her own remark.

Rather than go to trial and be exposed to more bad publicity for his car business, Big Erv pleaded no contest to a charge of child endangerment. Fortunately, his high-priced attorney saw to it that he served no jail time—sentencing was limited to a two-year probation and a hundred hours of community service. Big Erv, through his attorney, did argue that his car dealerships were a community service, but the judge wasn't biting.

To say little Troy wasn't nearly as resilient following the show grounds incident as his father had expected was a gross understatement. He went more than a year without speaking—to anyone—not even his sister. Katherine Haslett was devastated by her son's unnatural behavior. She cried constantly over what her son had become. Over

Katherine's objections, Big Erv took Troy to see neurologists and speech therapy specialists up and down the central coast in hopes of finding an answer to his silence. No luck. Katherine was furious at her husband for *making a sideshow out of her little boy.* Troy often took out his frustration on Rachel—oftentimes by striking her with his fists for no apparent reason. One time he whacked her with his mother's tennis racquet and gave her a black eye that was visible for several weeks. Troy's preschool teacher, a mother of two, was so baffled by her inability to bring Troy around to classroom normal that she ended up quitting the profession at the end of the year. "I've tried everything," she informed the Haslett's in a letter. He simply won't engage with his classmates. "I would strongly urge that you seek psychiatric help for your son."

Big Erv wasn't up for any son of his requiring a shrink—not at any age. So once more against Katherine's objections, he took Troy out of preschool and got him a private in-home tutor. That didn't work out longer than a month. The tutor, a young female graduate student who majored in surfing at University of California, Santa Barbara, threatened Erv with fake sexual assault charges if he didn't write her a check for a hundred thousand dollars. It took the woman, a kinky-haired redhead with a tan right out Hawaiian Tropic's catalog, only a short time to discern that Big Erv was vulnerable, still reeling both socially—he was kicked out of his Rotary Club—and financially—his car business sales were off 12 percent—from the fallout of the show grounds incident. She used the fact that she was attractive in a surfer girl way to her advantage. Who wouldn't consider trying to hit on her, she'd reasoned? Big Erv finally got rid of her for seventy-five thousand and a new Chevy El Camino.

Rachel went about her young life, acting as if she were an only child—the only one that mattered anyway. It didn't take her long to realize that for all intents and purposes, she had her dad all to herself, and she took advantage of it. There was some guilt associated with that but not enough to change her behavior. She filled the void of her brother's strange behavior by doing all the things that her dad would have wanted to do with his son—play catch with a baseball, shoot at squirrels with a pellet gun, watch pro wrestling on TV. It embarrassed her that Troy wouldn't speak to any of her friends. As payback the first year, she asked a department store Santa to bring her brother charcoal for Christmas. Katherine told Erv about the incident, and he just chuckled. "Girls got balls. I like that."

Katherine, a former college cheerleader—she met Ervin at Fresno State—who could still turn heads with an athletic figure, year-round rich tan and a wedge haircut that resembled that of figure skater Dorothy Hamill, closed her eyes and shook her head. "You're so goddamned insensitive, Ervin."

When little Troy finally began talking again, it was a compromise. He spoke only when spoken to for a couple of years. Troy was a handsome young boy with a dark complexion and a girl-magnet dimple on his chin. The result of good genes, he'd also developed an impressive physique. As a student, Troy was below average. Not once, kindergarten through high school, did he do anything to distinguish himself. He was a *C* minus student who didn't participate in school social activities. Sports were never a consideration. The only games he played were found on his portable video console. Super Mario became his sidekick.

Despite his good looks, he'd had only one girlfriend in his life, and that was in his sophomore year of high school. All they did was have lunch together in the cafeteria and talk about how depressed they were. Sex was never in the equation.

Peggy Walters was a pig-tailed cutie that, despite her good looks, was not popular because she was shy. She was afraid to talk to a mirror. She eventually broke up with Troy when she invited him to dinner with her parents, and he inexplicably slipped in to "no talk" mode. "You couldn't even say yes to my dad when he asked if you like me," Peggy had scolded him afterward.

Only in his junior year of high school did he try sports. He finally caved into his dad's constant nagging and tried out for baseball team and was given—his dad offered his coach a new car—a position on the squad as a utility infielder for San Marcos High School. He hit .116 primarily as a pinch hitter. He struck out twenty-two times in thirty at bats that season.

After high school, Troy entered Santa Barbara City College and majored in marijuana and Starbucks. He dropped out after his freshman year and took an olive branch seasonal job as a clubhouse attendant for his dad when he purchased the Santa Barbara Rancheros. He held the position for close to ten years—never doing enough to warrant a promotion even from his father, not to mention an occasional "good job, son."

Katherine never stopped blaming her husband for stealing her little boy's normal childhood away from her and turning him into a problem child of unfathomable proportions. "A social outcast" is how Katherine often referred to Troy to outsiders. Not long after the horse show incident, the two started taking separate vacations. Katherine and a couple of girl friends regularly went on shopping binges in New York, Paris, and London. Erv and an old college teammate would travel to the best fly-fishing rivers in North and South America and chase women in small town dive bars.

The carousel pony incident had shaped the Haslett's marriage. After the incident with Troy, they stopped smiling at each other, laughing together, or demonstrating any kind of affection for each other. When she became old enough to understand their marriage, Rachel had figured her parents relationship for rocky at best. She imagined their bedroom must have been like the inside of a Frigidaire. "You could store perishables in there," she'd once told a girl friend.

Both Big Erv and Katherine had made reckless statements about the other having an affair. In the days before she left him, Katherine had confided in a then teenage Rachel, saying she was certain Ervin was having an affair with his lone female sales person, a fortyish auburn-haired beauty with bedroom eyes that came equipped with a sleep number. And Ervin made it known that he was sure the cosmetic work Katherine had done on her eyelids was exclusively for the purpose of attracting men—specifically the tennis pro she credited with developing her two-hand backhand into a weapon that won her USTA singles fame at the Rio Laguna Tennis Club.

Despite the mutual suspicions of adultery, what finally brought the marriage down was something that neither has ever spoken of—to this day. Rachel never learned what triggered it. She remembered the split happening suddenly, but that was all. Her mom had cried every day for a week. Just when Rachel gathered the courage to ask her what was bothering her, she was gone—to another life.

CHAPTER THREE

Rachel Haslett's thoughts wandered as she sat cross-legged on a burgundy recliner in the home office of Eileen Lindholm, PhD. If she could be anywhere else on the planet, she would. It further pained her that she'd had to pass on a Katy Perry concert in LA because of the appointment. Dr. Eileen Lindholm's home office was richly appointed with fine leather. The respected psychologist had a Maplewood desk that was big enough to land executive jets. The office, in Rachel's mind, was excessively dark and created a kind of morose vibe. There were no windows, and only a small desk lamp was lit. Rachel, who preferred shorts, sandals, and loose fitting blouses for most occasions—her way of promoting her thoroughbred-like legs that had earned her a *Sports Illustrated* "Best Gams in Sports" award in 2013—kept her best assets under wraps for her seemingly straight-laced psychologist. She went business casual with dress slacks, a polo shirt, and a blue blazer.

After they exchanged frosty, fake greetings, an awkward silence ensued. Dr. Lindholm reviewed some notes she'd taken from their initial session a week ago, which was basically a tepid get-to-know-you hour. When she was done, she got up from her desk chair and moved to a twin recliner directly across Rachel. As the silence continued, Rachel curled a strand of her shoulder-length honey-blond hair into a little ball with her index finger—a nervous habit of hers. One moment, she found herself staring at the Thomas Kincade print behind the doctor's desk that depicted a fly fisherman standing in a river surrounded by snowcapped buttes; the next, she found herself examining the doctor's chinless face and protruding lips that appeared as a genetic shortcoming rather than a Botox job gone bad. Silently she wondered if the good doctor might have been a tropical fish in a previous life.

She wasn't surprised that the doctor wasn't wearing a wedding ring. Her wardrobe might have been the issue. She had on a maroon turtleneck and a wildly collared patchwork skirt that appeared to Rachel as if it might have been purchased at Goodwill. Odd for a woman so esteemed in her field.

The session with Dr. Lindholm was mandatory following a court order that directed that, as a condition of her probation, Rachel seek help with anger management. An ugly ABVP (Association of Beach Volleyball Professionals) postmatch assault on an opponent after an event in Huntington Beach a year ago had earned her a misdemeanor assault charge and conviction. It was an ugly incident that unfortunately for Rachel was captured by a KTLA-5 cameraman and played on the LA station that evening. He was shooting footage for a feature story on Rachel's playing partner Annie Eastbrook.

Earlier in the week, Annie had announced her retirement at the end of the Huntington Beach event. She was ending her twelfth year on the beach volleyball tour and planned to marry a doctor who was moving to Malawi, Africa, to help with the fight against aids there. Annie and Rachel, ABVP champions in 2008 and 2010, had won their semifinals match that day in a chippy contest, where trash talking had been at a premium. After the match that was won by Rachel and Annie, the two sides moved together for the customary handshake. The taller of the two opponents, who still had sand in her teeth from a desperation dig on match point, shook Annie's hand but not Rachel's. Instead, she got up in Rachel's face, her long nose almost touching Rachel's chin. Venom accompanied the words from her mouth. "Has anyone ever called you a cunt before, cunt?"

Rachel's eyes opened wide, and she bit into her upper lip. Every muscle in her body tensed. She quickly used the leverage provided by her five-foot-ten frame and decked the player with a sweeping right uppercut that broke her jaw.

Six months previous to that incident, she'd been having drinks in a Santa Monica bar with another female member of the tour when a forty-something guy, sweating at the temples and dressed in an LA Lakers jacket, stumbled to the bar and grabbed the chair next to her. He slobbered on himself when he spoke. "You've got great legs, lady. I hear they're always open." He laughed at his own stupid self. Rachel's knee jerk reaction caused her to accidentally spit out the beer in her mouth all over the bar. Then she grabbed her half-full beer mug and swung it as hard as she could, striking Mr. Laker upside his head. He was too dazed to retaliate. The blow must have burst a vessel is all Rachel could figure because in an instant, Mr. Laker was a bloody mess. When the cops arrived, only Rachel was arrested.

That incident, the volleyball tournament KO, and Annie's retirement played heavily on Rachel in the months that followed. After an intense period of gut-wrenching introspection, she too decided to retire at age thirty-five. Her decision was frustrating because she knew she still had a few years of good beach volleyball left in her. She rationalized that she could always coach volleyball at some level and had even followed that line of thinking by applying for the vacant job at Santa Barbara City College. A UCLA grad with teaching credentials beat her out.

Dr. Lindholm paused to put on a pair of horn-rimmed glasses that combined with her hair that was tied in a bun—made her look like everyone's high school librarian, the very kind the kids in Rachel's school loved to torment. "Tell me a little more about your dad." Her tone was passive.

Rachel finally uncrossed her legs "He's why I've never married."

Dr. Lindholm raised her penciled eyebrows, no doubt in some state of disbelief. The doctor didn't say anything for several seconds.

Rachel had already decided not to react too quickly. A wealthy friend who'd endured a lifetime of therapy had warned her not to grope for words just to keep a conversation going. "It's their little trick to evoke unfiltered thoughts," her friend had warned.

"He's the perfect man." Rachel broke the standoff.

Dr. Lindholm made a new note on her legal pad but said nothing, stubbornly waiting for Rachel to embellish her statement.

"He's honest to a fault which in the car business is a trait that is frequently on permanent sabbatical. And he's loyal—just ask any of his employees. He'd give them the shirt off his back. He's got a heart as big as Wyoming. He was a great parent. I called him MVP for Most Valuable Parent. When no one asked me to my high school senior prom because I was supposedly 'stuck up,' my dad took me. We had a great time. His love and care extended into adult life as well. When Annie Eastbrook and I won the tour championship, he threw a huge victory party for us at the Fox Arlington Theatre downtown. He'd hired a video crew at the beginning of the season to shoot a documentary on the two of us. They shot every match. My dad showed the video at the party. It was the greatest gift I had ever received." Rachel stopped talking but left the impression she had more good things to say about her dad.

"Go on, Rachel."

"He's funny too. He wouldn't let me play soccer—period, end of story. He said, 'Any sport whose signature moment was a player ripping off her jersey to reveal a sports bra wasn't a sport.' And oh my god, what he did to me on my first driving lesson when I was sixteen. He was riding with me in the passenger seat, and as soon as I pulled away from our driveway, I heard this police siren. I looked in the rearview mirror, and all I could see was a cop car flashing its lights. On his PA system, he ordered me to pull over. I was horrified. I was instantly certain that I would never get behind the wheel of a car again. I hadn't traveled four hundred feet. Turns out, the cop was a friend of my dad, and it was all a setup. My dad laughed about it for a week."

The doctor shifted in her recliner. "Sounds like you're a daddy's girl. Must be hard for any suitor to live up to his standard?"

Rachel smiled for the first time, revealing her perfect teeth that paired with her ocean blue eyes; honey blond shoulder length hair and classic jaw line made her a babe, as the boys in her high school called her. She was attractive enough to have snagged a lucrative swimwear modeling gig with Chicos. Her only physical blemish was a feint half-inch brown birthmark located just on her neck just below her left ear. Her mother had hired a graphic artist to Photoshop the mark out in every picture she'd had taken since Adobe came out with the software in the late eighties. Rachel would be the first to admit she wished she had bigger boobs but always understood that in the volleyball business, they would have been a detriment. During her years on the pro tour, she was often mistaken for super model Heidi Klum, in that both are head turners, tall, and blond.

"To answer your question, Doctor, I'm definitely daddy's girl. And I'm proud of it."

"Do you think you possess his same values?"

"Yes, and I guess I've got his temper to prove it." She tried to muzzle a laugh.

Dr. Lindholm pointed her pen directly at Rachel. "What are some examples of your dad's temper?"

Rachel tossed her head back and let out a muted laugh. "My mother should be the one to answer that. She's witnessed a lot more of his ugly tantrums than I have."

"It's the first time you've mentioned your mother." The doctor's brow furrowed with a look of surprise.

"She left him and us long ago. But then she bagged a guy who had three times the money my dad had and moved thirty miles away to San Ysidro where he grew avocados. He had two kids, and they have one together—a boy, who has something wrong with him. Not sure what it is. She did stay in touch with Troy, mostly by phone, even though she was close enough to visit. Once she left our house, I never heard from her. I think she always resented the fact my dad took more interest in me than her."

"Some would call that jealousy."

Rachel nodded. "I think you're right."

Dr. Lindholm held up a follow-up question. Awkward silence again.

"My dad once drove his brand-new Ford Mustang into the living room of a house where he thought my mother was sleeping with another man. The car came to a stop on the other side of what had been an ultra-expensive TV and sound system. Happened in the middle of the night. Fortunately, no one was home at the time. Turned out my mother had spent the night alone in a motel after they'd had a nasty fight over his spending money to buy both an airplane and a minor league baseball team. Years later, I learned the incident got my dad two months in jail—he lied to us about an extended business trip to Mexico to search out possible new franchises—and restitution nearly forced him into bankruptcy."

Dr. Lindholm locked her deep-set eyes on Rachel. "Is that how the perfect man acts?"

Rachel sat up straighter. "My mom deserved it. She was the classic flirt. She was an attractive woman. She knew it, and she let every man know it."

"Was jealousy at the root of his bad temper?"

Rachel put her clinched fist to her lips in thought. "No, his first big temper episode I'm told by his longtime college friends just happened out of the blue. It was classic. He was a football player at Fresno State—a pretty good one. He played defensive tackle. He was so strong he'd just pick blockers up and throw them around like they were made of rubber. He was nicknamed 'Erv the Eraser.' He was living on campus in the men's dorm. He'd just broken up with his girlfriend the day before. It was taco night at the dining hall. Long story short, the newly appointed ex came up to where he was seated with friends and fired a taco at him. It got him smack in the face—his lips were covered with guacamole. Well, he got pissed and grabbed every taco from every plate within his reach and fired them back at the girl. That triggered a major food fight that ended with guacamole and salsa dripping from every wall in the building and with ten guys getting expelled from school. Luckily, my dad was an important enough football player that the coach got him a reprieve. There was some good that came out of it though. One of the guys involved in the fight started a small Mexican fast-food business in his hometown. Inspired by the food fight, he called it Taco Mucho, and now he has 450 stores around the country. For a guy who didn't graduate college, it was a pretty impressive accomplishment, wouldn't you say?"

Dr. Lindholm didn't answer at first. She shuffled a stack of papers on her lap. "So how has your father influenced your quick temper?"

Rachel put the palm of her hand to her chin and paused for a second. "I guess I like how his reputation for having a temper keeps people on edge. It's a great defense mechanism in a harsh world. It allows him the upper hand at all times. I carried that line of thinking into my volleyball career. I came to every game with a mind-set to destroy, not just beat my opponents."

"What's harsh about your world, Rachel? You're recognized as a start athlete, and you've just been appointed CEO and general manager of a professional baseball team, have you not?"

Rachel produced only a blank stare.

"It would appear that you're in a unique and glamorous situation for a woman of your age."

Rachel got out of her recliner and circled behind it. She placed her hands on the headrest. "I don't buy glamorous. I'll constantly be under a microscope. Every decision I make will be scrutinized by my players, our fans, and the media." She paused and inhaled deeply. "And wait until minor league baseball hears that I've hired a complete staff of females. Those in baseball's 'good old boy' network are going crap in their pants. We'll have the first minor league ball club run entirely by women—from promotions and player personnel to team trainers. I plan to complete my hiring next week by stealing the AVP's marketing director. We'll make history."

Rachel let out a sigh as if she'd perhaps just realized the magnitude of her undertaking. "And if that's not enough, I've got a brand-new $25 million stadium I'm christening. All my dad's money went into it. The only outside revenue, he attached to naming rights. The stadium is called Erv Haslett TireCo Park. Yes, he's got an ego. I've shortened it to The Erv for marketing purposes. We have Montecito Village and

Cottage Healthcare bullpens, a Rusty's Pizza refreshment center, and a KISS radio souvenir stand. Even the restrooms were packaged with naming rights. Mini Towels has their logo over all men and women's toilet facilities."

Dr. Lindholm asked Rachel to sit back down. She did. "Interesting. Now how do you plan to deal with this harshness you speak of, Ms. Haslett?"

"Rachel, please. Ms. Haslett is way too formal."

"Rachel it is."

Rachel gently stroked her hair. "That's why I'm here, Doctor. I was hoping you'd figure that out for me. Isn't that what you do? Isn't that why the court referred me to you? Please tell me I'm not wasting my time sharing your office with you."

"Continue on, Rachel."

"I'm already getting heat from the league about my total lack of experience as a GM, and this columnist for the *Santa Barbara News-Press* roasted me for changing the name of the team to the Santa Barbara Charros."

Dr. Lindholm made a note of the name change. "Why Charros? Weren't they nicknamed the Rancheros for years?"

"Yes. I wanted Vaqueros, but the community college claimed title to the name. A charro is an elegantly attired horseman. A ranchero is an ordinary cowboy."

"It appears you researched your name change quite thoroughly?"

Rachel produced a faint smile. "I did, thank you. I'm a detail kind of person."

"What do you think will be your biggest challenge running a baseball team?" Dr. Lindholm asked while taking off her glasses for what appeared an unfiltered look at the patient sitting before her.

Rachel laughed. "Let's start with my brother."

"Explain, Rachel." Dr. Lindholm suddenly appeared more energized as if she had imagined she now had something substantive with which to work.

Rachel dropped her head slightly toward her chest and inhaled deeply before releasing what could only be described as a sigh. "He was devastated that Dad didn't turn the team over to him. He hasn't spoken to Dad or me since I was selected, which was five months ago. Since he got his own apartment near East Beach, we seldom see him—he no longer participates in family outings. My dad thinks it's about his drug problem and not rejection."

Dr. Lindholm again paused to make a note. "Being a male and having played baseball in high school, as you say he did for a short period, don't you think it's understandable that he might be angry and withdrawn over your dad's rejecting him? It must have been a pretty big blow to his masculinity. Baseball seems like such a manly game to me. Players spit, chew tobacco, fart at will, and hurl insults at one another. It's macho. To me, it doesn't seem like a suitable game for women. Just my opinion."

Rachel winced internally. She crossed her legs a second time and once more curled a strand of hair. Troy's too unreliable to run a baseball team. Outside of working for Dad, the longest he ever held a job was two months—at the Wherehouse. He's thirty-four years old, and he hasn't accomplished anything but successfully mooching off my dad."

"Have you considered that your brother might have been bothered by something other than his being passed over by your dad?"

Rachel pawed at the leather chair arm. "He hated that I didn't even offer him a job. I told him it was because he wasn't a female. He called my desire to hire only women 'a cheap ass publicity stunt.' He also was angry about my idea to change the name of the team."

"Can you expand on that?"

Rachel released her curl. "He called me a 'stupid bitch' and said I had no sense of tradition. Our team will always be the Rancheros. He'd screamed at me when he saw the announcement in the newspaper. He was convinced the name change was going to result in the team taking on even more debt than it has in recent years."

"So your team is running a deficit?" Dr. Lindholm moved out of her recliner and back to her desk. "Why is that?"

Rachel laughed. "Because our stadium was a dump—in a bad neighborhood. Our new stadium—it's at Cabrillo and Carrillo streets—will definitely help with attendance. My dad decided to build it after the city granted him the use of land that was a public park that had three softball diamonds. 'Softball Guy' was pissed about losing his fields, but he finally gave in. It will hold five thousand people and change. Bottom line, however, we've sucked for the last five years finishing with the worst record in the league each year. No one likes a perennial loser."

"And the reason for all the losing?"

"My dad got bored with running the team. He found a young girlfriend—a fitness trainer at the gym where he goes—and he stopped challenging San Diego management on the lack of talented players they were sending us. We've been affiliated with the Friars for ten years, and they've pretty much sent us their rejects for all those years. It got so bad that my dad demanded to have the right to recruit and sign free agents. It surprised everyone in minor league baseball when Friar's management agreed to make us the only semi-independent team in the California League's history. Team officials throughout the league were suspicious that the commissioner had taken a bribe from Dad. Two years ago, my dad found his eventual starting first baseman, playing semi-pro ball in Goleta. He signed him up, and he paid dividends by hitting .280 for the season."

"Bored doesn't sound like the hugely successful business man you've described to me."

"There's a health issue. He had a heart procedure last year where they placed stents in two clogged arteries. It's his go-to excuse." Rachel waved her hands like she was crossing out that excuse. "The real reason, however, for his diminished interest in the team is Jessie."

"Jessie?"

"She's the fitness trainer. She's a ginger with tight ringlet curls that flow to the middle of her back."

"Ginger?'

"Skin tone and hair color. I confess, she's got a world-class body. She's a workout maniac. She was a regular contestant in Southern California physique competitions. My dad had been single for a long time, and he blamed his decline in connecting with potential mates on his weight gain—especially around his middle. He was always pretty vain about his appearance. I used to bug him by calling him Homer Simpson. Pissed him off. Jessie weaned him off free weights and got him into any form of exercise that impacted his core. She also educated him on nutrition. His idea of a balanced meal was when his server arrived with his high-calorie meal on a tray and didn't spill anything. He lost two inches off his waist in six weeks and gained a sidekick who wouldn't let him out of her sight. She's ten years older than me, and I'm envious of her body. If you saw her, you'd understand why he spends so much time with her. He's with her constantly. He taught her how to fly his Cessna Skyhawk, and now she pilots the plane most of the time when my dad visits his car dealerships up and down the coast. He's taken her everywhere.

"There's hardly a five-star vacation spot in the world that they haven't visited—Bora Bora, Jamaica, Montenegro, Maiorca, the Greek Isles, you name it—all in a period of a couple years. And they're not tourists. They are doers. He took her to La Paz Baja to teach her how to saltwater fly fish. She actually caught a Dorado with fly-fishing gear. They just got back from ten days in New Zealand—a place called Queenstown. Jessie talked him into bungee jumping from the highest venue overlooking the town. He still hasn't stopped talking about the experience."

Dr. Lindholm smiled for the first time in an hour. "Is she, by any chance, the beneficiary on his life insurance policy?"

"Good point, Doctor. I don't know anymore."

"How do you two get along sharing the same man?"

"She hates me." Rachel put her fingers to her mouth to govern a smirk. "She sees me as her competition. A mutual friend told me she was pretty casual about throwing out dirt that portrayed me as a 'sleep-around girl.' She's lucky that hasn't gotten back to my dad, or she's 'gone girl.' She's part Latina and part gold digger, but if my dad's happy, why should I protest? Dad wanted me to join them on the New Zealand trip, but Jessie threw a shit fit. She told my dad that if it was to be a family outing, she was out. Dad caved."

Dr. Lindholm scratched out another note and then said, "Our time is up for today. Perhaps we can pick up right here next time."

"Same time, same station next week?" Rachel asked while rising to her feet.

"Yes. During the week, I want you to make a list of all the potential pitfalls you think you and your female staff might encounter as you begin your first season as head of the Charros. Pitfalls that would cause you to regress in your efforts to better control your anger. I don't think I have to remind you that another incidence of violence could result in a severe penalty for you—maybe even land you in prison."

"I'm well aware of that, Doctor."

"Sounds like I'm back in school and getting my homework assignment."

"Please don't be flip, Ms. Haslett?"

"It's Rachel. I told you. That's your homework, Doctor. Learn not to call me Ms. Haslett." Rachel put extra mustard into closing the doctor's office door as she exited.

CHAPTER FOUR

His two boys, Gary and Larry Greene, ages ten and twelve, were startled by their dad's snapping at them several times at the breakfast table for making too much noise while eating their cereal—Wheaties.

"This is not a pig feed, boys. Time you started learning some manners."

Contrary to his reprimand, Will Greene was generally what you'd expect of a car salesman at breakfast—bubbling with enthusiasm for the start of a new "bargain basement" sales day and eager to dissect the morning baseball box scores with his boys. He wanted them both to grow up to be the next Mike Trout, so he always had them check his stats first. His energetic wife, Becky, a forever high school "best personality" who still fashioned Cher-like bangs and long black hair that almost touched her waist, had tried to smooth over her husband's unusual behavior by telling the boys their dad was just a little edgy about a morning meeting with his boss and that they hadn't really done anything wrong.

Edgy would not have been the word Will would have used to describe his state. He was downright scared that his job as general manager of Haslett Ford, a position he'd held for thirteen years and one he revered, might be in jeopardy. The job had become who he was, a damn good card salesman.

In recent years, Erv Haslett had flown up to Eureka less often because as he'd put it to Will, "You've got this dealership under control. Your profit margin tops all my other dealerships." So it was disconcerting for Will when he'd taken a call last week from Big Erv asking for a meeting not about the car dealership but a personal matter. Since he'd received the call, Will had lost his appetite and dropped over five pounds from his frame of 220 pounds. Sleep had become a task. He carried bags under his eyes that looked like carry-ons. Add to Big Erv's impending appearance was the possibility that his assistant sales manager, who he'd fired a week ago for his chronic drinking on the job—three martini lunches had gone out with the Carter Administration—might have ratted him out for his marijuana dealings. He worried the two were connected—deep down he knew they were.

In his early fifties, Will Greene's hair had gone gray, almost silver. He sported a medium-size potbelly and a round face that featured a double chin that jiggled when he laughed. As a young man, he was never considered handsome; and as he aged, he hadn't been able to alter that perception. Now an oily complexion, along with a splotchy mustache and goatee, made him look like the stereotypical wheeler-dealer car salesman that he despised.

Fifteen years ago, to the surprise of just about everybody in both families and all her sorority sisters, Will had been able to convince Becky Holmes, the everything girl at Eureka High School—homecoming queen, senior class president, cheerleader, valedictorian—to marry him a week after they'd graduated college at Humboldt State. Along with a brother and two sisters he'd grown up in Eureka, a town known foremost for a nauseating smell that was emitted daily from the pulp mills and lingered in the citizens' senses like a bad cold. It was also a town that operated on the brink of economic disaster for most of its existence.

The logging industry had ruled Humboldt County—about a five-hour drive north up Highway 101 from San Francisco—for decades. But in the late sixties and early seventies, the entire county went through a radical shift in the structure of its economy. Humboldt County literally went to pot. Counterculture hippies moved north from San Francisco's Haight-Ashbury to a sparsely populated Redwood country attracted by cheap land and the opportunity to grow and smoke marijuana without much resistance from law enforcement. As the logging industry stalled out and loggers found themselves out of jobs, they turned to growing pot as well. Today Humboldt enjoys the reputation as the country's "weed haven", and its economy has become dependent on the illegal farming of marijuana.

For years, Will Greene had resisted abundant opportunities to become involved in the marijuana industry. In his mind, there was no need. He was making a decent living at Haslett Motors, pulling in $125,000 a year. For eight years, he'd served the community as an upstanding member of Eureka's five-person city council and, with his wife Becky, was a churchgoing regular. His reputation was spotless. He'd been a strong antimarijuana-growing advocate while on the council. He'd aggressively promoted the notion that becoming so reliant on something that was illegal was an e-ticket to economic disaster. He was praised for his stand by some residents but became public enemy number 1 of the marijuana growers.

Will's strong opposition to profiting from marijuana took a dramatic change when he lost a ton of money beginning with the 2007 recession—$200,000 worth of losses in stocks, a restaurant partnership that tanked, and his mother-in-law's health.

Becky's mother was diagnosed with lymphoma and, thanks to a drunken absentee husband, had no insurance—Medicare was a drop in the bucket—to pay for her treatment. Will was forced to do what he'd previously considered to be the unthinkable. He employed his car-selling skills to serve him as a conduit between the county's marijuana growers and dealers throughout Northern California. In just a couple of years, he'd become the biggest dealer in the county, raking in double the amount of cash he was making at the dealership. And he'd done it all under law enforcement's radar.

Big Erv had never been one to be wishy-washy over firing employees. Just last week, he'd axed his service manager at his Ventura dealership for allegedly making inappropriate gestures and statements to a female customer. Big Erv was doubly pissed by the incident after viewing a photo of the woman that showed her to be a slight, thin, with stringing dirty blond hair—ordinary looking at best. He was of a mind if you're stupid enough to stalk a woman, make sure she's got tits big enough to keep her afloat if her plane ever went down in water. When he made up his mind to let someone go, that was it.

Will Greene was the exception. He wanted to hear Will's side of the story and then take time to think it over. First, he felt obligated to meet face-to-face with Eddie Anderson, the recently fired assistant sales manager who'd called him about Will Greene's drug connection. After flying in the night before, he met with Anderson first thing the next morning. Their hellos were cordial, but Big Erv wasted little time on small talk.

"I want you tell me to my face what you told me on the phone, that your boss is dealing marijuana."

Anderson was well prepared. He'd hired a computer science student at Humboldt State to hack into Will's online banking account. He'd kept both his personal and business accounts on his office computer. He gave Big Erv names, dates, and he presented dollar amounts. The copies of transaction documents he turned over to Big Erv served as the knockout punch. Will Greene was a confirmed dope dealer.

Bouncing a general manager was a serious matter in the small empire Big Erv had built. He viewed his reputation as an extension of the reputations of his top employees. He'd axed a lot of employees over the years but never a general manager. In Will's case, he didn't have a suitable backup to take over the Eureka business.

After coffee with Eddie Anderson, Big Erv had a 10:30 a.m. sit-down with Will Greene. In the afternoon, he planned to play golf with his buddy and former USGA playing partner, Jim Hankins, a former Santa Barbara County sheriff's deputy who'd retired to Arcata, a neighboring city to Eureka.

After downing the strongest coffee he could buy at a neighboring Starbucks, Big Erv entered his dealership with his usual swagger and greeted Will with a firm handshake. He did, however, restrain himself from giving his employee his customary one-arm hug. He inquired about Will's wife and kids and complimented him on the neatness of the showroom.

"I like that you're featuring the F-150. This is the place to do it—big country."

Will asked if Jessie had made the trip.

Big Erv offered a terse no.

Will took his answer as an early indicator that this was not a pleasure trip for Big Erv. Jessie had accompanied him on his last half dozen visits.

They sat down in Will's office just off the showroom floor and next to the soda machines. It was painted in car dealership bland.

Will's desk and office chairs were *Office Place* cheap, but he'd kept them in first-rate condition. Plaques adorned all four walls. There were four saluting Will as the Haslett Motors general manager of the year, another recognizing his year as president of the Eureka Rotary Club, one with the mayor at a fun run, another with the little league team he sponsored, and plenty of family photos. There was even one with Will and Big Erv, arm in arm at a local golf tournament.

Big Erv slapped his hands on both of his thighs, his version of gaveling the meeting to order.

"I had a disturbing phone call from Eddie Anderson. I followed it up by meeting with him first thing this morning."

"What's this all about?" Perspiration appeared above Will's lip.

"You."

"I'm not surprised he'd retaliate against me." Will shifted in his chair. "He was pretty upset about being let loose. Keep in mind, he's a serial hothead."

"You know I'm not one to beat around the bush, Will. So is it true you're heavily involved in marijuana trafficking as this Anderson fellow described?"

Will inhaled deeply and then exhaled as if all the life had suddenly gone out of him and his soul had been bared. He nodded his head and dropped his chin to his chest.

"Yes. But I can explain." He choked on the words.

Big Erv got up from his chair. "It's not something you can explain away easily, Will. I have documents of your transactions." He placed his hands on Will's desk and bent at the waste to get a level look into Will's frightened eyes. "I will not allow that kind of activity sully my company's reputation. Those in this community might overlook your drug dealing. I imagine you're probably a local hero for keeping the economy afloat. But for Haslett Motors, the corporation, your involvement could result in a PR disaster." He turned and walked over to the picture of the Haslett Motors-sponsored little league team—last year's champions at that—and pulled it off the wall. Big Erv eyeballed the photo for a few awkward seconds. "I wonder, with all your dealing, if you've ever considered what impact that shit might have on the lives of these young kids. Thanks to you, they're all potential potheads."

Will started to cry. Tears raced down his cheeks. "I just—"

"You have been a good servant, Will. If it weren't for the fact that you've recently become my franchise sales leader, I'd fire you on the spot. Business is business, but—"

"I'm so sorry, Erv. I'll stop selling the stuff yesterday."

"Before I left for here, I promised myself I wouldn't do anything rash. Imagine me adopting that stance? The biggest hothead west of Al Sharpton."

Will shook his head.

"I will think this over and decide if yesterday is good enough. I'll let you know by the end of tomorrow whether it's an offense that warrants your termination."

Will was sobbing in his chair as Big Erv exited his office.

"I've done so much good in this town. Please take that into consideration."

That afternoon, Big Erv shot a ten-over-par eighty-two at the Eureka Country Club to beat his buddy Jim Hankins by six strokes. Big Erv never talked about the reason for his trip North. He just told Hankins it was business as usual. Big Erv had a well-earned reputation for being a combustible golfer. Jim Hankins was one of only a handful of golfers who dared to tease Big Erv about his temper. Each time they'd played together, Jim opened his golf bag and showed him the fire distinguisher that he always carried.

"It's in my bag only when I play with you, big fella," Hankins laughed.

Big Erv didn't disappoint this day. He was on his best behavior until he got to the first par three. It happened after he took a triple bogey six on the par three-sixth hole. It cost him his pitching wedge. Crazy mad over a 120-yard tee shot that hooked hard left over a sand trap and down a steep ravine, he snapped the wedge over his knee. It made a sound like a giant limb falling from a tree. Big Erv tossed both ends of the broken club into an adjacent pond without even watching them strike water.

In general though, Erv and Jim laughed, pounded beers, smoked cigars, and talked about life its own self for eighteen of the most enjoyable holes either had ever played. It turned out to be Big Erv's last moments of enjoyment.

CHAPTER FIVE

Mid-March wasn't supposed to produce morning frost in Arizona—not according to the Casa Grande Chamber of Commerce Web site. *Do all chambers lie,* Rachel asked herself? Santa Barbara claims to have the best climate in the United States, yet the city of Redwood City in Northern California uses the slogan "Weather Best by Government Test." The Casa Grande Chambers site reads, "The best climate in all of the Valley of the Sun." Casa Grande, a town of forty-eight thousand, was located halfway between Phoenix and Tucson. The unseasonable cold forced Rachel to wear khaki-colored embroidered crop pants and a V-neck sweater instead of her customary shorts and blouse. Because of her affiliation with Chicos, she's able to get all her casual clothes—her wardrobe staple—at a 30 percent discount.

She had come to Casa Grande three and a half weeks before the start of the Charros' season to get a firsthand look at the young prospects San Diego was considering for her Advanced A league affiliate. She also planned to meet with the new manager, Jenks Houghton, a former big league pitcher for the Rangers, Angels, and Padres and most recently, the bench coach for San Diego's Arizona League team. Jenks was Rachel's top priority. She wanted to make it clear to him from day one that she wanted to win. "Nobody remembers who finished second at anything" was her philosophy for life. They met at a Starbucks that was located a couple of blocks away from the Friars' spring training home, Grande Sports World—which also served as a spring training home for soccer teams.

Rachel had used the time during a flight stopover in LA to research her manager. Google presented an uninspiring portrait of a "baseball lifer" who'd had very little success as a minor league pitching coach for four different organizations. Rachel stumbled on a two-year-old newspaper story from the *Albuquerque Journal* that reported his arrest for soliciting a prostitute. It was his second such arrest within a year's time.

Jenks was quick to recognize Rachel as she entered the coffee shop. He whistled at her. It was a sound she'd expect to hear coming from a baseball dugout. *Bad beginning,* she thought to herself after ordering a coffee and sitting down next to him. She immediately didn't like the way he was dressed for a meeting with his new boss— soiled jeans, a "Grateful Dead" T-shirt from decades past and flip-flops. He was slumped in his chair and didn't stand up to greet her. Plus, he smelled of alcohol.

"Recognized you from your picture on the Charros' Web site, darlin'. Been waiting for you, 'little lady.'"

Rachel's stern glare suggested she was irritated by her appointed manager's lack of polish.

"Two things to know about me, Mr. Houghton. You don't call me darlin' or little lady. Ever."

Jenks sat up straight in his chair and pawed at his dirty, unwashed shoulder-length brown hair. His first impressions of his boss ranged from "a potentially great fuck to what-does-she-know-about-baseball to an assertive bitch."

"Now where were we?" Rachel asked.

Jenks tugged at the whiskers from his full beard.

"Have you been drinking this morning?"

Jenks smiled. "Depends on what you consider morning. Not to worry. It's a spring training ritual that anyone who's not playing the next day can get hammered at night. I haven't played in twenty years. So I get hammered most nights, and sometimes it extends into the morning hours."

Despite all his hair, Rachel actually considered him to be a good-looking guy with a rectangular face, sturdy jaw line, deep-set brown eyes, and a good set of teeth that would have been perfect if it weren't for the chewing tobacco stains.

Rachel took a long sip of her coffee. "You really know how to impress a girl, Jenks."

Jenks slapped at his modest belly with an open hand.

"I've got a decent track record in that department, little—"

"Nice catch."

"Boy, I'm gonna have to watch it around you, ma'am."

"There's something else that bothers me about you, Jenks." Rachel leaned forward in her chair. "I don't like your look. I want my manager to look like a professional—clean cut, Yankee-like—not an out-of-work rock star."

Jenks eyes opened wide. "But—"

"Clean yourself up or find another club to manage, Mr. Jenks." Rachel popped her half-empty paper cup on the table that made a distinct gavel-like sound—end of discussion.

Jenks got up from his chair and pushed it under the table. By the flash of his bloodshot eyes, Rachel realized he was angry.

"You don't pay me, Ms. Rachel. The Friars do. And they're paying me to manage your team. It's not your call, little lady. What you see is what you're going to get. Understood? See you opening night."

Rachel's fresh but lightly applied makeup couldn't hide the red in her face. In one motion, she grabbed her coffee and tossed it at Jenks, hitting him squarely in the chest. A stain the size of Arizona covered Jerry Garcia's image on Jenks's T-shirt.

A final statement punctuated Jenks's exit from the coffee shop. "You're a fucking psycho, darlin'."

It wasn't nine thirty yet—the anticipated thaw hadn't taken hold as frost still appeared on anything green—but Rachel, who was plenty hot on the inside, had new business to take care of. Jenks Houghton was not going to be the Charros' manager.

From the coffee shop, she elected to walk directly to the Friars' facility within the Grande Sports World complex passing by perhaps the longest single row—three blocks worth—of fast-food outlets she'd ever seen. There were two Chipotles two blocks apart. One served only bowls, the other only burritos. It took her about five minutes to negotiate the route, not long enough for her to completely cool her anger.

The Friars' business office was located adjacent to the left field foul pole. She had to ask directions from a young man who appeared to be a grounds keeper. He wore a guilty look on his dark brown face as if he might have been returning from sneaking a toke under the grandstand. As soon as she entered the office, she made a direct line for the general manager's office, bypassing an energetic-appearing, pigtailed secretary who was too slow on the trigger to inform her she would have to make an appointment to see Mr. Braxton.

Devin Braxton was startled to see his office door swing open and to find an attractive female stranger stepping toward his desk. He did a quick visual study of his unexpected visitor. He apparently liked what he saw because he tempered his greeting.

"I haven't had the pleasure," he greeted Rachel, his hand extended.

"Be sure and comfort your deer-in-the-headlights secretary that I don't need an appointment for your trying to saddle me with that slime ball of a manager." She flipped her business card in front of the startled general manager. "In case I forget. Hello. Pleasure to meet you."

Impeccably dressed in a blue blazer with the Friars' logo located over the left pocket, Devin adjusted his tie while he studied the card he was presented. Rachel used the awkward moment to take a stab at the cologne he was wearing.

"I'm going to guess, Polo Red by Ralph Lauren."

"You're good, miss. A boyfriend?" Devin Braxton's eyes were still on the business card.

"Former."

"Oh, I get it now." Devin raised his eyebrows as he glanced up from the business card. "You're Big Erv's girl. I heard you were taking over the Santa Barbara club. By all means, have a seat." He pointed to the rich leather chair opposite his desk. "It's a pleasure to meet you. I used to hear about all your volleyball achievements from your dad. You were a tour champion as I recall."

Rachel nodded and smiled for the first time—an everything-is-okay-now smile it wasn't.

"He was very proud of you."

"Forgive me, Mr. Braxton, but you were informed of our management change six months ago, and I have to bust in here like a dessert storm to get an introduction to you."

Devin sat up straight as if he'd taken offense at the statement. He was a handsome black man with distinctive hazel eyes, close-cropped hair, and delicate facial features that were contrary to the big, meaty hands he displayed as he wrote on a notepad. With those hands, according to Rachel's research, he'd banged out 389 home runs over a fifteen-year span as the Friars' anchor at first base.

"You have my sincere apology, Ms. Haslett. I've been so tied up with negotiations with our newest addition, a Cuban outfielder that hooked up with my worst nightmare of an agent. The agent wants sixty million over four years. The kid was great in Cuba, but even so at that price tag, it's a crapshoot. As a result, I've let a lot of administrative things slip."

Rachel reclined slightly in her chair and crossed her legs. "You haven't really ignored our organization, Mr. Braxton. You've pretty much acted like we don't exist. We're raising your kids that you've paid good money for, and you don't even acknowledge a major shift in the direction we're taking?"

Devin got up from his desk, took off his blazer, walked across the room to a mini kitchen, and poured a cup of coffee for himself and offered Rachel the same. Rachel was impressed with his fitness—a tight ass on a guy always got her attention. He looked as if he could make the Friars' lineup even after seven years in retirement. She made a mental note of his not wearing a wedding ring.

"If it's any consolation, Ms. Haslett, we have the best crop of players in years that we're sending your way."

"Call me Rachel." She smiled.

"Of course, Rachel. I hope you can appreciate my commitment to quality players for you. It will make up for my regrettable little snub. One of the kids I'm sending you is Austin Grant. He's a center fielder from Pierce Community College in LA. He's a cinch future major leaguer if there ever was one—a five-tool player. He's got great power for a twenty-one year-old, and he runs like the wind. I just hope he's not too good, and we have to move him to double *A* before you're season is over."

Rachel got out of her chair and wandered over to the big glass window that featured a spectacular view of the three baseball diamonds that made up the complex.

"Nice view."

"I don't have to leave my office to evaluate our talent. It's pretty sweet, I must admit."

Rachel walked back to her chair. "My priority in booking a three-day stay here in Casa Grande was twofold—to get a look at the players likely to be assigned to the Charros and to meet with the manager you assigned to us."

"I heard you've already visited with your manager." Devin wore a slight grin that displayed a perfect set of shiny white teeth.

Rachel had a surprised look on her face. "News travels fast in the dessert. Must get caught up in the blowing dust."

"He texted me, Rachel. He just said it didn't go well and that you don't want him managing your team."

Rachel studied the fingernails she was never allowed to grow as a volleyball player. "He came off like a complete A-hole."

"He's a little rough around the edges, I'll have to admit."

"What you have to admit is that you made a mistake in assigning him to us. And you need to find someone else. I want this team to be a winner. I've been a winner all my life. I don't intend to stop now. I've taken the risk of assembling an all-female management and training staff—unique to all of baseball. Jenks Houghton would bring down our infrastructure in a week."

Devin Braxton raised his thin eyebrows. "I'm afraid he's yours for the long haul, Rachel. I was under strict orders to promote him to A ball as a manager. He did very well with our Winter League entry as a bench coach. He's a personality. He will boost your marketing in Santa Barbara. I guarantee it."

"The only thing he'll boost in Santa Barbara is the crime rate. I've read all about him, Mr. Braxton. He doesn't fit my mold. Christ, he came to our meeting to learn how bad I want him to win a crown, and he smells like Crown Royal. You're going to let this guy lead your young men?"

Devin placed his hand on the phone next to him. "If I could, I'd put in a call to Mr. Zeller right now and demand he change his mind on Houghton. I honestly don't know if Houghton has something on Zeller—he's only owned the team for two years—but there's a strong allegiance to Houghton coming from the top of the food chain."

Rachel stood up and placed her hands on her hips. "I can't believe a guy, with your big league credentials as a power hitter, could be such a weeny as an administrator."

As soon as the words left her mouth, Rachel conceded to herself that they may have been too harsh. Oh, well.

Devin shook his head. "I can't make my $20,000 a month alimony payments, if I don't have a job, Rachel. I'm sorry, but my hands are tied. All I can promise you is that I will get him into AA and make sure they provide him with a live-in sponsor. I'm told that when he's sober, he is a solid baseball man."

Devin stood up and extended his hand in Rachel's direction. "I have an offer for you," he said, shaking Rachel's hand. "I would love for you to be my dinner guest tonight as a kind of 'make-good' gesture. I'll give you some advice on how to make it work with Houghton, and you can bring me up to speed on how you expect an all-female organization to operate a game for young men."

Rachel smiled and turned toward Devin's office door. She spoke as she walked. "I'd probably grab a burger at In-N-Out and have dinner in my room, so you're offer is accepted, Mr. Braxton."

Braxton smiled. "I didn't think that would be so easy."

Rachel smirked. "It's the only thing that'll be easy with me."

They dined at the Iron Gate, a four-star steak place in Downtown Casa Grande. It appeared to Rachel, who'd chosen to wear the only cocktail dress she'd packed for the trip—a sleek black Guess Illusion Lace—that everyone in the place knew Devin Braxton. It took the two of them five minutes to move from the hostess stand to their table.

"How are we going to do this year?" Most wanted to know. To his credit, Devin graciously shook every extended hand and smiled for any number of selfies.

"You're a popular guy, Mr. Braxton."

Devin politely pulled her chair out from the table. "When you spend as much time in this town as I do and you don't cook—well, you get the picture."

"Bachelor, are you?" Rachel gave herself a mental pat on the back for strategically casting for an explanation of his empty ring finger.

"Going on four years." Devin shook his head, suggesting his own disbelief.

Before he addressed his menu, Devin took some papers out of a manila folder he'd been carrying. He shuffled them into a neat stack and then handed them to Rachel.

"This is my evaluation of every single Friars' player who I think could end up with your club in Santa Barbara. It's so detailed it identifies whether they sleep on their stomachs or on their backs. I felt so bad about my corporate slight of your franchise that I sat down and wrote these player assessments out after you left my office this morning."

Rachel's eyes lit up. "Wow. Now I don't have to stay here for three days to catch these guys in action. I can get back home and deal with the thousands of items on my plate before opening night. Thank you so much. That was very thoughtful." Rachel placed her hand on top of Devin's and looked him squarely in his eyes. "You're not such a bad guy after all." She patted the top of his hand.

Devin laughed. "I wish everybody thought that way—especially agents. I swear, some of those guys would eat flies off dead people to get another year on a client's contract."

After Devin enjoyed a Macallan 12 single-malt scotch and Rachel, a Cosmopolitan, they both ordered the house specialty, $40 steak Diane's.

"Tell me about yourself, Devin. Not the baseball part. I read about that this afternoon in your media guide. The *you* part—hometown, mom, dad, ex-wife, kids. I'm always interested in what makes a person successful."

Devin leaned back in his chair and tugged at his chin with his hand. "I didn't see this coming. But I'll try. Perhaps we should wait until after our meal?"

Rachel smiled and shook her head. "Now."

"I grew up in Longview, Texas. My father was a Methodist minister. Mom was a seamstress with her own little business. I was an only child—probably a little on the spoiled side. My dad was a huge baseball fan. Chicago teams all the way. The only time I remember him using a swear word was when my uncle said the team known as the Go, Go Sox were overrated.

"He used to take me with him to Chicago when he visited his parents, and we'd always go to either a White Sox or Cubs game. I became a huge Greg Luzinski fan—the White Sox leftfielder and home run hitter. His nickname was The Bull. I started imitating his batting stance in junior high school and stuck with it throughout my career. I made all state in division five in high school. I played first base and hit thirty-one home runs my senior year. San Diego drafted me with the number 13 pick in the 1993 draft. What else?"

Rachel cocked her head and smiled a teasing look. "The married part?"

"I got married to my high school sweetheart. We have a teenage daughter who is the prettiest sixteen-year-old in all of East Texas. Unfortunately, that's a long way from San Diego. But we Skype each other regularly."

"And the reason for your divorce?"

"This feels like an interview. You're relentless, Ms. Haslett."

Rachel shook her head and pointed her index finger at Devin. "Rachel."

Devin Braxton spanked his own hand. "Sorry. Whew!" He paused momentarily, leaving the impression he was collecting his thoughts. He wanted to make sure Rachel would walk away with a good impression of him.

"The divorce was my fault. I loved Jackie Lynn with all my heart, but I morphed into *Testosterone Tommy* my fourth year in the league. I started playing around. It's not hard to do in the big leagues. There are women in every big league city that prey on professional athletes. And then I got involved in an off-and-on yearlong thing with a gorgeous white woman who was the marketing director for a major San Diego hotel—we meant at a Boys Club fundraiser at the hotel. She made many a road trip. We were pretty clandestine. She'd fly alone into a city where we were playing, get her own hotel suite somewhere other than where the team was staying. I'd spend every night with her. I'm not proud of what I did. Wasn't at the time either, but I just kept doing it. I guess it was because I could.

"Jackie Lynn found out from the wife of one of my teammates, and that was it for us. She called me the cheat that I was and took our daughter and went home to Texas, leaving me steeped in so much guilt I thought I might kill myself."

Devin took a napkin and wiped off the perspiration that had accumulated on his brow during his lengthy monologue.

"That does it for me. How about you?"

Rachel played with a curl as she had done with Dr. Lindholm.

"I grew up in Santa Barbara. I was a tomboy. I surfed with the boys in high school and really got into beach volleyball on weekends. My dad, you know about. My mom, kind of missing in my life. She married a richer guy after she divorced my dad, and I haven't had much contact with her since, which is close to fifteen years. I think she preferred his two kids to her own—sad but true. They eventually had a child together.

"Let's see, I attended UCSB for a year but had no interest in getting a college degree. I damn near flunked bonehead English, and I quickly realized I wasn't going to be anybody who worked at a desk in an office full of insecure and entitled college graduates. About thirteen years ago, I had a female friend who encouraged me to team up with her and become beach volleyball professionals. When I committed, I went whole hog. I started lifting weights and built up my legs to where I recorded a thirty-two-inch vertical leap—very important for spiking in sand."

Devin sat back. "Wow, my best is thirty-one."

"I'm not lying." Rachel wore a confident smile.

"Oh, I believe you."

"After playing in a number of amateur events throughout Southern California, we earned enough points to participate in a qualifying ABVP tournament that was held in Santa Barbara. We made it to the semifinals and qualified to join the tour. In 2009, a year after my partner Annie Eastbrook and I won the tour championship, I was voted to head the female players union. I founded the union—over margaritas at Sloppy Joes Pub and Restaurant in Ventura—so I was a logical choice to head it. It was a small group of twenty women. At that time, we were making a third of what the men were taking home. With the union's blessing, I hired a marketing firm to survey the ABVP to determine who—men or women—was driving attendance. It was close, but the women won the war of statistics 55 percent to 45 percent for the men. We were the bigger attraction. I jumped on those numbers like cream in a latte and lobbied hard with our commissioner. We came this close to going on strike," Rachel said, placing her thumb and index finger together.

"The effort upped our scale to within 10 percent of what the men were getting in prize money. I had become public enemy number 1 to the men on tour, but we, women, got what was coming to us, what we'd earned. Of course, the guys cried foul, claiming we were selling sex with our skimpy bikinis, but I made it known that sex works in Hollywood. Why not on the beach? I'm more proud of what our union accomplished of than I am of any of the trophies I've won."

Devin ordered a second scotch. Rachel passed on a Cosmo refill.

"Men?" Devin asked, his brow stretching upward.

"Whew! No one at the moment."

"As attractive as you are, I find that hard to believe."

"On tour, I got the reputation as a ball buster. All flirt and nothing but hurt." Rachel lightly bit into her lower lip and served up look that read *sorry*. "I've had two relationships. One was a guy, the other, a woman."

Try as he did, Devin couldn't keep his eyes from opening wide.

"Women in any all-female sport are subject to being roped into lesbian relationships. It's viewed as a cultural rite of passage. On tour, it's like if you don't participate, you're a social outcast. It breeds mistrust between teammates and can radically affect one's playing performance. I tried it and quickly—as in a month's time—learned it wasn't me. She was a diva. If I borrowed her toothpaste without asking—crisis. If I did the grocery shopping and didn't buy organic veggies—crisis. And every time I looked twice at a good-looking guy on the beach, Tara, that was her name, would go into a funk. She scared me one night when she pulled a carving knife on me after I'd flirted in front of her with a handsome surfer friend at a beach coffee shop. That freaked me out so that I ended the relationship on the spot.

"The guy, he was strictly a case good looks outweighing everything including my common sense. He was vice president of a drinking water company that sponsored the volleyball tour. He would travel with the tour, and I'd naturally hook up with him at each stop. He was drop-dead gorgeous with curly blond hair and an all-season's tan, but I quickly found that when I wasn't around, he was whoring after any decent-looking woman he could find. We lasted six months—until the end of my fifth year on the tour. He actually admitted to me that sex was his biggest enjoyment in life, and because of it, he would never be able to commit to a single woman. According to what mutual friends have told me, he's ended up being hit with two paternity suits."

Rachel, who appeared to Devin to be uncomfortable telling her story, sat back quickly when the food arrived.

"That's my story. Not a lot of success in the romance department. Now let's eat."

They did talk some business over dinner. Devin alerted Rachel to a young woman pitcher who'd traveled to Casa Grande with her parents in hopes of getting a camp tryout.

"Our director of player personnel watched her throw in what amounted to an abbreviated bullpen session but denied her request to pitch in a live game because he felt there wasn't enough time for our pitching coaches to audition and unknown quantity."

"How disappointed was she?"

"Extremely."

"If I'm not mistaken, I believe the Charros have the right to sign free agents."

Rachel nodded. "Thanks to my dad."

"You might want to stay an extra day and give her a look. Her name is Jacqui Davenport. She's a spindly but very athletic African-American who, I'm told, has a pretty good slider and a fastball that lives at or around eighty miles per hour. She played on the boy's team at Union High School in Tucson. Her senior year, she was four and three with a 2.97 ERA. You might be able to use her as a reliever. It would surely authenticate your all female brand if you signed the first woman to pitch in a professional baseball game."

Rachel took out her smart phone and entered the girl's name in her Notes app.

"I can e-mail you her contact information if you like."

"I'd like. But I can't stay the extra day."

"Can't fault a guy for trying."

Rachel blushed at the comment. Nearly three hours after they'd sat down, they said their good-byes. Devin departed, convinced he'd been forgiven for his neglect of the Charros, and Rachel left, certain Devin would honor his promise to visit the Charros and their new general manager on occasion.

CHAPTER SIX

The Ojai Valley Inn and Spa was a forty-five-minute ride from Santa Barbara. Much of the journey featured the Pacific Ocean as a traveling companion off to the west. For the Charros ladies, it was a scenic bus ride if you didn't count the offshore oil platforms that looked like prehistoric creatures rising from the deep. Rachel had gone ahead of her staff to attend to their arrival.

Dressed her usual casual with running shoes instead of sandals, Rachel stood in front of the resort's registration center anxiously anticipating the arrival of the Happy Trails bus she'd rented to carry her thirty-five employees. She was convinced a two-day retreat ten days before the start of the season would produce the necessary bonding between her employees to ready themselves for the difficult task ahead—operating a minor league baseball team.

When the bus finally arrived, Rachel made it a point to hug every one of her lady employees as they stepped down to the sidewalk. She also treated each one to a bottle of Silver Oak cabernet.

Rachel graciously gave all credit for the retreat idea to Adrienne Telfair, vice president of marketing and media relations. Out of appreciation, Rachel allowed Adrienne to put the program for the two-day event together. The agenda consisted of golf, tennis, hiking, biking, and lots of spa time. The only real seminar on the schedule was a three-hour session on how to meditate taught by an instructor at the College of Holistic Study located in Montecito—just outside the Santa Barbara city limits.

Adrienne had convinced Rachel to spend the extra thousand dollars to hire the instructor, saying, "All of us embarking on this journey will need to learn how to decompress from time to time."

The first order of business was a welcome from the general manager. It was held precisely at 4:00 p.m. in the spiritual center, a Spanish ranch-style room with a decorated marble floor and wooded overhead beams arching seemingly to the heavens. The only male in the room was a *Santa Barbara News-Press* sports columnist, who answered to the byline of Miles Rooney. He looked like the last person on earth to cover sports. He was fat, probably fifty pounds overweight for someone five feet eight. His arms were fleshy and showed no definition. His black hair was spiked. He'd requested media presence at the retreat, and Rachel, after consulting with her media director, okayed it. As he promised, he stayed in the background the whole three hours he was present.

Five minutes after the group had assembled, Rachel walked to the podium to a chorus of "Rachel, Rachel" chants and applause.

"I want to thank all of you for coming," Rachel began. "It's a statement about your commitment to this organization that we have 100 percent attendance." More applause. "We want the next two days to be fun, and hopefully, they will provide us the opportunity to get to know one another in preparation for the challenge ahead. I'm convinced that having gone through the hiring process with each of you that we have the smart, strength, and character to get the job done. As I stated when I hired each of you, we're not here to be window dressing or to become a cute little feature story on the network news. We're here to win a California League championship this year and in years to come and to set league attendance records. It will take a well-oiled machine on and off the field to accomplish that. I think you all have the right stuff to get it done. You are the best of the best at your skill sets, handpicked from minor league teams operating in the Western states. I want success for my father who had the courage to turn this franchise over to an unproven leader and to accept my desire to have an all-female staff. He propped this franchise up for fifteen years and exited by providing us with a new state-of-the-art stadium. I want to reward him with a championship." Raucous applause followed Rachel's pep talk.

Rachel followed with a PowerPoint presentation that featured photos and the previous season statistics of each of the forty minor league players Devin Braxton had identified as possibly being sent to the Charros for the start of the 2015 campaign.

"Get to know them. They'll be our kids. We need to support them in the best manner possible."

Before adjourning the session, Rachel asked all employees to stand and talk a little about themselves. The highlight of that requirement was new ballpark operations director Connie Martinez recounting her discovery on her initial tour of the new stadium of a city worker—he was wearing his city jacket—and a sleazy-looking young lady half his age having sex in the shed where the Charros' new groundkeeper had stored the tractor that groomed the playing field. When she asked what they were doing, the man said, "She's looking for foul balls." Everyone in attendance cracked up.

Before adjourning the session, Rachel asked if anyone had any questions about their responsibilities. Robbie Sparks, director of player personnel, asked if she could invite corporate sponsors to a barbecue at the stadium the Saturday before the Monday home opener. Rachel said yes.

Then Marci Williams, the assistant trainer spoke up. "I'm told I should be anticipating a lot of groin injuries the first week, and I'm not sure how to handle it." There were a few snickers in the audience.

Rachel quickly addressed the issue. "Just have them get in the hot tub and direct them to point the jet in the vicinity of the injury. If it hurts something else, too bad." Thirty-five women roared their approval.

On her way to a gym workout the following afternoon, Rachel stopped at the registration center to ask the resort manager if they could move their cocktail hour onto the patio instead of having it indoors. The weather was perfect—in the midseventies. Before she could ask to speak with the manager, she spotted a stack of the afternoon edition of the *Santa Barbara News-Press* sitting on the marble-topped front desk for the convenience of spa guests. Rachel picked one up.

Miles Rooney's column was positioned on the front page, not in its customary position in the sports section. The headline to *Rooney's Rants* column stunned Rachel. Her immediate response was a thundering "SHIT!"

Honeyball Comes to Santa Barbara
Miles Rooney

Santa Barbara—April 7 will mark the start of the twenty-fifth season of class A baseball in our town—not that anyone would notice anymore. The Advanced A league affiliate of the San Diego Friars hasn't had a winning season since its first in 1990. And if you're wondering why they aren't the Rancheros anymore, their media guide says it's because a charro is a higher-class horseman than a ranchero—as if that has anything to do with winning baseball games—a difficult task when the Friars offer up their annual collection of anemic hitters, whose averages almost always fail to clear the Mendoza line of .215. This season, however, the first at the new Erv Haslett TireCo Park promises to be like no other. First and foremost, women are running the entire operation—from the CEO and general manager, Rachel Haslett, to teenage ball girls. There's not a single male employee on the Charros' organizational chart. Even the radio announcer uses lipstick. It's definitely a first for any baseball league in America, and in my humble opinion, it's a blueprint for disaster. What do a bunch of women know about running a baseball team? The new Charros' GM was a volleyball player (a damn good one) who has zero experience in baseball and whose daddy ran off Bill Howser who'd operated the team seemingly quite efficiently the past five years. Big Erv Haslett, who kept a pretty tight leash on Howser and was privy to all things Rancheros, upped and quit the team he purchased fifteen years ago in favor—rumor has it—of romancing a young woman who's only slightly older than his daughter. The aforementioned daughter, unfortunately, wouldn't know saber metrics (the statistical analysis system of measuring a player's performance that was the basis for the book and movie Moneyball) from a saber-toothed tiger. And how will the Charros' two-women training staff effectively operate among a roster of teens and a few twenty-year-olds with juiced-up hormones? They should place cameras in the Charros' locker room this season. They'd generate a viral video a day. Maybe they could get Victoria's Secret to sponsor it. Yesterday General Manager Haslett held the first of a two-day retreat for all her employees. On the program agenda was a meditation session. In my humble opinion, the Charros' ladies are going to need a stronger stress reliever in the months ahead than humming a mantra for twenty minutes at a time. I'm all for equal opportunity, but if Rachel Haslett punctuates this season with a California League championship as she is forecasting, then she should immediately take over running the parent club without having to interview for the job. Prediction: Charros 40 wins, 100 losses. Average attendance: 250.

Rachel was noticeably absent from the five-o-clock cocktail hour. Several in the group tried to reach her cell phone—no answer. Adrienne Telfair tried knocking on the door to her suite. That got a firm "Not now!" from behind the suite's expansive double doors.

"It's me—Adrienne. We're missing you on the patio. They're serving a Pinot from New Zealand to die for."

No response from inside.

"Are you okay, Rachel?"

After a minute or more of silence, Rachel finally opened the door. Adrienne could tell by her puffy eyes that she'd been crying.

"What's going on with you?"

Rachel picked up the *News-Press* from her bed and handed it to Adrienne. She waited patiently for her media director's response to the Honeyball article. When Adrienne finished Miles Riley's column, she had a blank look on her round face.

"No reaction, Adrienne?"

"I don't think it's a bad thing if that's what you're asking me."

Rachel flopped her backside onto the bed and placed both arms under her head for support. Her eyes were directed at a ceiling fan that was making an annoying cranking sound.

"That asshole made us look like a bunch of bimbos, Adrienne. Putting the Honeyball tag on us means we're going to have to work harder than ever to earn the baseball community's respect. Shit! This undertaking is going to be hard enough that we don't need to be starting at minus zero."

Adrienne sat down in a chair opposite Rachel's bed. She cupped her hands in front of her face to suggest she had an idea.

"I haven't had but a few minutes to noodle this in my brain, but I think we can take this Honeyball moniker and run with it—turn it into a mega-positive."

Rachel issued what could only be interpreted as a sarcastic laugh and turned her head away from where Adrienne was sitting.

"I'm all ears."

"I've been racking my brain for weeks for some kind of clever marketing slogan to hang on the coming season. Nothing has worked. The best I've been able to come up with so far is 'These Charros don't horse around.'"

Rachel shrieked and quickly sat up in bed. "That is so god-awful, Adrienne! It's a good thing you never proposed it to me."

Adrienne laughed and nervously played with her hair. Next to Rachel, she was probably the most attractive of the women on staff, with her short rust-colored haircut, twin cheek dimples, and perfectly shaped butt.

"*Honeyball* is perfect, Rachel. We should pay that asshole a creative fee, introduce him on opening night, and give him a gold-plated press pass. I can visualize a graphic. Stay with me on this." Adrienne paused for effect. "It takes us back to the Hollywood pinup girl era. We have the Charros' logo positioned opposite a cartoon drawing of a woman in short shorts and heels, hands on hips, looking back at the camera Betty Grable style. We stamp a slogan on it, maybe 'Honeyball happens here!'"

Rachel raised her eyebrows like she might be buying Adrienne's brainstorming idea. "So you're saying we should sell sex—our sex?"

Adrienne got to her feet and executed a vigorous fist pump. "*Yes!* Exactly. Our marketing of the team could only be as effective as how well they played—wins and losses. We have no control over that. But we can sell sex. That, along with a new stadium, will attract a younger crowd—a whole new patron. Last year's demographics showed that the average age of our season ticket holders was fifty-six. We've got to put younger fannies in our seats. The beer sales alone would increase dramatically."

Rachel got to her feet and began pacing the length of her suite. It was another nervous habit of hers. She paced the court boundaries for five minutes before every volleyball match.

"But exactly how do we market sex?"

Adrienne laughed. "We start with you. We make you Betty Grable. Your legs—not the pimply face of some unknown second baseman—would become the face of Charros' baseball. Don't you see, Rachel? You are Honeyball."

Rachel stopped pacing and stood before a floor-length mirror and examined herself.

"I spent my entire volleyball career battling against the sexist notion that women were only included on the ABVP tour because they looked good in skimpy two-piece beach outfits. I'm sure you remember my pissing match with Bill O'Reilly on his Fox TV show when he declared women volleyball players were glorified bikini models with sand in their toes. This is kind of counter to who I am. But . . . I love it." Rachel motioned for Adrienne to stand up. She stepped in front of her and gave her a giant hug. "That's great thinking, Adrienne. I knew, when I hired you, I was bringing aboard a star."

Adrienne's eyes became misty. "Thank you. That means a lot coming from you."

"I want to run this past all our ladies at tonight's dinner. I want to make sure everyone's on board with the concept."

That night, at the closing of the retreat following dinner, Rachel had Adrienne detail her marketing plan. It won unanimous approval. On the bus ride back to Santa Barbara the next morning, Maci Erickson, the manager of corporate partnerships, passed out sheets of paper that contained her revised lyrics to Bobby Goldsboro's 1968 hit "Honey." All thirty-five women aboard sang out loud as one:

> See the team,
> How good is grown,
> But, fans, it hasn't been too long,
> They weren't good . . .

> Fans laughed at them,
> And we got sad.
> The first day that she managed it,
> It drove fans mad . . .

Then the franchise changed,
And she stepped up to lead the way
So it wouldn't die.

Honeyball, we salute you,
You made us good,
And we're all with you
Because we all should.

CHAPTER SEVEN

Exhausted was the only way to describe Rachel's mental and physical state as she got off the bus from Ojai in the parking lot at The Erv.

The retreat had been a monumental success from a morale standpoint, but she conceded to herself that the task ahead—making Honeyball work—was going to be more stressful than she could have imagined.

In the days immediately following the retreat, the Honeyball concept blew up on social media. Baseball purists were the most vocal. A Facebook fan page called the Minor Leagues labeled Honeyball the worst promotion since Saint Louis Browns GM Bill Veeck inserted a midget, Eddie Gaedel, into his lineup to pitch-hit in 1951. Twitter was buzzing with tweets that ranged from "ridiculous idea" to "heading West for a Honeyball vacation."

Overnight, Rachel was in great demand by the nation's sports media. In her first national TV appearance, Rachel appeared on *Baseball Now*, a Fox sports pregame show. She'd joined a panel of former major league executives. The program's lead topic was "Is Honeyball good for the game?"

The show's host, Ryan Chrisman, a former major league pitcher with Minnesota and later San Francisco, started the program by asking Rachel why she'd sought an all-female organization.

Rachel, who'd driven two hours to be at the Fox studios in Los Angeles to accommodate the show's producer, was quick to respond.

"To empower women everywhere. To show that women can work together and be successful at anything they attempt."

"So you had an agenda, and this is more of a women's movement issue played out in the name of baseball," Chrisman said. His tone was borderline combative.

"Not at all." Rachel pawed at her hair and caught herself about to play with a curl. "It's about women, pulling as one, trying to be the best at what they do. This is no different than what I experienced on the beach volleyball tour. The women constantly strived to prove they were just as much an attraction as the men. This isn't a stunt. We got into this to win a championship and sell tickets. The Charros' organization has no interest or intention of becoming a political arm of any women's movement."

Rachel could feel the stickiness of perspiration accumulating under her arms. She prayed she could keep moisture from showing above her lip.

Allan Sinclair, a former GM with Baltimore, was the first panelist to speak from his remote location at Camden Yard.

"Ms. Haslett, this is the biggest stunt since Chicago staged Disco Demolition Night in 1979. Assigning female trainers to care for young men still combating acne is a stunt. I don't care what kind of ribbon you want to put on it."

Rachel straightened in her studio chair. Suddenly, she became aware of the heat being generated by the studio lights.

"If it was a stunt, I'd have gone to the local gentlemen's club and hired lap dancers to run the organization. I did exhaustive searches from the West Coast to the Midwest and even beyond to find the best women in the baseball industry. No minor league team in America has a better staff than the Santa Barbara Charros."

Tom Langersham, promotions director for the Seattle entry in the American League West, jumped into the conversation. "Am I to actually believe this Honeyball idea isn't about selling sex? Because it definitely appears that way. What happened to promoting your team—the players, the manager, the coaches? The word in baseball circles is that you, whom I'm told enjoy exposing your world-class gams by sporting mostly shorts and T-shirts in your daily attire, are going to be provocatively featured in the team's marketing campaign. Is that true?"

Rachel took a sip from a water glass that had been provided for her by the only woman in the studio crew.

"I'm not at liberty to disclose that, Mr. Langershame." The pronunciation was intentional. "Any comment would be premature."

Last up was Atlanta's media relations director Stanley Roberts, a black man with a dark outlook on women in baseball.

"You should consider having your Honeyball organization join the circus in the off season. You could easily generate some extra income by riding elephants and lighting flames for torch swallowers. This is nothing more than an attention-seeking concept that will alienate a male audience in numbers I don't think you fully realize."

By the time the fifteen-minute segment concluded, Rachel felt as if she'd been placed on trial and convicted of inflicting great damage on the game of baseball. She clearly had not swayed any on the panel that Honeyball was a fresh idea that would give young women everywhere the incentive to be the best at whatever they attempted.

When she reached her studio dressing quarters, she released the tears that she'd been desperately hiding from a national TV audience. For the first time since she'd started on her baseball journey, she wondered in silence if she'd made a mistake. She stayed in the room for a full hour before wiping away her smudged mascara and heading out on the return trip home.

CHAPTER EIGHT

It took Rachel several days to recover from the emotional strain of her Fox TV experience. The support of her Honeyball staff helped her keep her head high, even though at times she felt like she was having difficulty staying afloat.

"We're very proud of you," Adrienne Telfair told her prior to a meeting of the team's executive staff. Applause followed her statement.

Rachel spent most of her day declining an avalanche of media requests. The exercise itself was physically and emotionally draining. Rachel decided to leave her office early. She felt an afternoon nap might help her restore her energy.

From her office, she walked the two blocks to her West Beach oceanfront condo, allowing a crisp ocean breeze to help refresh her mind. When she arrived at her front door, she was surprised and startled to find it unlocked. Her heart suddenly began to race. She slowly pushed open the door, mentally preparing to encounter and intruder. Instead, sitting on her living room couch—her prized Darlings of Chelsea handcrafted in Italy white leather couch—with his hands cupped and resting on his lap was an unshaven Troy Haslett. He wore a soiled Rancheros baseball cap that covered his shoulder-length brown-and-blond streaked hair and was dressed in a worn sweat outfit. His face was blank. He stared straight ahead, refusing to acknowledge his sister's presence. She assumed him to be in a drug-induced fog.

Her first instinct was to ask him to get off the couch before he dirtied it, but she bit her tongue and decided against it. Rachel advanced toward her brother and stopped just short of where he was sitting.

"Question. How did you get in here?"

Still staring straight ahead, Troy pulled his driver's license out of his wallet and mimed jimmying a lock. Then he unloaded the awful news on his sister. "Dad's plane is missing." His voice was monotone.

Rachel's face reddened. "This had better not be some sick joke, Troy."

It wouldn't have been the first time that Troy had fabricated a story about a family member meeting some catastrophic fate. He'd once informed his parents that he had taken a phone message from his grandmother detailing how his grandfather had been diagnosed with Alzheimer's. It wasn't true. He just made it up. It was all in the interest of his gaining attention.

Troy shook his head.

Rachel fell backward into her living room love seat. "How do you know this?"

The phone rang while I was here. It went to your voicemail message, and then someone from the sheriff's department started to leave a message. I picked up."

"What did they say?"

Troy's eyes pointed down. He spoke softly but still without a hint of emotion. "It was a she. She said he hadn't completed his instrument flight rules plan from Eureka back to Santa Barbara. He was due back in Santa Barbara four hours ago. His last radar contact from some air traffic control outfit placed him over the Pacific near Pismo Beach. There was no 'Mayday' message. Nothing."

Rachel cried out, "GOD, NO! Please, God." She burst into tears and then buried her head in a pillow that was lying next to her.

Several minutes passed. Neither sibling stirred. Still crying, Rachel released the pillow and flashed a death stare at her brother.

"How can you be so emotionless, Troy? He's our dad. Don't you care?"

Troy got up to leave.

As he passed by Rachel, she pulled her head from out of the pillow and asked, "What the fuck were you doing here in the first place?"

"I came to see if you had anything of value I could steal, but you didn't."

"Christ, Troy. Run short of drug money?"

Before closing the front door, Troy turned to face Rachel. "As a matter of fact." The door shut behind him.

Rachel was left with many more questions of her now departed brother. As usual, it was up to her to do the heavy lifting. At that moment, she was filled with instant rage at her useless brother and horror over the disappearance of her father's plane. Her insides churned like a cheap washing machine. She found herself wishing it had been her brother who'd gone missing.

Her dad's fate, however, quickly reclaimed her thought process. The memories of being his copilot on so many flights flooded her consciousness. How could she ever forget flying over migrating whales near Point Reyes and buzzing Neverland at the height of Michael Jackson's popularity? The memory of him placing his large hand on her shoulder when she was at the controls had refused to go away over the years.

Rachel snapped out of her fog and quickly jumped to her feet, crossed her living room, and hit the replay button on her voicemail machine. She wanted the name of the deputy who'd called. Sgt. Mary Ziegler was the voice on the machine.

After being taken on a circuitous route to Sergeant Ziegler's phone extension, Rachel was more than a little agitated by the sheriff department's bureaucracy. When she finally reached Sergeant Ziegler, Rachel was stressed.

"God," she greeted the sergeant. "I bet I could get a faster response at the Pentagon."

Sergeant Ziegler didn't say anything.

"Can you tell me anything about my father?" There was a pause on the sergeant's end. Rachel quickly realized she'd forgotten to identify herself. "Oh! Haslett. Ervin Haslett," she blurted out. "You reported his plane missing to my brother over an hour ago. He was flying his Cessna from Eureka back to Santa Barbara."

"Yes, yes. I'm up to speed with you now. Unfortunately, all our information came from out of the Oakland Air Route Traffic Control Center in Fremont. All we're hearing is that he is now five hours behind his estimated arrival time."

Rachel fought back tears on her end of the conversation. "Forgive me, Sergeant, this is such an unexpected shock."

"I understand, Ms. Haslett."

Rachel paused to gather herself as she felt a crying binge coming on.

"Take your time, Ms. Haslett. What I can do for you is give you a coast guard contact. Usually when a plane goes down in the ocean, the coast guard is immediately dispatched to search for survivors and to rescue any remnants of the downed aircraft. They will have the very latest information for you if in fact your father's plane did go down."

Rachel gasped for air. "He always flew just off the coastline. He didn't like the turbulence near the mountain ranges. I've flown the route with him so many times."

"All the more reason for you to stay in touch with the coast guard. I can only pray for you and your family at this point."

Rachel hung up the phone, dropped to her knees, and cried until there were no more tears.

Hours passed with no word of Big Erv's whereabouts—only that his flight plan documents did not mention a passenger. Rachel stayed in hourly contact with the coast guard station out of Morro Bay, located along the central California coast not far from San Luis Obispo. They were the station that responded with both a cutter and a helicopter for the ocean search.

When nightfall arrived and a dense fog covered the coastline, the mission had to be put on hold until daybreak. By that time, Big Erv's plane would have been missing some twenty hours. Just before noon the next day, as Rachel was completing details by phone to rent her own search boat out of Avila Beach, she received a call from her coast guard contact in Morro Bay.

The caller identified himself as Executive Officer Aaron Kirkland.

"I regret to inform you, Ms. Haslett, that we have located pieces of the wreckage of your father's plane, and there are no survivors. My deepest—"

Rachel dropped the phone to her home office floor. "No, Daddy!" she screamed over and over.

CHAPTER NINE

The memorial for Ervin Wesley Haslett produced a boatload of surprises for Rachel. The attendance at the service topped two thousand—mostly dealership employees and customers. The greatest number was made up of fans—many of them longtime season ticket holders. Noticeable in their absence were both Troy and Jessie. The ex didn't show either. *DNA*—did not attend—was the mental note Rachel made upon discovery.

Will Greene had made it with his family and several employees from his Eureka dealership in tow. He made a point to have a brief private conversation with Rachel. He expressed his deepest admiration for her father, but as Rachel had learned over the years, car salesmen don't always come off as being 100 percent genuine, and that's how she categorized his outreach.

Devin Braxton brought two female Friars' employees from San Diego to help as temps with the logistics of opening night and for as long as they were needed, and he also guaranteed her that Austin Grant would stay with the Charros for the entire season, no matter if he produced numbers that were off the charts.

Rachel was grateful for his bending over backward to help out in a difficult time. She worried she wouldn't know how to express it to him.

Rachel generated tears by the bucket loads with her eulogy. She had the mourners on her first sentence.

"I'm single at thirty-five, and that's because no man I've ever met could match up to my dad. Not even close. He was bigger than life. He was my compass as I passed from childhood to becoming a woman. Making him proud of me fueled my very existence, whether it was through volleyball or making his favorite cherry pie. I'm indebted to him for everything I've accomplished in life."

She kept the eulogy to ten minutes so that his lifelong hunting and fishing buddy, Matt Overfelt, could have ample time to remember Big Erv. He was Big Erv's roommate and teammate at Fresno State. He was the first to start addressing him as Big Erv.

Together, they'd won twenty-eight football games and created more havoc on campus than two young men had the right to without being caught. They'd orchestrated a panty raid a year in the girl's dormitory, which made local TV news each time, and they'd organized a dozen or more fellow students to slit the tires on San Diego State's team bus prior to a night game at Fresno State. San Diego State's coaches, along with their players, were so pissed off they had to wait two and a half hours after losing the game to Fresno State to get all new tires that they later threatened to end the home-and-away series with Fresno that had gone on for twenty years.

The two of them also claimed the two-man world record for most cans of Olympia beer consumed in a twenty-four-hour period—201. Guinness, however, refused to give them credit. They were drunk for forty-eight hours. They learned that hair will grow on teeth after that many Olys.

Matt had recently undergone a hip replacement, and it took him some time to get to the stage that was located on home plate. He'd lost most of his hair by his thirties that resulted in him being one of the early pioneers of a shaved heads for men. He wore glasses, even though he didn't really need them. "It makes me look smart" was how he explained it.

His comments produced another round of tears everywhere you looked. He embellished the stories of his adventures with Big Erv and recalled with fondness and a huge smile their greatest achievement.

"It was on a school night," he began but then stopped to catch himself from starting on a laughing spell. "We recruited about half a dozen teammates and picked up a flatbed truck from one of their dads. We rode in the truck out to this milk farm outside of Fresno, near Clovis. Now the guy who owned it was not a football fan—quite the opposite. He'd started a campaign in town to eliminate football at Fresno State. He claimed money for scholarships would be better spent on starting a school of veterinary medicine at the college, claiming that with all the farmers in the San Joaquin Valley, it would serve a greater need than cheering someone scoring a touchback—his words. He appeared on the local TV news every other week, stirring up stuff. We called it something different then," Matt said, unable to prevent a belly laugh from escaping. "Well, we jumped out of the truck like a bunch of commandos and started tipping cows that were standing around near the feed area. In all, I bet we knocked over forty cows. The cows made so much noise trying to get back to their feet that the owner heard the commotion and came running out of his house firing a shotgun, not in the air but directly at us. Our fine offensive guard, forget his name today, took some buckshot in his ass and missed the rest of the season, but we all made it safely back to campus just ahead of the police."

Laughter filled the park.

With Rachel in tears of joy backstage, Matt wrapped up with one final observation. "Back in the day, teammates called him Eraser. As fast as you could snap your fingers, he could erase another student's negative impression of him just as he could help the Bulldogs win a football game by erasing opposition blockers like they were made out of papier-mâché. He was tough as nails on the football field and a real softy in life. He had more cars than any dealer west of the Mississippi and more friends than the IRS has enemies."

He closed the service by pointing to the sky, saying, "If you folks that are entering the Pearly Gates need a good ride for getting around, look up Big Erv. He'll have a steal of a deal with your name on it."

CHAPTER TEN

Rather than return to her condo after the memorial and allow her depression to consume her, Rachel reached out to Devin Braxton and asked him if he had time for a drink before he returned to San Diego. He surprised her again by saying he wasn't going back to San Diego until after the Charros' season opener.

Rachel rode in Devin's rental car and directed him south on 101 to the Olive Road exit and eventually onto Village Coast Road where the hotel was located. The Montecito Inn had been a popular escape destination for hundreds of Hollywood stars over the years. In recent years, it had been promoted as the inn that Charlie Chaplin built. There were silhouette images of Chaplin everywhere on the grounds. Rachel took Devin by the hand and directed the two of them to the cozy café bar that was a patio and garden fountain removed from the hotel's main dining room. Even there, a couple of patrons recognized the former San Diego slugger and asked him to take selfies with them.

"You can't go anywhere without being recognized, can you?"

Devin shook his head. He wore a look of resignation.

"I didn't know you were that big of a star in your day. But then, I didn't follow baseball all that closely."

Devin presented a sheepish grin. "I'll let you off the hook. You were too focused on your volleyball career."

Rachel changed the subject. "I can't tell you how much I appreciate what you're doing for the Charros." She raised her gin and tonic to salute her guest. "It's above and beyond."

Devin waved her off. "I owe it to you for saddling you with Jenks."

"You're right. You do owe me for that," Rachel smiled. "I'd forgotten all about him what with all that's happened in the last week."

Devin swirled his scotch. "There's something new on that front. He's been bounced from the organization."

"No?"

"He had two hookers visit his hotel room this last week of training camp. Jenks and the women got into an argument over payment, and he struck both of them multiple times with his fists. Both women filed complaints with Casa Grande Police. Old man Zeller said that's enough and eighty-sixed him two days ago."

"I can't say I'm disappointed that I don't have to babysit an abusive alcoholic for an entire season." Rachel pretended to wipe sweat off her brow.

Devin leaned back in his chair and produced a pained look on his face. "I'm not sure his replacement is someone you'll want to go steady with either."

"Oh?"

"His name's Dom Benedetti. He's very Italian and very intense— old-school baseball guy. Played for the Chicago White Sox for a couple of years as a utility infielder. He joined the Friars' major league club two years ago as a bullpen coach. He's been bugging me ever since to give him a shot at managing. I finally caved. I liked the way he handled the young players during spring training. He's an accountability guy. Young players as a rule aren't used to being held accountable for their level of play. Hell, they're not used to being accountable for doing their own laundry."

That got a chuckle from Rachel.

"He'll be here Saturday. You should probably sit down with him and lay out your expectations for the team."

The two had managed to go through three rounds of drinks over a period approaching two hours. Rachel wanted to know his opinion of her Honeyball marketing campaign.

Devin produced a broad smile. "A lot of the young players who expected to be sent to Santa Barbara talked about it a lot last week. I think they're all in."

"What about you?"

"As long as it doesn't interfere with the task of developing young baseball talent, I'm all for it. I think it's a great idea. Yours?"

"I wish I could claim it. My marketing director is a budding genius. I was reluctant at first to adopt the campaign, but if it puts butts in the seats, I'm in. It will be interesting to see the response opening night."

Devin put on his reading glasses to peek at the menu. "What motivated you to try the female-only approach? As some of my colleagues in the Friars' front office have said, 'The girls got moxy.'"

Rachel laughed. "I can understand that. While I was still playing volleyball and my dad was starting to make noises about stepping away from his baseball team, I bought tickets to a 'Women Now' expo at the Staples Center in LA. They had some amazing speakers including Hillary Clinton and the Yahoo CEO Marissa Mayer. But the woman who influenced me most was a black woman who'd built a cookie business that she'd started in her home and now has 150 locations in the Midwest. She did it in three years. She preached that if women wanted an equal footing in business or government, they'd have to accept taking risks, and they'd have to accomplish something where the odds were stacked soundly against them." The smile that crossed Rachel's face was wide and warm. "That was the genesis of Honeyball."

The talk eventually moved away from baseball. They laughed over silly things like body tattoos in exotic places. Both of them confessed to having at least one such form of body art but refused to disclose locations. Rachel did confess to getting hers at a body paint expo in Los Angeles. They both agreed that Prius drivers were the worst on the planet—always slowing traffic and uncertain of their direction—and that the Kardashians had one upped the American Dream by becoming famous for doing nothing remotely close to the things that make people famous.

Before embarking on another round of drinks, they decided to have dinner and simply moved across the patio to a crowded café. Once again, Devin was besieged by at least three admirers—all of them men in their sixties.

Devin dined on New York pepper steaks and cognac, while Rachel settled on a seafood salad. They shared a bottle of Silver Oak cabernet.

"What do people around here do for excitement on a Friday night?" Devin asked, taking a last sip of wine.

Rachel was surprised by the suggestion that Devin might want to extend the evening. She closed her eyes while she searched her mind for an answer.

"Ever do karaoke?"

"Once, I tried to do Al Green's 'Let's Stay Together' after Obama tried it, and I crashed and burned." Devin broke into song. "You make me feel so brand new—" He stopped there, and they both laughed loud enough to attract attention from some of the other diners. "Sorry," Devin apologized to those sitting to the couple's immediate left.

Rachel directed Devin to drive back to Santa Barbara to the Red Roof hotel where she knew they held a karaoke night every Friday night. They each ordered an after-dinner drink and watched close to five amateur acts before Rachel said, "We have to do one song."

Devin waved off the suggestion with both hands and a wide-eyed look.

"I dare you." She took him by the hand and forced him to get up from their drink table. "What's your choice, Mr. Home Run Hitter?"

Devin again tried to wave off the idea but was unsuccessful. "You've Lost That Lovin' Feeling." He failed to appear bold about his selection. They performed it as a duo. Devin assumed the role of the deep-voiced Bill Medley—Rachel sang Bobby Hatfield's high parts. They got a very nice round of applause from the assembled hotel guests and partiers when they finished. Someone held up a white paper placemat that contained a handwritten number 10.

By the time they traveled back to Rachel's condo, both were feeling pretty good. They'd consumed enough alcohol that Rachel recommended that Devin not drive back to his hotel.

"I've got a futon in my den. You can sleep there." Rachel started to get out of the passenger door when she felt Devin's meaty hand grab her arm. She instinctively flinched and thought about resisting but didn't. He leaned toward her and then, at the same time, pulled her toward him. He kissed her. Rachel closed her eyes. It was a long and wet kiss. She felt her skin tingle.

Devin suddenly pulled back. "I apologize." His voice was soft. "That was inappropriate."

Rachel smiled and looked directly into Devin's dark eyes. "It wasn't inappropriate, Devin. It was just premature. I need to process it. While I do, the futon is an option for you."

Devin shook his head. "I'm a gentleman. I'll be okay driving back to my hotel."

"Just be careful. I might want to reprise that kiss sometime soon."

CHAPTER ELEVEN

Rachel took lots of deep breaths as she walked up the steps to Dr. Lindholm's two-story Mediterranean-style home to prepare her for the one thing she didn't want to do in the wake of her dad's memorial—sit down again with Dr. Lindholm. She'd taken to wearing a Charros hoodie so that the doctor's neighbors wouldn't recognize her either coming or going. She hated wasting time on things that didn't motivate her. Spending an hour once a week with the doctor was clearly not enlightening her about her inner self, as the doctor had promised during their first meeting.

Dr. Lindholm was late arriving to her office that was located in the back of the house. Rachel waited impatiently in a small room just opposite of her office. When the doctor did arrive ten minutes late, there was not a hint of an apology. Dr. Lindholm wore the exact same patchwork dress as the last time, only this session she went with a white-laced granny top. It only cemented Rachel's earlier conclusion that the good doctor was not a fashion setter—more like a fashion assassin. Rachel made herself a promise that she would never lose touch with clothing trends like Dr. Lindholm.

The first spoken words between the two irritated Rachel.

"Did you complete your homework?" The doctor was not one for small talk.

Rachel had gone with her super casual look—shorts and sandals. It was her way of establishing her turf. It was a statement that said, *I am who I am, and this is how I dress. Live with it.*

She stared directly at the doctor, barely stopping to blink, after taking a seat in the patient's recliner. "I'll be honest with you. I never gave it a thought, Doctor."

Dr. Lindholm slumped back in her chair and raised her eyebrows in a look of mild disgust. "I'm disappointed. You know I can't help you if you don't want to do the work, Rachel. You're wasting my time and yours when you don't follow up on the things I request of you. Is that clear?"

Rachel got to her feet and walked behind her chair and stood with her hands on the headrest. She could tell by the doctor's glare that she was agitated even more.

"Do you have any idea what kind of week I've had?" The veins in Rachel's neck protruded. She realized she was about to unload on the doctor, but she couldn't restrain herself.

Dr. Lindholm exhibited a stoic look. "Perhaps you should enlighten me, Ms. Haslett."

"Rachel, Doctor. Apparently you passed on your homework assignment as well." Rachel took a couple of deep breaths. She was hopeful it would help calm her. "Perhaps you should read the newspaper or watch TV news, Doctor. Even check the local headlines on your smart phone. You know, keep up on current events."

Dr. Lindholm got out of her recliner and walked back to her desk. She sat down on its edge.

"This is not about me. If you're going to be combative, Ms. Haslett, there is no need to proceed today or in the weeks ahead. I thought I'd already made that abundantly clear. You must understand that I have the authority to suspend any court-mandated therapy if the patient is uncooperative. I'll be candid with you. Right now, I'm leaning in that direction. Consider yourself on doctor's probation."

Rachel walked to where the doctor was sitting and got up in her face—their noses almost touching. She raised her voice.

"My father was fucking killed in a fucking plane crash. Haven't you fucking heard?"

Dr. Lindholm remained expressionless and held her composure. "Please sit back down, Ms. Haslett."

Rachel turned and walked back to her recliner and sat on the edge of the seat. "And keep it up with the 'Ms. Haslett' thing if you really want to piss me off."

The doctor pulled out her desk chair and sat down, increasing the distance between the two.

"That little outburst tells me we haven't made much progress with managing your anger. I'm disappointed. I sense your regressing to the angry woman who first walked into this office."

Rachel laughed. "You're right, Doctor. My anger is on steroids at the moment."

"You shouldn't allow your anger over your father's passing to consume you. The pain caused by his death will pass with time. It's incumbent on you to find closure and move on. Only you can give the pain permission to stoke your anger. It's time for you to step up, Rachel."

Rachel laughed again. "I beg to differ with you. My anger won't go away until I find out what happened to my father. It gnaws at me." She described to the doctor the three things she believed could have caused his death.

Dr. Lindholm paused to make some notes on a legal pad. "Do you favor one of the possibilities you've mentioned over the other?" Dr.

Lindholm asked. "It would help me if you could pinpoint the source of your anger for me."

Rachel pushed her body back into the recliner and extended the chair's footrest. "I have three suspects I think could have had a reason to tamper with his plane's engine or who might have hired someone do it for them."

Dr. Lindholm sat up straight and put on her reading glasses as she prepared to make more notes. "So you're leaning in the direction of someone tampering with the plane's engine over pilot error or a physical problem experienced by the pilot?"

Rachel nodded.

"The names of your suspects would be helpful to me. I guessing your brother is one."

"What? Why?"

Dr. Lindholm picked up her notepad as if she were preparing to write down the three names. "The names would never be revealed. I religiously adhere to doctor-patient privilege. Nothing you tell me leaves this room. Ever. But learning who they are might better help me guide you through your troubling crisis."

Rachel immediately shook her head. Her whole face tightened. "Let me see if I have this correct. You want me to reveal the names of individuals who could be suspects if foul play was involved?"

"Yes, that's what I'm asking. Actually, I'm insisting that you do this."

Rachel produced a sarcastic sounding grunt. "Why would I tell you that? That is solely a police matter. Pardon me if I don't appear appreciative of your invasive nature. I can't believe you would ask me that." Rachel stood up. "I think I'm done here, Doctor."

"For today?"

"For good."

Dr. Lindholm put her notepad away in her desk drawer—a sure sign the session was over.

"Even had you not announced your disengagement from me, I don't believe there would have been any reason for me to continue seeing you, Ms. Haslett. You're clearly at odds with my attempts to help you with your issues. You give off the impression that your being here is punishment. In three sessions you've yet to express any remorse for the actions that got you here. Of course, you know what I'm obligated to do once you walk out that door. I will have to notify your probation officer that you are off my grid. You could end up in jail. But that's for you to deal with."

"It's been a pleasure." Rachel words dripped with sarcasm. She gathered her purse and headed for the office exit. "I must have gained some hold on my anger, Doctor, because I have the ammunition to bury your practice on social media, but I won't."

Rachel left the doctor's house with a giant sense of relief. Little did she suspect she would soon regret ditching the respected doctor.

CHAPTER TWELVE

Opening night produced a sensual overload for Rachel, her Honeyball ladies, and the astonishing five thousand fans that attended the game against the San Jose Giants. Three hours before the game, as Rachel approached The Erv on foot, she couldn't help notice the abundance of bunting hanging from everywhere imaginable—parking lot light poles, grandstand railings, stadium light banks, and the merchandise store. It excited her beyond her imagination. It occurred to her that the Charros were suddenly an event and not an afterthought as in past years. Her dad's dream of a new ballpark was all dressed up and pretty and just waiting to be admired by a new generation of Charros' fans.

Upon approaching the ticket window, Rachel was greeted by a group of twenty or more men carrying protest signs, reading, "Singles, not Sex," and chanting, "Baseball, not Honeyball." Most of the men looked to be in their late sixties or early seventies. There was one white-haired man in a walker. Someone later told Rachel they were all from a senior league softball team in town. As soon as the group recognized Rachel, who was wearing the same cutoff shorts that she'd worn in the Honeyball billboard pictures that appeared at five locations around town, they ratcheted up their volume. Rachel clapped for their effort in the hope of diffusing any real animosity among members. She went a step further by speaking with the women running the ticket office and telling them to allow each of the protesters in for free. As a thank-you, the protestors gathered in a group and applauded a smiling Rachel.

Because of all things Erv Haslett and because she'd had to spend most of her day trying to convince her probation officer not to have her locked up for quitting Dr. Lindholm—she was given a week to find a new therapist—Rachel had not found time to meet with her players or her new manager. She actually had an hour that she could have worked them both into her schedule, but she'd taken the time to grab a latte at Starbucks and process the conversation she'd just had with her probation officer. His name was Bernard Coffee. He was in his late thirties. He looked like he had some Pacific Islander in his genes. He was big guy—250 pounds, Rachel guessed—with an ego to match.

From day one, he'd come across as creepy. Rachel felt like he was constantly undressing her with his deep-seeded, shifty dark eyes. He'd often brought an ex-girlfriend's name into their conversations. Claimed she was a porn star he'd met on a trip to San Fernando Valley to visit a friend. On two occasions, he'd actually asked Rachel to come watch his band play at the Ranch House, a honky-tonk bar off Haley Street. He said he was a drummer for The Bad Boyz.

Before heading to the ballpark, Rachel Googled his name, which only confirmed her instincts. She found he'd been placed on a six-month probation after being accused of groping a female client five years ago. He was never formally charged with a crime. From that point on, Rachel vowed never to wear shorts in his presence.

Once at the park, Rachel met first with manager Dom Benedetti. She found him seated in his locker room office wearing the bottom half of his uniform and flip-flops. He was bare-chested and engrossed in filling out his lineup card. He appeared to Rachel to be in great shape for a man in his late fifties. His muscle tone was that of someone who regularly worked out with weights. He was unshaven and his jet-black hair looked like he'd just gotten out of bed.

Rachel popped her head in the office doorway. "Got a minute?"

Benedetti looked up from his lineup card and smiled. He jumped to his feet. "For the boss. You bet."

They exchanged handshakes, and Dom offered her the only other chair in the small room. "Nice new digs, here."

Rachel nodded. "I hope our guys like it. The dressing quarters are twice the size of the old ballpark, and we've got three Jacuzzis. What I'm most proud of is our training center. It was my idea. Every athlete today, no matter the sport, needs to be on a steady regime of in-season weight and fitness training. My training staff is second to none. The head trainer, Angie Rheinhard, worked as an assistant trainer with the Cleveland Indians before I lured her away. And our fitness instructor, Lydia Gregory, is a former Miss *Muscle* Magazine. She got started in training with the Alabama football team. She knows her stuff."

"My boys will love them, ma'am. Figuratively, that is. I can guarantee it."

"Please call me Rachel." The new team general manager took about five minutes to explain to her manager that she was "in it to win it." She told Dom that she had never played a volleyball game that she didn't intend to win, and she wanted that attitude to be the team's mantra in the coming season.

"The Charros are no different. My staff is prepared to foster a winning atmosphere by doing their jobs to the best of their capabilities, and I want to see that carry over to the players."

Dom shook his head in agreement.

Rachel then asked to speak to the players.

The Charros' manager whistled for his players—each in some form of undress—to get clothed and gather around in the main room. After a few awkward moments for Rachel, waiting and watching as the twenty-five players completed the task of dressing for the game, the team finally stood as one in a semicircle ready to meet the boss.

"Welcome to Santa Barbara, guys. It's not the worst place in the world to spend spring and summer—temperatures in the seventies and eighties and plenty of pretty beach girls in bikinis."

"Do you provide maps to Isla Vista?" one of the players, a left-handed relief pitcher asked.

Rachel smiled and shook her head. "You guys learn quick. A word of caution: Stay out of that community if you don't want to become a parent after you leave here in September." She began to pace the room, a sure sign she was pumped for the season to begin. "I know you'll like our new stadium and playing field. Everything that surrounds you while you're here is state-of-the-art. You'll notice when you're taking batting practice that we even have a scoreboard that plays video. Not many class A minor league teams can say that."

She went on to tell them about how she wants a winner and how she wants the player's to carry themselves as professionals on the field and in the community.

"Our personnel director, Robie Sparks, will be taking groups of you to schools throughout the area to interact with young students. You'll be charged with trying to motivate them to do their best in school. Figure on a couple of these field trips a week." Then she addressed the Honeyball marketing campaign and the all-female staff. "In no way is our Honeyball campaign to be perceived as a reflection on you as players. A sports radio talk show guy here in Santa Barbara wrongly surmised the other day—notice I didn't call him an idiot—that our franchise was concealing the image of a perennially lousy baseball team with a tits-and-ass, dog-and-pony show, nothing could be further from the truth. I'm sure you all know by now about our all-female organization. We're committed to making Charros' baseball something special in this town. You do your job on the field, and we'll take care of the rest."

A player raised his hand. His long sandy hair hung to his shoulders. Rachel recognized him from the team's recently taken profile photos as Austin Grant. After seeing him in person—uniform top off, revealing a bare chest with large pecs that appeared to dance when he spoke—she told herself if ever a young athlete had movie star looks and a superstar body, it was this kid.

"Is there some kind of ban on dating any of your ladies, or even you?"

Everyone in the room did their best to cover their laughter in their jersey sleeves.

Rachel smiled. "We're all off-limits, guys."

A groan could be heard coming from Austin Grant and a couple of his teammates standing near him.

"Cocks on locks, fellas!" Dom Benedetti hollered. "Violators will ride the pine," he said, pointing his finger directly at Austin. Laughter swelled throughout the clubhouse.

Rachel dropped her head toward her chest in an effort to bury her smile. "That's one way of putting it." Her face revealed more than a modest blush.

CHAPTER THIRTEEN

The pregame ceremony was spectacular. After both teams had been introduced and had positioned themselves along both baselines, the female public addresser announcer, a morning DJ on KISS radio, called everyone's attention to center field. On cue, a two-foot-by-two-foot RJI drone suddenly appeared, climbing above the outfield fence into the night sky. Once the drone reached a hundred feet, it switched its direction and moved toward home plate.

The woman on the PA enhanced the drama. "Ladies and gentlemen, please welcome Demon the Drone to The Erv."

There was a vigorous applause for the drone. As the object approached home plate and started its descent, fans realized it was carrying a baseball in its underbelly. At that moment, Hector Fuentes, the Charros' catcher, trotted out to home plate and stuck out his catcher's mitt as Demon the Drone dropped the baseball into his glove from a distance of ten feet.

The PA announcer milked the moment. "Charros' fans, you've just witnessed the first drone to ever throw out the first pitch of a baseball season anywhere in America. Let's hear it for history." The sellout crowd went nuts as fireworks crackled and reached for the sky from behind the same center field wall that had concealed the drone.

The game was a crowd pleaser as well, but the result was not what Rachel and her crew had hoped it would be. Austin Grant hit two home runs—one a 410-foot blast to dead center to account for all four of the Charros' runs, but the Giants lit up Santa Barbara closer Winston Sparrow for four runs in the top of the ninth and won it when right fielder Rodney Ellison ignored his cutoff man between first and second on a single by the Giants' number 2 hitter and sailed the ball over Hector Fuentes's head all the way to the backstop. It proved to be the winning run. 5-4 Giants.

Nothing in Rachel's mind could compensate for a win, but beer sales eased the pain. Food and Beverage Director Mimi Scarborough reported her total at just over $15,000.

"Must have been the Isla Vista contingent."

Known as one of the great college party communities in the country, Isla Vista was located right next to the UCSB campus. At least a thousand kids in attendance rocked UCSB sweatshirts or caps. Mimi couldn't contain her excitement. She pumped her fist.

"If we can continue to attract that crowd, we'll be rolling in the black before the all-star break."

After the final out, Rachel decided to pay a visit to the Charros' clubhouse, something she vowed not to make a regular practice—opening night would be her exception. What she found startled her. Most of the players were already dressed and had started to head out. Rachel wore a perplexed look on her face as she passed by Austin Grant.

"Tough loss, but you guys will bounce back."

Austin smirked. "Tell that to your locker room attendant." He pointed in the direction of the players' lounge. Rachel followed his lead and entered the room. She was shocked to see what looked like the aftermath of an earthquake—a 7.3, she guesstimated. Three serving tables were upside down, and there was macaroni and cheese, potato salad, and a fresh fruit salad all over the brand-new carpet.

"Skip's got a temper." It was a voice from outside the door to the lounge. "He hates mental mistakes."

"Where is he?"

"Long gone." Austin had made his way into the lounge.

"Maybe, next time, we'll just leave you guys cookies and milk. This is unacceptable."

Rachel's mood was *not all it could be* as she liked to say as she exited the clubhouse. To her surprise and delight, she found Devin Braxton waiting for her. He was wearing a Friars windbreaker, tight-fitting slacks, and a pair of Nike running shoes. She so wanted to stick him in the Charros' lineup for tomorrow night's game. That's how good he looked. She found his broad, welcoming smile comforting.

"Late night spirits?"

Rachel nodded an emphatic yes. "After what went down in there, I need a wagon load of spirits."

"What happened?" Devin asked, as the two walked toward his rental car in the parking lot.

"Your replacement manager went ballistic over Rodney Ellison's failure to throw to the cutoff man in the ninth inning. The only way the players could have eaten their after game meal was with a dustpan. I'm all for the guy wanting to win, but I can't replace the carpet in there every time we lose a game."

"Despite the loss and despite Dom Benedetti's tantrum, you have to be very pleased with how things went tonight, Rachel."

"There were a couple of glitches with our radio play-by-play person. Her name is Melanie Sandberg. I hired straight out of San Francisco State College where the signal from campus broadcasts barely reaches the student dorms. She's such a cutie. I'll introduce you to her first chance I get. She always has her hair in a ponytail. Her hair is black, but she dyed her bangs blue—team colors. She'd done play-by-play of basketball and football in school but never baseball. I honestly only renewed our contract with KYO because my dad insisted on having a radio presence, even though there were often more people in our restrooms at any given time than were listening at home or in their cars."

"What kind of glitches?"

"I had downloaded the Charros' app, which allowed me to listen in from time to time to Melanie's call on my smart phone. Each time there was a home run, she had a distinctive but eyebrow-raising call. On Austin Grant's rocket homer to left, she said, 'They show in-flight movies on that, baby.' On his blast to center that must have gone 430 feet, she said, 'That ball is high and deep and will arrive at the Sea of Tranquility momentarily.' Not your standard calls. Even I know that."

Devin laughed. "I like it. She's fresh and certainly original."

Rachel smiled. "And she ended the broadcast by saying, 'Thanks for listening. Our final here tonight, Giants, 5. Charros, 4. Shit!"

With Devin still laughing at Rachel's announcer, they headed out on a ten-minute drive to the bar at the Four Seasons Biltmore, Santa Barbara's most exclusive hotel where Devin had been staying.

"That was a great opener," Devin reminded her again. "There was an electricity in the place tonight unlike anything I'd ever seen at the old ballpark."

"I appreciate your thoughts." Rachel ordered the same Rodney Strong Merlot as Devin. "Austin Grant is his own built-in electricity generator. Please tell me again that I can have him for the whole season."

"I don't go back on a promise. He's yours. Just watch out for him. Word is, he's quite the ladies' man."

Rachel laughed. "He's a boy."

"And you're an attractive woman."

Rachel inhaled deeply before taking another sip of wine. She wasn't quite sure how to process his remark. "So you're back to the grind tomorrow."

"Yep." Devin loosened his tie. "We open in Denver in two days. I need to be there. Are you going to be all right with all that's going on in your life?"

Rachel dropped her chin toward her chest for a second and then glanced back up at Devin, catching his eyes directly in line with hers.

"I have to. There's too much at stake here. Perhaps when we get on the road to Visalia next week, I can catch my breath."

Devin ordered a second round of wine for the two of them.

"Do you think you'll be able to put your father's death on the back burner anytime soon?"

Rachel started to tear up, and her voice turned shaky. "Never. I have to find out why he crashed and died. It's keeping me up nights. I don't know how I'm going to do it, but I'm going to do it."

Devin turned and squared himself in front of Rachel on their respective bar stools. He reached for and took her hands in his.

"You have my two administrative assistants as long as you want them. It's just a little something I can do to help with your burden."

Rachel exhaled deeply again and smiled softly. "Would you consider repeating your inappropriate behavior with me this evening?" She surprised herself with her candor.

Devin's eyebrows rose. "Whew, in a heartbeat. My place or yours?"

Rachel took him by the elbow. "We're already at yours."

They finished their wine and retired to Devin's suite where they made love until sun up.

CHAPTER FOURTEEN

Troy Haslett was wound pretty tight after two nights without sleep, thanks to a weekend-long cocaine binge with an old buddy from city college who'd gone on to become a respected assistant director in Hollywood. Troy had always been reluctant to hang out with anyone who'd become successful in life, but Richard Hurley had been the exception largely because he didn't take himself or what he'd accomplished too seriously. He'd recently passed up the opportunity to attend the Golden Globe Awards for a movie he'd worked on to go surfing in Chile.

Troy had already smoked a half pack of cigarettes, Marlboro red, and it wasn't yet ten in the morning. His lungs felt like someone had reached inside him and put a strangle hold on them. He'd chosen to walk south along East Beach as a warm-up to his next scheduled stop—Jessie Santiago's Montecito bungalow.

His long, now mostly blond hair—he'd bleached it himself—lofted in the breeze blowing in from the Channel Islands to the west as he wandered south along the beach, dodging the foamy residue of incoming waves as he went. He'd headed in the direction of a long section of cliffs where most beach goers didn't walk because of the massive amounts of seaweed that always seemed to come ashore there. It provided him the privacy he sought. His thoughts, as he stopped occasionally to skip seashells off the incoming broken waves, were immersed in his seemingly never-ending dilemma of what to do with his life. He'd come to the concession that it was time for him to grow up and become a productive member of society. He just struggled with the idea of how. He had no foundation on which to build.

About a mile into his walk, his cargo shorts soaked from the surf, he turned around and headed back toward his starting point. He was disturbed that he still hadn't managed to capture the ocean's healing vibe and get his head completely straight. He really wanted to have a sharp mind when he met with Jessie. They had both agreed it would not be a good idea to be seen meeting in a public place so soon after his father's death.

They weren't strangers to one another. During a dinner out six months ago with Erv and Troy, Jessie talked Erv into letting her train Troy. She'd promised Erv—she never liked the notion of calling him Big Erv—she could, through a good fitness regimen, help get him on a positive track with life.

"A fit body makes for a fit mind" was how she put it. Another of her favorite sayings was "The body is the temple of the spirit." Erv agreed and paid for Jessie to work with Troy for an hour at a time three days a week. Troy didn't scoff at the opportunity to observe Jessie's killer body firsthand. After a week of her sessions, he was sure he got more exercise fighting off a hard-on than he did from the drills she'd put him through. Oftentimes, when they'd worked out together, Troy would try to image being in his dad's skin having sex with Jessie. He was mesmerized by the sexual aura she produced. Everything about her—her deep-set hazel eyes, full lips, killer figure, and most important, her vibrant body language—all said "fuck me" to Troy.

In one his few seemingly lighter moments in the company of his dad, Troy asked Big Erv if he could fill in one time with Jessie. Big Erv struck him with his fist. It was a miracle he hadn't broken his son's nose.

Jessie had called Troy earlier in the week saying she had something to discuss with him and that it pertained to his father. Troy was a little nervous as he rang the doorbell to her bungalow which was located just a couple of blocks from the Four Season's Biltmore. Troy didn't know Jessie all that well, but he did know that she was fond of saying, "I live not far from Oprah." In truth, Oprah couldn't store her beauty aids in a place the size of Jessie's.

Once inside the tiny bungalow, Troy was surprised to find more workout equipment than furniture—a treadmill, elliptic trainer, and step climber. The step climber exhibited fresh sweat stains. She later told him that she didn't like working out in front of clients at the gym.

"Too many creepy eyes on me. I had one guy actually grab my ass while I was doing pull-ups. 'I've been dreaming about doing that since I became a member' was his justification."

Jessie had a bottle of Argentine Malbec waiting for the two of them. It would not serve as a remedy for the condition in which Troy found himself.

"I'd take you on a tour of my home, but this is it." She smiled, waving an open-faced palm at her cramped living room.

Even for an innocuous business meeting, Jessie couldn't or wouldn't—Troy wasn't sure which—hide her sexy. She wore cutoff jeans an old UCSB T-shirt and sandals, filling out her rather skimpy attire in all the right places. Troy was instantly self-conscious of being caught staring at her firm nipples that seemed to be aggressively pressing against her T-shirt for recognition.

"So what's this all about, Jessie?" He was still upset that his mind wasn't 100 percent drug free.

Jessie poured Troy's wine glass half full then took a seat at the opposite end of her brown leather couch.

"It's business, Troy." Jessie paused to inhale. "I wanted to let you know, before you heard about it from somebody else, that your dad had me listed as the sole beneficiary in his life insurance policy. I met with his attorney yesterday, and he gave me a copy of the documents." She reached for a handful of papers that had been placed on the end table next to her. "You can see for yourself—the amount, $300,000."

Troy's sleepy eyes lit up. "All to you? But—"

"Yes, but I have a plan that will reward you as well."

"What about my sister?"

"Someone has to lose out. It's her. She's fully capable of taking care of her own financial well-being. That's your dad's thinking, not mine. Besides, he told me she'd set herself a salary of $150,000 to run the baseball club."

Troy placed his untouched glass on Jessie's coffee table that was constructed out of driftwood she'd retrieved from the beach near the Coral Casino, a forties era pool and spa that had attracted many a Hollywood celebrity in its heyday.

"I could have made some money there if she hadn't decided on hiring skirts for every single aspect of the organization. I'm a really good graphic artist. I could have helped with marketing. Nooo! She calls it Honeyball. I call it dikes and spikes."

Jessie laughed and got up from the couch and started pacing the small room—end to end. "Here's what I want to do with that money and how it involves you."

Troy smiled for the first time since he'd arrived. "You have my undivided attention, Ms. Jessie."

Jessie turned her nose up at his reference to miss. "Don't call me that again," she said. "It makes me feel old." She had a way of unnerving anyone when she put on her stern face.

"Okay," Troy said meekly.

"All right, here's my concept. I want to create a TV fitness show that is cohosted by a male and female. No one else does that. I'm going to call it *Slo-Go Fit* after the growing fad of lifting weights in ultraslow motion. This new method burns fat at a far faster rate than traditional weight lifting. *Slo-Go* calls for reps that last twenty seconds as opposed to from two to six seconds for the traditional rep. Going slow fatigues a greater number of muscle fibers, and that's the key to the concept's success. It increases a person's metabolism, which causes you to burn more fats and calories all day long."

Troy was struck by the energy Jessie expended just talking about her new concept. He wiped the back of his hand across his forehead to get rid of the sweat his body was experiencing just listening to her.

"It's a killer workout that lasts twenty minutes, and a person only needs to do it twice a week. And the best part is you can do it at home, thus the TV show. I passed my certification test last week in San Diego. That's why I couldn't make your dad's memorial."

"I didn't either."

"That's a discussion for another time, Troy." Jessie propped herself up on the seat of spinning bike which he hadn't noticed before. "I have a former client who's now vice president of Langly-Hoffman in LA. His company produces and syndicates shows to TV stations throughout the country. He's on board with my concept. Truthfully, I think he believes he's going to get in my shorts in return for putting up the money for the show."

Troy's eyebrows had climbed up his forehead. "Why me?"

"Because there isn't a fitness show out there with a male and female host. Hey, I don't mind sharing celebrity. And when I get through with you in the next series of training sessions, you'll be the most handsome, most cut, most tanned guy on TV. You'll wet women's pussies from Long Beach to Long Island and that young man, translates into ratings."

"What's in it for me besides exposure? You can't live off being good-looking."

Jessie laughed. "Not that you haven't done that so far."

Troy did not smile at her attempt at humor.

"I'll pay you a salary the same as your sister is paying herself."

"One fifty?"

"Yes? Deal?"

Troy got off the couch and walked to the front window. He stared out at the traffic on 101 for a moment.

"Deal. What have I got to lose?"

Jessie got off the bike, shook Troy's hand, and then gave him a giant hug. "I thought you'd see it that way."

Troy held onto the hug longer than he knew he should have.

CHAPTER FIFTEEN

Comfortable in a Charros windbreaker, shorts, and sandals, Rachel occupied her customary box seat directly behind home plate for the second game of the four-game set with the Giants. She was rapidly approaching celebrity status in her hometown as fans continuously recognized her and approached her box seeking autographs. She was enjoying a beer and basking in the thrill of a second straight sellout crowd. The woman largely responsible for the robust attendance, promotions director Holly Redman, was seated next to her. The two girls Devin Braxton had loaned the Friars sat in the remaining two seats in the box. A pregame "Smash for Cash" promotion had again brought out a young crowd—again, many wearing UCSB gear.

Before the start of the game, a beat-up Chevy truck, nineties vintage, was brought out, and three fans with lucky ticket numbers were invited to throw a baseball at the front headlights of the truck from a distance of sixty feet. Each contestant got two tosses. Each time a headlight was shattered, the contestant would receive a hundred dollars. A short hefty young woman, who identified herself as a PE teacher at Santa Maria High School, seventy miles from Santa Barbara, knocked out both headlights and picked up a check for $200. The crowd cheered her wildly.

Everyone in Rachel's box was happy. It was only the fourth inning, and the Charros had built a 5-0 lead, chasing the Giants' starting pitcher in the process, despite his being timed on the radar gun at ninety-eight miles per hour a couple of times. Austin Grant had blasted another monster home run to drive in three. In less than eighteen innings, he'd become a hometown hero. After his home run, Madeline Rossberg, in concessions, reported that a dozen of his number 4 jerseys had been sold between innings.

Just prior to the start of the fifth inning, Rachel received a text from the head of ballpark security.

"Ur brother is here. No tix. Belligerent."

Rachel quickly excused herself and made her way to the main ticket window at the entrance to the stadium. There, she found Troy, a tattooed female friend whose exposed arms looked like murals, and Security Chief Bad News Brown—he preferred that to Charles. Rachel immediately assessed that Troy was high on something. His eyes were glossy, and his balance was compromised.

"So you're refusing to pay, little brother?" Rachel reached out and grabbed him by his open jacket.

"Get your hands off me, sis."

Bad News stepped closer to Troy undoubtedly, anticipating that things might get physical.

Rachel released her hands from Troy's jacket and placed them on her hips while getting her face up in his.

"We have a complimentary ticket policy here. You, as my only sibling, can attend anytime you want, but you must request your tickets twenty-four hours in advance just like everyone else. I've yet to see such a request cross my desk. You and your circus lady will have to come back another night. Please, Bad News, escort these two out."

Troy flipped off his sister and, with an assist from Bad News's meaty hand on his jacket collar, headed in the direction of the front gate.

"I didn't come to see your sorry-ass-team lose. Just came to tell you I got a job. Jessica Santiago is using Dad's insurance settlement to pay me."

By the time Troy was finished with his bombshell, he and his lady friend had reached the parking lot. Rachel considered chasing after them to get a better understanding of what he'd said, but she decided against it when she heard the home crowd roar over what she figured was something good happening for the Charros.

The final score was 9-0 as Santa Barbara registered its first-ever win under the Charros' banner. Number 2 pitcher, Joe Bledsoe, had tossed eight innings of two hit balls, and the Charros had touched five Giants' pitchers for thirteen hits. Rachel visited the locker room to give both the team and manager, Dom Benedetti, a shout out and then quietly disappeared from the complex with the sole intention of going home and sorting out what Troy had said about her dad's insurance situation. She couldn't be sure that even after a couple of glasses of merlot that she would be able to get her head around the reality of Jessie receiving her dad's blessings over her. Or was Troy just messing with her again and making up the story?

CHAPTER SIXTEEN

In recent years, Rachel had taken a disliking to having to weave her way through the homeless to walk the sidewalks of State Street, but her dad's attorney's office was located right in the heart of Downtown Santa Barbara at State and Figueroa, second floor, the law firm of Sutton, Satterfield, and Pennington. Despite the city's efforts to reduce the numbers—mostly men—on the street, the homeless problem had only gotten worse in recent years. To Rachel, it felt like they were everywhere, mumbling, talking, and sometimes yelling mostly at imaginary passersby. The city had put in a number of benches along the street's sidewalks for the comfort of shoppers, but the homeless had commandeered them as beds in the evenings and pulpits for their innocuous rantings in the daytime.

"Mr. Sutton will be with you in a minute," the young woman at the front desk advised Rachel shortly after she pushed through the heavy glass door to the law firm's suite. Rachel assumed the girl was the office secretary. She wore tinted glasses and had jet-black hair with the ends dyed pink. Rachel thought she was a bit too millennial for the button-down Andrew Sutton.

Rachel broke with custom and wore a bright orange sundress for the occasion. She figured her dad would want her dressed respectfully for a man of Sutton's stature. She nervously fidgeted with her purse as she sat directly across the secretary who was busy texting someone on her phone. When she finally got the okay that Andrew Sutton was ready for her, she took a deep breath and moved in the direction of the door to his office.

Andrew Sutton was standing in front of his large cherrywood desk. He greeted her with open arms as if he had every intention of hugging Rachel. He did, and then after the hug, he continued to hold onto her shoulders.

"How long has it been since I last saw you in here with your dad? Fifteen years? Twenty?"

Rachel smiled, a little taken aback by the warmth of his greeting. "At least twenty-five." Rachel purposely backed away from his outstretched arms. "I know I was ten, and my dad wanted you to represent me against some surfing competition promoter who hadn't let me compete in the city championships because I was too young."

The attorney motioned for her to take a chair directly in front of his desk.

"I do remember that now that you mention it, Rachel. Is it okay if I call you Rachel? It always used to be 'young lady'."

"Rachel's fine."

"I thought it would be." He adjusted his rather sedate-looking brown and tan tie. Andrew Sutton was in his midsixties and had gray hair that was closely cropped—Ivy League style. He wore a stylish pair of reading glasses and looked to Rachel as if he were in great physical shape—no belly popping through his dress shirt and no suggestion of a second chin.

"I wish you were here under better circumstances," he said, fumbling through a manila folder stacked full of documents.

"How much better?"

"Considerably."

"I think I'm afraid to find out, Mr. Sutton."

Andrew Sutton moved behind his desk and sat down. "I believe you should sit down as well, Rachel." His eyes were now focused on the documents, and the pleasantness was gone from his face.

Rachel crossed her legs and sighed loud enough for Andrew Sutton to notice. "Did Jessie get everything?"

Andrew Sutton took off his glasses and sat back in his chair. "Just about, Rachel. Your dad's estate was recently valued at close to $45 million. His will calls for Jessie Santiago to receive almost everything." He studied Rachel for a response—nothing at first. "He didn't leave Troy anything either."

Rachel put her hand to her mouth to block a gasp. She shook her head and then tossed her hair back. "And his life insurance?"

"Ms. Santiago." Sutton wore a sheepish look.

"Did he leave me anything?" Her voice cracked as she spoke.

Andrew Sutton drew his fingers on his chin. "Some stocks and this letter." He handed the one-page letter to Rachel, who read it immediately.

Dearest Rachel,

I'm hoping you won't be upset when you learn the contents of my will, but I would understand if that was, in fact, the case. I'm hoping that, in the end, you will take the small amount I'm leaving you as a compliment. You are most capable of sustaining yourself financially of all those named in my will. I've never worried about your surviving in this sometimes difficult world. What I'm leaving you is one more challenge—I know it's what drives you. I'm hoping that what I'm certain you will perceive as a slight will motivate you to accomplish even greater things.

I left your brother out completely. Maybe it will motivate him to become somebody. He is the biggest disappointment of my life. Jessie is a fitness trainer barely making enough to survive on her own. Money may be the reason she's hooked up with me, but I truly do love her, and she has made the autumn of my life a joy beyond words.

I'm leaving you my small stock portfolio and, of course, the baseball team. I know you'll convert the Charros into a money-making enterprise, which will draw a much more decent price tag in the future should you decide to sell it.

Please know that you are my pride and joy. I only wish it would be you to carry on the Haslett name. Be strong, my princess, and go with your incredible determination into a bright new and promising future.

Love always,
Dad

Rachel crumbled the letter in both hands and bit hard on her lip to prevent herself from crying in the presence of Andrew Sutton.

"Would you like to contest the will, Rachel? I think giving everything to a nonfamily member would be regarded by any probate judge as unusual and worthy of a challenge."

Rachel reached for her purse and stood to leave. "I'm a fighter, Mr. Sutton. If Jessie Santiago doesn't know that by now, she's in for a surprise."

CHAPTER SEVENTEEN

Rachel was so depressed from learning the details of her dad's will that she called in sick for the Charros' final game of their eight-game home stand. She'd never had a sick day in her life—not in school, not on the volleyball tour. She just wanted to be at home, alone. She pulled down all the curtains in her condo and silenced her perpetually active DVD player. She sat in her lone love seat and cried until she eventually fell asleep.

It was an inopportune time for her to go MIA. The Charros had a six-game winning streak going, and the excitement over their outstanding play had generated two more sellout crowds. Austin Grant had upped his home run total to six in seven games, and the Alpha Chi Omega sorority from UCSB had started an Austin Grant Fan Club. They brought multiple signs to the Charros' most recent games that read, "Please *Grant* Us *Austin* for a Night."

Rachel had been anxious for the final game of the four-game set against High Desert because Holly Redman was running out a unique promotion. It was publicized as a free transistor radio night, and she'd been looking forward to seeing how it played out. Rachel had wanted it to make it a free radio app night for mobile devices, but Holly had talked her into buying five hundred transistor radios—she'd found them for the rock bottom price of $5 on eBay—as part of a "Throwback Thursday Night" event.

"We're going old school," Holly told top Honeyball staff members. She predicted the transistor radios would be a hit because only a few old folks in attendance would have ever owned one. "Dinosaurs are us," she'd said to the *Santa Barbara Independent* reporter, who'd previewed the giveaway in the entertainment section the day before.

Rachel awoke from her sleep not long before the seven thirty start of the Charros-High Desert game. Her first order of business was to gather herself emotionally. She opened all the curtains thinking light would help bring her out of her darkness, but the sun had gone down, and it was near dark outside. Her long cry had helped, and she tapped her seldom-used Xanax prescription to help bring her the rest of the way back. She checked the time on her microwave and tuned into KYO for the broadcast.

Melanie proved to be in rare form. Rachel figured her slightly outrageous observations might have been sparked by the fact so many fans in the stands were tuned in. Rachel could hear the crowd's response to her in the background. The first three innings of the broadcast alone produced a half dozen "what did she just say" moments. When Dom Benedetti pulled his shortstop, Omar Escobar aside in the dugout after he'd been picked off first base, Melanie said, "Boy, the Charros' skipper is ripping Omar a new one. Somebody get out the Johnson and Johnson."

After the High Desert leadoff man poked a single between first and second base, she said, "That seeing-eye grounder was basically a bitch slap hit." In the background, Rachel could hear the crowd laughing. Shortly after Charros' catcher, Hector Fuentes, took a fastball in the dirt to his privates, she said, "After that shot, Hector's cohunes will float in water." On a fly ball to left field where the

Charros' Brad LeClaire had difficulty judging and turned back and forth on the ball twice while running it down, she said, "LeClaire just went through more change of directions than a pizza delivery guy." That got the biggest response from the young crowd.

Rachel figured it was time to get dressed and get over to the ballpark. She was determined to reel in Melanie before sponsors started blowing up her phone with their objections. What she found surprised her no end. In between the fourth inning, a dozen or so young people had gathered in front of Melanie's open-air booth and were requesting her autograph on her picture in the Charros' program. This continued during every half inning until the game ended. Melanie Sandberg had become an icon in the two hours and forty minutes it took her to broadcast another Charros' victory.

The only sponsor calls Rachel took the next day were from those who wanted permission to use Melanie's voice in future radio ads. One phone inquiry about Melanie stood out from the rest. It was Jessie Santiago. She'd begun with an apology of sorts.

"I'm so sorry your dad was so stingy to you and Troy in his will. I really don't know what to say to you."

And OJ's still searching for the real killer, Rachel thought to herself. "You're calling about—"

"Your radio announcer. She's great. I'm looking for a female voice over announcer for my new TV show, and I think she'd be perfect."

Rachel was now fully convinced she was lying about Melanie and using her as an opportunity to stick a knife deep into her back. Rachel pretended she had an incoming call and had to take it. She hung up, not wanting to ever hear more from Jessie ever.

"Bitch."

CHAPTER EIGHTEEN

Rachel viewed the Charros' first road trip—eight games in nine days—as a blessing. She'd decided to step back from all things Charros and stay home. She desperately wanted to focus on trying to find a strategy for finding out what had caused her dad's plane to crash. With so much of his estate going to Jessie, Rachel had an uneasy feeling in the pit of her stomach. It had found a resting place there and wouldn't give it up.

Did she have something to do with his crash? She'd wondered more than once. *And why hadn't she gone with him on his trip to Eureka? She'd made almost every one of his trips since they started dating.* Those thoughts had been haunting her ever since her visit with Andrew Sutton.

Her day started with a healthy breakfast of fresh cut fruit and a voice mail from Adrienne Telfair.

"We're on the road, and all is well" was the message she left. Shortly after that, she received a much-appreciated text from Devin Braxton.

"Great start. Can't wait to see u again."

The words gave Rachel goose bumps. She couldn't wait to see him again either. The sex at the Biltmore had been the best Rachel had ever experienced. She couldn't deny it if she'd wanted to. Even though he was an admitted adulterer, she wanted more of Devin Braxton and soon. He represented what she'd long thought a man should be. He was a powerful man who could be soft when soft was needed.

It wasn't nine o'clock yet, and Rachel was still in her white terrycloth bathrobe that carried the ABVP logo on the left pocket when the phone rang. She recognized the number on her caller ID as being a Denver area code. Her mom's sister lived there. Surely it wasn't her calling. Not even her mom had recognized her former husband's tragic death.

A woman spoke. "I'm calling for Rachel Elizabeth Haslett," she said, sounding very much like someone with a smoker's voice.

"This is she."

"Good. I'm Virginia Westphall with the National Transportation's Safety Board regional office in Denver." A deep cough caused her to pause.

"Yes." Rachel couldn't think of anything else to say.

"I'm calling to inform you that in the next three to five business days, you will be receiving a forty-page accident report on the crash that took your father's—"

Rachel interrupted the caller. "But you didn't authorize a salvage mission to find his plane's fuselage."

"Please let me finish. Our report includes airplane components, systems and records, meteorological information, communications, pilot response, pilot's fitness, flight tracking, and post-accident safety actions."

The woman sounded as if she were imitating those robotic phone calls that annoyed Rachel so much during elections. Her voice volume went up a notch as her frustration became apparent.

"Without the fuselage, how can you tell me anything I don't already know, Ms.—"

"Westphall. It's impossible for us to conduct a salvage operation on every plane crash. We don't have the necessary financial resources. Usually, salvage operations are conducted only in the cases of commercial air carriers and private planes with multiple passengers."

"So again, you're calling me to tell me what I already know."

The caller paused for a second. "To the contrary, I'm calling to tell you that each year we place single fatality plane crashes into a kind of lottery database. Twice each year, we do a random drawing of five case numbers for fulfillment. Your father's case number has been selected, and I'm pleased to tell you that a U.S. Coast Guard salvage boat currently based in San Francisco, equipped with the very latest sonar equipment, will be dispatched within the coming weeks to attempt to locate the wreckage. We're committed to helping determine what went wrong. We have a splashdown coordinates that will give the salvage ship a pretty strong indication of where the craft went down." Ms. Westphall paused again. "Do you have any questions?"

Rachel was silent for a few seconds. "How will I know when this is taking place, and how long after the fuselage is recovered will you have information for me?"

"You'll be notified by me as soon as a recovery is completed. The study to determine cause takes a few weeks or so. I promise to keep you abreast of our process."

"Can I rent a boat and shadow the salvage boat so I have a firsthand account of the effort?"

"It's not recommended."

"Neither is nose diving into the Pacific Ocean."

"I've never been asked that question before. I'll have to get back to you on a ruling from the coast guard."

Ms. Westphall again paused for more than a few seconds. "I was hopeful you would be overjoyed with the news I've just provided you, Ms. Haslett, but you don't give me the impression that you are."

Rachel's voice started to quiver. "Please don't take me wrong. I do appreciate what the NTSB is offering. It's just that I never expected it. Thank you."

Rachel began to cry and apologized for it before hanging up.

CHAPTER NINETEEN

Bad news seemed to be on an equal footing with good news for Rachel. After meticulously checking herself out in her bedroom mirror (black shorts, red bikini top, Foster Grants, and Charros baseball cap), she pronounced herself set for a long mentally rehabilitating run on the beach.

Just as she was about to exit the front door to her condo, the doorbell rang. It startled her as she was not accustomed to many visitors and hated solicitors. After peering through the door's peephole, she reluctantly opened it.

"Mr. Coffee." Rachel wore an embarrassed look. She asked for a few minutes to change out of her running attire into jeans and a Charros jersey. When she was dressed, she let Mr. Coffee in the front door. He took up almost all the door space.

"No, I haven't found a new therapist yet, sir," Rachel confessed first thing. She dropped her head toward her chest, accentuating her failing.

Bernard Coffee was informally dressed—muscle shirt, jeans, and sandals. The shirt accented his huge biceps. Previously he'd always worn a suit. His appearance served as a red flag for Rachel. Mr. Coffee fashioned a smirk as he addressed Rachel.

"I gave you a week to find another therapist, Ms. Haslett. I thought I made it clear that I'm not playing games."

Rachel shook her head. "You did. I just haven't had a spare moment. But now that the team is on the road, I'm planning on taking care of that oversight, Mr. Coffee." Without carefully editing her words, Rachel laughed and said, "Wasn't Joe DiMaggio the original Mr. Coffee, Mr. Coffee?"

Bernard Coffee pushed out a laugh, his big chest expanding. "Do you realize how many times I've had that asked of me?"

"Sorry," Rachel said. "It was just me being silly. Listen, I have a Dr. Thomas Marmar on my 'to call' list. He's a referral from one of the women who works for my baseball team. I'll get to it as soon as we're done talking. I promise." Rachel invited Coffee to take a seat on her couch. He was already in the process of doing just that without the invitation.

Coffee then turned the tables and motioned for Rachel to have a seat. Rachel was taken aback by his boldness.

"I have a proposition for you, Ms. Haslett. How about we strike a deal?"

"Deal?"

Beads of sweat suddenly appeared on Coffee's forehead, and his accelerated breathing was noticeable.

"How about I report your three visits with that other shrink as the required ten? I'll make up dates reflecting that you satisfactorily completed your court-ordered requirement. It's just a paperwork issue."

Rachel leaned back against the arm of her couch and advanced a puzzled look on her face. "In exchange for?"

Coffee grinned, readjusted himself in his seat, produced a sheepish grin, and then pointed with his index finger at the area where his cock resided.

"Fifteen minutes sucking on this guy should seal the deal." He patted his crotch with his big right hand. "It's bigger than a railroad spike and spits out pure protein. You should look upon it as a health product."

Rachel laughed sarcastically as she stood up. "Do you realize how many times that's been asked of me?"

Coffee stood up as well, an indication he figured he wasn't going to get what he'd come for. "I doubt anyone else had the hammer that I have, Ms. Rachel."

"In a million years I wouldn't put my mouth on you, Coffee, unless it was to bite off your limb."

Coffee executed a false grimace.

"And what's to prevent me from reporting this to your supervisor?"

"Who do you think staff is going to believe? Me or someone whose been convicted of assault and has not completed her mandated anger management treatment?"

Rachel reached in her back pocket for her cell phone. "You've got ten seconds, and I hit 911."

Coffee didn't flinch and instead sauntered to the door, smiling as he moved. He even chuckled a bit to himself.

"Better give that Dr. Marmar a ring soon, girl."

Rachel was sickened by Bernard Coffee's attempted bribe. Her skin felt slimy; her face burned, and she had a case of instant cottonmouth. Only one other time had she felt so violated, and that was year's ago at her high school's Harvest Moon dance. Her date, who was a freshman in college—two years her senior—threatened to drop her off in the foothills, miles from her home, if she wouldn't have sex with him in his car in the school parking lot. Rachel escaped from his car by striking him directly on his member with her fist and running back to the school cafeteria where the dance was being held. She told a chaperone who called police. They investigated but eventually said they had no case based on evidence.

Frustrated and feeling psychologically abused, Rachel made a phone call that a couple of weeks ago she'd never have considered making. She rang Devin Baxter and asked if he'd mind her hanging out with him for a couple of days. She said she needed a friend, and he told her she'd called the right number.

"I'll arrive at six o'clock on Southwest," she said, giving away the telling fact that she'd already booked a flight.

"I'll be at the ballpark at that time, Rachel, but I'll have one of the gals in my office pick you up and bring you to my suite." Devin paused for a second. "I'm so glad you called. I can't wait to see you."

"Me too. I'll have my fingers crossed your game tonight doesn't go extra innings."

The taxi ride to Santa Barbara Airport wasn't fast enough for Rachel's liking. "Can you step on it?" she asked the driver who was Indian and spoke poor English.

"Am go limit. No faster."

"I have to be on my plane in fifteen minutes, so please hurry."

The taxi driver waved his hand to indicate he would not comply with her wish. Once her taxi finally reached the terminal, Rachel jumped out of the cab and tossed two $20 bills at the driver through the passenger window. She sprinted into the building and was thrilled to find the line at security was only a couple of passengers deep. She quickly whipped out her ID card and presented it along with her boarding pass to a short portly TSA agent. He inspected it carefully.

"Please hurry. They're boarding my plane."

No sooner had she finished her sentence than a Santa Barbara County sheriff's deputy confronted her from behind. "Are you Rachel Elizabeth Haslett?" the deputy, who was broad shouldered and buffed, asked.

"I am. Why?"

The deputy grabbed Rachel by her arm. "I have a warrant for your arrest, miss."

"For?"

"A violation of probation. You'll have to come with me."

Rachel used her purse to cover as much of her face as possible as she was escorted to a waiting sheriff's vehicle outside the terminal.

"You've got to be kidding!" It was all Rachel could think to say to the deputy.

As the deputy pushed down on her head to clear the door space for his prisoner, the deputy said, "Do I look like a kidder to you, ma'am?"

CHAPTER TWENTY

Troy figured Jessie's credit cards must have been sizzling inside the wallet she carried in her fanny pack—a novelty travel item that had recently become passé. The cards, Troy learned had only been issued two days ago. Not only had she covered the down payment on a new burgundy Mercedes AMG GT S—she used three separate cards for that—but she'd also purchased a complete line of UjENA beachwear and booked and paid for flights to Puerto Vallarta for herself, Troy, and Halleck Stanley, her former client and the current vice president of the Hollywood TV production company that was interested in producing and distributing her show *Slo-Go Fit*. She had also made reservations for the three of them at the Four Seasons Resort in Punta Mita, a world-class five-star hotel located some forty-five miles north of Puerto Vallarta International Airport, that featured a golf course that boasts the world's only natural island green. Hole 3B requires a watercraft to putt out.

Why not mix pleasure with business? That was how Jessie's thought process had worked recently—ever since she'd seen her name in Ervin Haslett's will. She was able to advance the car purchase only after showing the general manager of the Mercedes dealership her legal documents.

Troy had pushed the Mercedes's passenger seat back as far as it would go to where he was lounging for the better part of a two-hour ride from Montecito to LA. Jessie had chosen to drive to the airport in LA rather than take a late afternoon flight—one of only a couple scheduled out that day—from Santa Barbara's small airport.

Troy, who was being entertained by his smart phone music selections—mostly John Mayer stuff and for nostalgia, Neil Diamond—desperately wanted to smoke a joint, but he feared that would ruin the Mercedes's new car smell, which he knew wouldn't go over well with Jessie or any new car buyer for that matter. He also figured he'd have to sneak his *maryjo* consumption during the entire trip so as to not alert Jessie to the fact that he wasn't as serious as she would want him to be about his fitness training and overall fitness in general.

"What if my sister contests my dad's will?" Troy asked as Jessie guided her shiny new car up the Conejo Grade just south of Camarillo on Highway 101. "You're laying out all this money like that could never happen, but I know my sister. She's always been up for a fight whether it was for a wave, a volleyball game, or who got the biggest slice of the birthday cake. I remember when she was in middle school somebody stole her bike. She hunted for that bike for a month, from one end of town to the other, and damned if she didn't find it abandoned in a bike rack out on Stearns' Wharf."

Jessie smiled and placed her hand on Troy's bare thigh just below his shorts. "Those documents are golden, Troy. I had my attorney review them inside out, and he tells me their full proof. I'm just borrowing on the good times that are sure to come." She checked the rearview mirror for a CHP vehicle as she had her speedometer pegged at eighty-five miles an hour.

The AeroMéxico flight to Puerto Vallarta was uneventful, save for a flight attendant who inexplicably passed out while serving peanuts and for the nanosecond that the plane was over the Baja peninsula when Jessie turned in her seat toward Troy, leaned her head on his shoulder, and confidently slid her hand over his crotch. She squeezed his package ever so briefly and then took her hand away.

Jessie's act gave Troy a hard-on that he seriously worried would last more than four hours. He squirmed in his seat and then unfastened and fastened his seat belt in an attempt to deflect attention from the giant bulge in his pants. She had lit a fire in him, and he knew it would burn for the entire trip if he didn't do something about it. Jerking off was not an immediate option. He finally conceded that all he'd had to do was look at her amazing body, and an erection was sure to result. He silently wondered if this Mexican trip would see him wind up with the worst case of "blue balls" he'd ever experienced— the kind that sends a guy to ER. He even tried to picture what an ER would look like in Mexico. "Would the drugs be delivered by burros?" he asked himself.

Upon arriving by taxi at their destination set comfortably on the Pacific Ocean with giant palm trees dotting the landscape as far as one could see, they were greeted by attendants who took their luggage and offered them margaritas in decretive glasses. Troy tossed his down in two gulps, a sure sign he was a little nervous about how the accommodations would be arranged, plus he was a little intimidated by the atmosphere of a five-star resort. He'd never stayed at anything fancier than a Holiday Inn Express largely because his dad had never taken him anywhere.

Jessie had another surprise for Troy. At the resorts registration desk, only two rooms were assigned to her reservation—one for Halleck Stanley and one for her.

"What about me?" Troy asked as he stood next to her opposite the clerk.

"You're with me, young fella." She slid her hip up against his. "You're taking the place of your father."

Troy gasped for air, which upset him because it was an obvious sign that he'd failed to keep his cool.

Their room wasn't just a room; it was a Mexican-style casita complete with a living area furnished with a high-end teakwood couch and love seat, a seventy-inch flat screen TV, and lavish floral arrangements at every turn. A hammock with a luxurious view of the ocean decorated the patio.

As soon as they settled in their room and put away clothing articles from their suitcases, Jessie excused herself, announcing she planned on a change of clothes. Troy busied himself with the TV remote, checking the menu for adult movies. There were ten listed, including the classic *All Summer Long* starring Summer Reign.

When Jessie finally came out of the bathroom, she noted that Troy was still scanning the porn menu. "You won't need any of those, Troy. You have me." She flashed him by opening her bathrobe and revealing nothing but her delicious-looking flesh. Her nipples were hard and inviting.

Troy's eyes rolled deep into their sockets. "Whooh!" he could hear himself say.

Having released her robe to the floor, Jessie walked toward Troy, who was sitting on the king-size bed. She motioned for him to get to his feet. When he did, she immediately began unbuttoning his Tommy Bahama shirt and then his shorts. Once he was naked, Jessie put her hand on his chest and pushed him onto his back on the bed. They made love for hours.

Sex, for Jessie, was like her workouts; she never seemed to be able to get enough. Her physicality slightly intimidated Troy at first, but he was determined to prove he was the equal of any man, his dad in particular; and in the end, he was pretty sure he had.

Exhausted and sweating like he'd come from a steam bath, Troy whispered in Jessie's ear, "Was I as good as my dad?"

Jessie smiled and nodded. "Oh yeah! Oh yeah! Way better! And bigger."

Troy sat up in bed and struck a vigorous fist-pump pose. "That's the first time in my life I've ever been told I did something better that Big Erv Haslett."

Jessie laughed and clapped her hands repeatedly. "Your dad is why you're here. This is my way of keeping him with me even after he's gone. I hope you can deal with that."

"I can." Troy wasn't sure he appreciated Jessie's thinking. "You sure this isn't about making my sister crazy—you winning over two Haslett men and all?"

Jessie shot up in bed and tossed the covers aside. She quickly trained her eyes on a surprised Troy. "Don't ever go there again. Understood?"

By the time they departed Punta Mita for the return home, Troy had counted a half dozen skin-clutching, deep-penetrating sessions similar to the first. Sex with Jessie had been the greatest. That he had one-upped his father was frosting on the cake.

When they weren't romping in the sheets, Jessie and Troy did manage a business meeting with Halleck Stanley. The married father of three had connected with a Mexican cutie that worked in the golf pro shop and didn't mind his free time.

"I may move here," he'd said to Jessie during a chance meeting in the fitness center. "Her name is Mia Hinojosa. Her eyes are like magnets. They draw me in with one look."

Jessie laughed. "I'd better get you out of here before you end up having to pay for child support. If that's your ultimate fate, please don't blame me for placing you in harm's way. FYI, I hate to admit it, but harm's got a better ass than me. Nice choice."

It took only one three-hour meeting for all the parties to decide that *Slo-Go Fit* would roll out in syndication in two months, just in time for the summer bathing-suit season, when most people were the most self-conscious about their look. *Weight Stoppers* had agreed to be the title sponsor at $55,000 per episode for a total of forty episodes. The contract called for two seasons worth of shows. Production costs and Langly-Hoffman's share of the profits were projected at $35,000 per show. That would leave Jessie—at her agreed-upon take of 75 percent—fifteen thousand per show. Troy's 25 percent would earn him five thousand per episode and a total of two hundred thousand for the season. It came out to slightly more than Jessie had promised him.

More than the money, Troy was being given the opportunity to become more of a national celebrity than his sister. He'd had a lifetime of playing second fiddle to both his dad and Rachel. This would be his coming out party. It was late in coming, but he was determined to make the most of it.

As he pondered his sudden good fortune over a joint he'd sneaked out with him to a protective cove on the other side of the resorts beach jetty, he was, for the first time he could remember, a genuinely happy soul. His life had changed completely in just four days.

CHAPTER TWENTY-ONE

The telephone voice of Friars' owner Irving Zeller was distinctive. It was a cross between a growl and a chortle; thus, he always sounded to Devin Braxton to be happily pissed off. This time, his voice appeared to be more of a growl.

"You heard what's going on with that Haslett woman in Santa Barbara?"

"She's got a winning team for a change. That's all I know. Or are you referencing her Honeyball campaign?"

"Damn, Baxter, that's one of my biggest complaints about you. I can't get you to stay on top of all the things that are under your charge. Here it is ten o'clock in the morning, and you don't know squat about her little episode?"

Devin held his phone at arm's length like he didn't want to hear anymore.

"Did you hear me?"

"I'm in charge of baseball operations for you, Mr. Zeller, not the personal lives of those who have a loose affiliation with the Friars."

Zeller, who made his money developing tract homes throughout the Western states—few in the expansive region will ever forget his "Be a Zeller Dewler" TV commercials—was okay with the Honeyball promotion, although his wife chastised him for allowing it in an in-depth interview in the *San Diego Union*.

"I think it's demeaning to women rather than empowering," Ethel Zeller was quoted as saying. "Hollywood markets sex. Baseball markets home runs, shutouts, and hot dogs."

"You need to be in charge of everything, Baxter. The Honeyball thing is the same as my Zeller-Dewler marketing campaign. It's all about good marketing . . ." He paused briefly. "I'm talking about her arrest."

Devin's antenna started sparking. "What arrest?"

"My good friend and former vice president of sales for Zeller Construction, Ernie Schmidt, retired in Santa Barbara, and he told me it was all over the local news channel last night. She was arrested on a probation violation. He told me she went to great lengths to conceal her identity from the one TV camera that showed up at the county jail. He said, by covering her face with her jacket, she gave the perception that she'd done something wrong. He actually advised me to wipe his hands clean of the woman. 'Publicity like this you don't need,' he told me."

Devin took a deep breath on his end. "I'm sure she's capable of making any bail amount. Her dad had plenty of money."

"How well do you know her?"

Devin inhaled. He didn't want his boss to have the slightest inkling that he knew Rachel intimately. Even though Zeller was far removed from the Friars' organization at the time, there are still those on the payroll who remembered the negative publicity Devin and the Friars received when it was discovered by the *San Diego Union*'s gossip columnist that the Friars' superstar had been cheating on his wife with a white hotel executive.

"I've only known her briefly, sir. She's really doing a great job of revitalizing baseball in that town. She's had six out of seven sellouts already."

"Well, Devin, this kind of shit gives our entire franchise a bad name. I mean, a woman owner going to jail for violating probation on misdemeanor assault charges is not something I want to brag about. This clearly impacts my campaign to promote you for MLB executive of the year honors."

"That's news to me."

"Don't mess in your shorts. If you get the award, I get the recognition for keeping you on as GM, despite our shitty record over the last two years. Good publicity steers my wagon, Devin. I'm just worried the Baseball Writers Association of America will make a point that her transgression happened on your watch. So I want you to get your ass to Santa Barbara as quickly as possible and get her out of jail and out of the headlines for the wrong reasons. I'd like for you to force her to quit and turn the club over to a real baseball person. Bring back the GM that the woman's dad ran off. I want you to take my personal attorney, Samuel Firestone, with you and report back to me in three days."

The click of the phone disconnecting on Zeller's end appeared to be louder than normal to Devin. In a rare fit of anger, Devin reached up to the top of the richly paneled section of his office where he showcased his memorabilia, grabbed the bat that he'd hit his three-hundredth homer with, and hurled it across his office. The bat whirred like helicopter blades until it crashed into the bigger-than-life portrait of Irving Zeller, duplicates of which he'd posted in the offices of every Friars' executive.

CHAPTER TWENTY-TWO

Even without makeup, little sleep, her hair matted, and dressed in an unflattering orange county jail jumpsuit, Rachel Haslett was still the same tantalizingly attractive woman Devin Baxter had held in his arms for hours that night at the Biltmore. The two were positioned directly across each other at one of a half dozen prisoners' phone stations located on the second floor of the county jail. A thick bulletproof glass partition separated them physically.

"Thank you for coming," Rachel said, jumpstarting the conversation. "It means a lot to me."

Devin dipped his chin slightly. "I was so worried about you. I couldn't understand why I hadn't heard from you, why you hadn't showed up. Now I know."

Rachel pulled her stringy hair back, pulled it together, and tied it in a ponytail with the help of a rubber band the guards had missed during a previsitation security check.

"I'm so sorry. They took my phone away from me the minute I was placed in a squad car."

Devin had a trace of a smile. "Well, not to worry. I have Irving Zeller's personal attorney working on your bail at this very moment. He's at some bail bonds office across the street."

Rachel sniffled, and tears formed in her eyes. "I'm on a bail hold, Devin."

"What does that mean?"

"It means I can't post bail. It's an automatic court-ordered hold. I'm at the mercy of the court. I could be here six months or more." Rachel started to cry and quickly checked herself by placing her hand over her face and inhaling deeply.

Devin's face locked up. "Not good."

"Please don't stress yourself over this, Devin. Adrienne Telfair is as capable as I am of running the team if not more."

Devin asked how her arrest came to be. Rachel explained in detail how her probation officer had tried to bribe her. At the end of his limited ten-minute visit, Devin asked for the probation officers name and wrote it down on a piece of paper he kept in his wallet.

As she prepared to depart the phone station, Rachel placed her palm flat against the glass that separated them, and Devin matched it with his palm.

"Keep strong."

"I will. You know that." Rachel quickly turned away and was immediately intercepted by an attending sheriff's deputy who escorted her back to her cell.

Less than twenty-four hours after Devin had relayed Rachel's account of her encounter with Bernard Coffee, Samuel Firestone had secured an appointment with county probation department chief Oren Weatherford. Devin attended as well and was greatly impressed by Mr. Firestone's command of the situation. Firestone not only detailed Bernard Coffee's visit and his illicit proposition, but he also lied to Weatherford.

"Ms. Haslett has a home security system."

Weatherford's expression changed from casual to concerned.

"It doesn't have audio, but the video clearly shows Mr. Coffee pointing his index finger directly in the vicinity of his genitals and gesturing with his hand what could only be assumed to be an invitation to perform a sex act on him."

Weatherford twisted uncomfortably in his desk chair. "That's borderline circumstantial evidence, Mr. Firestone."

Firestone exhibited the trace of a smile for the first time since they'd begun their meeting. "Perhaps we'll throw that puppy up on YouTube, Mr. Weatherford, where we would expect it to go borderline viral in a matter of hours."

"What are you asking for, Mr. Firestone?" Weatherford's face had gone blank.

"We want Rachel Haslett out of jail by noon and Bernard Coffee gone from your department by five o'clock this afternoon."

Weatherford got out of his chair and walked to a wall-mounted picture of himself standing next to former president George W. Bush.

"I've held this department to the highest standards for the past twenty years, gentlemen. I won't have it tarnished by a misguided probation officer. I will grant you your wishes once I have the security video in my possession."

Firestone immediately reached into his briefcase and pulled out at tiny SD card and handed it over to the probation department chief.

"I have an appointment in half an hour with superior court judge Thomas Fujita. I want you to call him and request he drop his probation hold on my client, and I want her released."

Weatherford cocked his head and paused for a second. "I'll do my best to honor your time frame."

The three men shook hands, and as soon as Devin and Mr. Firestone had cleared the office door, Devin asked, "How did you get Rachel's security video? We haven't even been to her place."

Firestone put his hands on Devin's shoulder as they walked toward the parking lot. "You're familiar with the age-old hidden ball trick in baseball, I assume?"

Devin nodded that he had.

"Well, this is not the hidden video trick. It's the nonexistent video trick." Firestone quickened his stride as if he'd experienced a sudden burst of energy.

Devin's brow knitted. "But the deal was contingent on your turning over the tape to him."

Firestone stopped in his tracks and laughed. "The SD card I gave him is blank. And it's also an outdated SanDisk format. By the time Weatherford figures out he can't play it on any device currently on the market, Ms. Haslett is free, and Mr. Coffee is looking for a job as a barista."

Devin shook his head. "You, sir, have balls of steel."

"I'll take that as a compliment, Mr. Braxton."

Samuel Firestone didn't stop with his shell game triumph. After he successfully secured Judge Fujita's authorization to release Rachel from the county jail, he contacted Santa Barbara's small sampling of media outlets and announced a two-o-clock news conference at The Erv.

With a two-hour window to work with, Devin picked up Rachel from the county jail and offered her the option of lunch at the Harbor Restaurant on Stearns' Wharf or home. She chose home.

"I have to clean up for the news conference. I wouldn't show up for one of those 'mudder' events looking like I do now."

Firestone excused himself in order to find a Starbucks where he could review his strategy for the news conference.

TV crews from KEYT-TV in Santa Barbara and KSBY-TV in San Luis Obispo joined reporters from the *Santa Barbara News-Press* and the *Santa Barbara Independent* in a grandstand section behind home plate. A handful of radio reporters were also in attendance. At precisely two o'clock, Samuel Firestone began his prepared statement. He looked every bit the high-priced lawyer—$2,000 Armani suit, $1,000 Salvatore Ferragamo shoes, a Huber watch big enough to display in the town square, and $500 Ray-Bans.

"I'm here to rectify the unfathomable public relations harm that has been done to my client, Rachel Haslett, by an agent of Santa Barbara County's Probation Department. First, I'd like to bring you up to speed on why my client was on probation in the first place." Firestone continued on, masterfully outlining the progression of Rachel's "nightmare"—his words. When he got to the part where he detailed Coffee's request for oral copulation, Rachel, who was sitting next to him at a small table, stood up and asked to be excused from the session.

Firestone played his sympathy card. "I understand, Rachel. Take your time. You've been through a lot." Rachel fought back tears as she exited the news conference. Firestone, who would later admit he couldn't have choreographed the news conference any better, continued on. "Because my client is a public figure in this community and because her reputation—all important in an entertainment business—has been defamed to the degree that it has, I will be heading over to the courthouse later this afternoon to file a defamation suit against the county's probation department."

Borrowing a chapter from his experience as a once flamboyant defense attorney, Firestone paused to take a drink from a bottle of water that allowed his statement about filing a civil action hang in the air in the interest of generating impact.

Sound bites from Firestone's news conference led the six-o-clock newscasts on both TV stations that had been in attendance. An enterprising KEYT-TV reporter expanded on the news conference by adding several additional elements to her story. Mary Fairchild's report included a comment from Santa Barbara County Sheriff Robert Cox.

"I'm extremely embarrassed for everyone in my department for carrying out an arrest that wasn't warranted." She also included a sound bite from psychologist Thomas Marmar indicating that Rachel Haslett had in fact attempted, via a voice mail message, to arrange for his treatment services. Sheriff Cox was tepid in his TV interview compared to what he had to say to the *News-Press* reporter.

However, by the time he did his interview with the newspaper reporter probation, Chief Oren Weatherford had admitted to Judge Fujita's office that he had been duped.

"There was no security video," he said to the judge by phone. "Ms. Haslett's attorney deceived me." Sheriff Cox was livid over the news. "How in god's name does the administrator of a county department that has a $3 million budget bungle a probation hold the way Weatherford did? It's all the more embarrassing for my department. First, the woman is remanded to my jail, and then she isn't. Now, I have to start the arrest process all over again. It's a colossal waste of taxpayers' dollars." The sheriff's public pushback prompted Oren Weatherford to resign his position the next morning.

That night, Devin and Rachel put Samuel Firestone on a plane back to San Diego and then returned to Rachel's condo for pizza and beer while keeping an ear to Melanie Sandberg's call of the Charros' 5-4 road win over the Inland Empire 66ers.

As midnight approached, Rachel repeated the evening's common theme. "I know I'm being redundant, but I'm so grateful for you, Devin," she said, cuddling next to him on her expensive couch. "Without your help, everything I've tried to build with the Charros would have come tumbling down." She kissed him on the cheek. That led to an embrace and then a follow-up, more sensual kiss on the lips.

Moments later, they retired to Rachel's bed. Unlike the first time, or at any time in her life, Rachel felt as if she were making love, not just having sex. The feeling was exhilarating. She could feel her nerves standing at attention. For hours, they mixed ferocious lovemaking with periods of tender caressing—each excited by the touch of the other's firm, athletic body.

When they awoke in the morning, Rachel felt overwhelmingly fulfilled. She turned under the covers to face Devin and put her lips against his cheek and whispered, "Is this the beginning of a romance?"

Devin smiled big. "It sure feels like."

CHAPTER TWENTY-THREE

Two days after Rachel's release, the Charros returned home for an eleven-game home stand with Bakersfield, Inland Empire, and Visalia. The team was off to its best start (9-2) in franchise history. Austin Grant was getting national attention on ESPN.com for his amazing start—nine home runs, twenty-two runs-batted-ins, and a .378 average in eleven games.

After her orange jumpsuit exile of three days, Rachel was excited to get back to The Erv and watch both her team succeed and her organization pull in fans at an astonishing pace. She wouldn't admit to being nervous about fan acceptance after her criminal history had been paraded before the public by what she believed to be a sensationalistic local media, but she was.

Rachel clearly had her game face on when she arrived at the ballpark. At first she was reluctant to put on anything resembling a happy face, but it proved to be all for naught. The entire Honeyball staff presented her with a large chocolate mousse cake (her favorite). The cake read, "Welcome Back." It was decorated with a Monopoly "get out of jail" card. Kisses and hugs for all her employees followed the cutting of the cake. The fans were equally accepting. One of the few elderly men in the crowd, a fixture at games for a decade, played the theme song from the TV show *Welcome Back Kotter* on his accordion.

With the notion of nurturing the Honeyball brand, Holly Redman had scheduled a "short shorts night" with a female voted "best in shorts" by fan applause to receive a weekend stay at the Four Seasons Biltmore. Rachel told Holly just before the start of the contest that if she hadn't been in jail, she wouldn't have approved the promotion.

"Too sexist, but it's too late now."

Ten minutes prior to the first pitch, Rachel followed her instructions and walked from the Charros' dugout to a temporary stage that had been set up at home plate and kicked off the contest. Seven out of twenty females had passed Holly's visual auditions that were conducted in a little used woman's restroom located near the visiting team's bullpen. The finalists were standing by in the Charros' otherwise empty dugout to show off their stuff—the players having been directed to retreat to their clubhouse.

As Rachel cleared the dugout steps and walked toward the stage in her best Chico's beach shorts—the same ones she used to model for the Honeyball billboards—a humongous roar went up from a section of mostly young people (college students) behind the visitor's dugout. Whistles of every variety were abundant throughout Rachel's attempt on the PA system to explain the judging. Once she'd managed to emphasize that the voting would be determined by the amount of noise for each candidate, she called the first contestant to the stage.

"Pleases welcome, Dina from Buellton."

Dina from Buellton wore tan cutoffs and wowed the crowd with a body builder's legs. She looked as if she could squat a VW bug. Her downfall turned out to be her too-short frame.

Bridgette from Montecito came next and showed off the shortest pair of Levi's this side of anybody named Daisy. She had legs that didn't quit but lacked the sufficient Southern California tan for voters to take her over the top.

The loudest applause was reserved for Kyra, a black restaurant hostess from Santa Maria. She strutted out her prodigious but perfectly shaped booty in a black-and-white patterned Tribal Aztec number. When she shook her booty like a porn star, a riotous crowd induced area Richter Scale into panic mode. Kyra jumped like a kangaroo when she was declared the winner. She hugged Rachel and thanked her homies for "making all that beautiful noise."

At the close of the contest, Rachel got a standing ovation for announcing—a spur-of-the-moment decision—that the July 4 game against Lake Elsinore would be a "short shorts bobblehead night," featuring a Kyra model who would, in her words, "rock the bobblehead industry." Again, the applause was deafening. "You're going to want to be among the first three thousand fans to enter the stadium that night. We'll have a bigger Fourth of July celebration than the 'Star-Spangled Banner.'" She also proclaimed every Thursday night, until the end of the season, "short shorts night."

The Charros helped make "short shorts night" complete with a 1-0 victory over Bakersfield to push their record to 10-2, tied with Rancho Cucamonga for the league's best record. Austin Grant was responsible for the lone run in the game by ripping a solo home run to the opposite field—a display of pure power if there ever was one. Melanie Sandberg's home run call came from somewhere back in the seventies. She said, "Sky Rocket in flight . . . after dark delight."

In his postgame visit with sports writers from three newspapers, Dom Benedetti made a point to make sure confetti wasn't thrown at Austin Grant alone. He'd already expressed to his lead assistant coach that he was concerned Austin was developing an industrial strength ego citing the fact he blew off a pregame interview request from a local KEYT-TV reporter but gave the reporter from KNBC-TV in Los Angeles a good ten minutes of his time.

"I can't have any player 'big timing' it," he'd told all his coaches, following the incident. After the game, he was effusive in his praise for his starting pitcher. "Kevin Sargent tossed the best eight innings of ball I've seen in a long time at this level. My hat is off to Kevin. His sinker tonight was a real 'gopher getter.' And our defense was first rate. The play Jesus Velarde made on that screamer down the third place line in the fourth inning with a runner on second was 'big league' in every way."

CHAPTER TWENTY-FOUR

Rachel was emotionally drained from the 1-0 win. She wondered how many tight games could she take in a long season. As she left the park on foot, the lights from the stadium haloed her from behind. Rachel couldn't help thinking how much better things were now that she was back in her environment—back with her team and her Honeyball crew. Jail had been the low point in her life. She never experienced depression like what had beset her, sharing a cell with Ms. Molly, a wiry-haired, emaciated shell of a woman. Rachel guessed her to be forty years old going on sixty. Ms. Molly was an admitted meth head that was jailed and awaiting trial for trying to light her boyfriend on fire while he was sleeping. Rachel couldn't forget how she'd become short of breath the first time she'd had to join the other inmates in the eating area, and every single one of them—mostly tattooed head to foot—ogled her like she was fresh meat.

As she turned the corner from the ballpark and entered the sidewalk on Cabrillo Boulevard, she stopped momentarily and looked back at the ballpark. She felt a sudden surge of pride in knowing she'd created something very exciting for the people in her hometown— something to make them even more proud to be residents of the great city of Santa Barbara.

By the time she'd reached her condo, Rachel was ready for a glass of wine and an episode of *House of Cards* that she'd downloaded from Netflix. She was so ready for a shutdown.

The instant she opened the door to her condo, her instincts told her something wasn't right. The power light from her DirecTV satellite box was on. That wasn't her MO to leave it powered up whenever she left the home. The throw rug that she'd placed under her dining table was flipped over on one side. As she stepped further into her condo, she noticed the light above the kitchen sink was on—again, not her MO. She could feel her breathing becoming more rapid. Her skin started to tingle.

Was there someone in the house, she wondered. *Or had they been here and gone?* Out of the corner of her eye, she saw the figure of a large man dressed entirely in black, including a ski cap, step down from the bedroom stairs and into the living room area. She flinched and gasped at the same time. It was him—Bernard Coffee.

"Greetings." Coffee affected a maniacal Jack Nicholson-like grin. "You probably weren't expecting me."

Rachel felt an immediate adrenalin surge. Her flight-or-fight response was boarding at gate *S* for scared.

"What do you want?" Her voice was shaky.

Slowly, Bernard Coffee moved in Rachel's direction, one size 15 shoe step at a time "That last time I was here, I asked for sexual favors. This time I'm not asking."

Fortunately, Rachel was still carrying her mobile in her hand—a habit she'd adopted when walking home from the ballpark at night. She reached in her shorts pocket for it and punched the 911 speed dial icon. That only angered her would-be assailant. He reached for and got hold of her arm with his big claw of a hand and pulled her toward him. He tried to kiss her on the lips, but she briefly spun free of his grip. Rachel was terrified by the anger in his eyes. She knew she had to buy time for an emergency response to her call. Frustrated by her temporary escape, Coffee charged after her like an angry bull and tackled her next to her living room couch. Rachel went down hard on her right shoulder, releasing a shriek of pain upon contact with her hardwood floor. Coffee immediately pinned her to the floor with the weight of his large body.

"The 911 call went through," Rachel groaned. "They can track where it originated, fool."

Rachel's warning only seemed to aggravate Coffee more. He executed an arm bar across her neck and shoulders and then with his free hand reached inside both her shorts and panties and ripped at them with a violent tug. Rachel winced as one of his fingernails scraped across her left cheek. She immediately felt a stinging pain.

In Rachel's mind, he wasn't going to stop there. She had to get away from him. Somehow she was able to free her left arm just enough to rip her elbow into her attacker's side. She dug it in as deep as she was capable of doing. He winced and grabbed at spot of his pain just above his kidney. It was enough of a movement for Rachel to struggle to her knees, shed his bulk, and eventually get to her feet.

"I will fuck your brains out, Ms. Honeyball," Coffee said as he struggled to upload his big frame to a standing position.

Rachel could see Coffee was still grimacing from the blow to his side. Free of him for the moment, Rachel scrambled to her den. She had a purpose. She'd remembered storing a Louisville Slugger baseball bat in a wastebasket next to her desk. It was a souvenir model signed by Austin Grant. It was smaller in size than a regular bat.

She'd been considering it as a promotional giveaway at one of the Charros' upcoming games.

In one motion, Rachel reached for and grabbed the bat with her right hand. When she turned toward the open door of her den, Coffee was only a few feet away. His forehead was drenched in sweat. Instinctively, she raised the bat to ear level and violently swung it forward with all her strength, crashing it against Coffee's temple.

The sound of the wood bat hitting Coffee's skull was horrific. He groaned and dropped to the floor like he'd been shot, his head banging against a large decorative ceramic flowerpot in the process. His eyes rolled back in his head. Blood oozed from his wound. Rachel believed him to be unconscious and then was suddenly relieved to hear police sirens off in the distance. She told herself she would hit Coffee again with her bat if he showed even the slightest movement.

While she cautiously watched over her wounded assailant on one knee, Rachel tried to help stop his bleeding by putting pressure on his wound with her hand. Suddenly, two uniformed Santa Barbara police officers arrived on the scene. With guns at the ready, they burst through the slightly open front door. Quickly they surveyed the scene. The taller of the two cops immediately radioed for an EMT.

"What happened here?" the other cop with the round face asked.

Rachel took her hand away from Coffee's wound and got to her feet. She placed her hand over her mouth and started to cry, her hand only partially muzzling the sound.

"He was going to rape me."

The round-faced cop asked Rachel to recall in as much detail as possible what had happened. She did her best while still shaking, and the cop took detailed notes on an iPad.

During her recall exercise, a pair of EMTs arrived, immediately checked Coffee for his vital signs, comforted him as he began regaining consciousness, and eventually placed him onto a gurney for a ride to Cottage Hospital about ten minutes away.

Shortly after Coffee had been transported into an awaiting ambulance, the officer with the round face reentered Rachel's condo. His lips were tight, and there was the hint of perspiration just under the hairline of his police baseball cap.

"I'm afraid I have to take you with me, Ms. Haslett."

Rachel eyes searched the officer's eyes for an explanation. "I just told you everything I know. Why do I have to go anywhere with you? I'm the victim."

The officer—O'Banion, his nametag read—cleared his throat. "They actually want us to transport you to the county jail, miss. We were just told by our dispatcher that the sheriff's office is exercising an old probation hold against you. I'm sorry, but that's all the information I have."

Rachel's eyes lasered the officers. "NO!" she screamed. "I'm not going. This can't be happening to me again."

Immediately, Officer O'Banion radioed his partner outside for help. Within seconds, he arrived back in the condo where he helped his partner pin Rachel to the floor and handcuff her. Rachel was then escorted, kicking and screaming on the way to the squad car for the ride to county jail.

As her head was being pushed downward, forcing her into the backseat of the police car—a déjà vu moment—Rachel's mobile pinged, indicating she'd received a text. Once she arrived at the jail's intake area, Officer O'Banion confiscated her mobile.

Rachel asked him for a favor as he took possession of the mobile. "Can you just show me the last text I received?"

O'Banion thought about it for a second and then held the phone up so Rachel could retrieve and read it. She was hoping it was from Devin Baxter. It was instead from the woman at the NTSB's Denver office. It read: "Salvage begins tomorrow."

Rachel cried out. "There is a god!"

CHAPTER TWENTY-FIVE

Rachel's rearrest was again headline news: "HONEYBALL GIRL BACK IN SLAMMER," read the *Independent*. "HONEYBALL GM VICTIM OF ATTACK BUT RETURNED TO JAIL" was how the *News-Press*'s banner headline read. County Sheriff Robert Cox, up for reelection in a year, worked her incarceration in his jail for all it was worth and more. He was all over KEYT-TV's local coverage and even appeared live on a San Diego TV station because of the Charros' connection to the Friars. During his interview, he implied that the Santa Barbara Charros' CEO-GM would be detained in his facility for a period of at least sixty days, awaiting a court appearance.

"We're investigating a possible sexual assault case, in which she appeared to be a victim, but we can't ignore that she was originally released from a probation hold, the result of her counsel's legal shenanigans presenting probation with a bogus security tape." He also added that at his insistence, the district attorney was looking into filing charges against Friars' legal counsel, Samuel Firestone, for indirectly but purposely introducing fraudulent documents to the court.

Rachel's first phone call was to Adrienne Telfair. She asked for Adrienne to visit her at her first opportunity and told her to prepare to take notes when she arrived. Rachel was ashamed at the thought of again facing her top employee wearing prison garb. In the hours before the jail's visiting period, she desperately tried to fight off what she recognized as another bout of depression. It manifested itself in a darkness that seemed to permeate her mind and vision. She recalled only one other time that she'd been hit with depression, and that was when her parents got divorced. Like many children of divorced parents, she went through a period where she was certain she was the reason for the split. She recalled running away to Los Angeles for two days to stay with an older cousin.

When a deputy eventually advised her she had a visitor, she experienced a brief spell of dizziness. That prompted her to request a few minutes to meditate. She tried to utilize the techniques she'd learned at the Charros' Ojai retreat, but they didn't calm her like she'd hoped.

Rachel couldn't muster a smile for Adrienne when their eyes met across the glass partition. Adrienne didn't know how to act in her boss's presence. She nervously bowed her head before addressing Rachel.

"I'm so sorry for you, Rachel."

"Please don't pity me. I have no one to blame for this but myself. I was too arrogant. I thought it was below me to go through the anger management process."

"Why did your shrink turn you in?" Adrienne asked.

"She was a control freak, but she couldn't get me under her thumb. We had bad vibes for each other from day one."

"Still? Jail?"

"She was obligated by law. That's all I want to say about it. End of subject."

Adrienne did ask that Rachel not share the details of Bernard Coffee's assault. "I've been in that situation. I can't handle a refresher on that experience."

Aware that her time with Adrienne was limited, Rachel quickly dispensed any further small talk and rattled off her "to do" list. The first order of business was for Adrienne to take over the reins of the team.

Rachel was matter of fact about her status. "I could be in here as long as ninety days, Adrienne. As of this moment going forward, you're running the Charros' show."

Adrienne swallowed and bit her lower lip. "That's a lot of trust in me, Rachel."

Rachel, whose eyes appeared swollen from too little sleep and too many tears, pointed her index finger at the glass partition.

"You are the consummate multitasker. I know you can handle it. In fact, I'm giving you an additional assignment that has nothing to do with the Charros."

Adrienne sat back in her chair and raised her eyebrows. "What is it?"

"I need you to keep me posted as best you can on the salvage operation on my dad's plane. I got a text that they were scheduled to start today."

"How do I do that?"

"Call the NTSB's Denver office and ask for—god, I've forgotten the woman's name—Virginia, I think." She shook her head in a form of self-disgust. "Can't remember the last name. But how many Virginias work for the NTSB in Denver?"

"Not to worry. I'll get to the right person."

"You've got to tell her I'm in jail and can't communicate with anyone other than through letters or postcards and, if I'm lucky, by making a collect phone call on the only damn phone on my floor. See if she'll brief you, and then you can tell me the latest when you visit."

Adrienne promised to do her best to fulfill Rachel's request. Before she left, she told Rachel the remaining seven games of the home stand have been sold out.

"That's the best news of the day," Rachel said, tears suddenly rushing from her eyes as she dropped her head to her chest and placed a palm on the glass partition.

Adrienne teared up as well at her good-bye. "Find your peace, Rachel." She quickly hung up her phone and departed the visiting area.

Rachel silently wondered if she'd ever again be able to do that.

CHAPTER TWENTY-SIX

The Charros upped their record to 21–4 over the next couple of weeks and pushed their lead over Rancho Cucamonga to two games. It clearly appeared it would be a two-team race for the league's first half championship. The next closest teams in the standings, San Jose and Visalia, were already eight games back. The Charros had become a hot item, nationally as well as locally. *The Ticket* cable network sent a crew to Santa Barbara to do a feature on the Honeyball team for the following month's hour-long show. With the way the Charros were selling out games, they had become the talk of minor league baseball.

Wilson van Landingham, a retired two-time twenty-game winning pitcher with Saint Louis, was assigned to be the reporter for the story. He'd joined *The Ticket* just this TV season. He'd been assigned to only baseball-related stories since joining the cable giant. He was handsome, tall, tanned, and full of himself. He insisted on a jailhouse interview with Rachel, or he'd pull his crew and head back to New York without a story.

Rachel's attorney, Jackson Pennington, a partner in Andrew Sutton's law firm advised her not to do any interview. He was of the opinion that Rachel and the Charros had nothing to gain from her appearing in a jail cell setting.

"Why derail a positive story with a negative?" Pennington advised.

At Rachel's suggestion, Pennington put in a call to Devin Braxton to see if he would do the interview as the big league representative for the Charros' franchise.

Devin responded immediately. "Of course, I'd be happy to represent the Charros." They agreed upon a time of six thirty in the general manager's ballpark office.

Early afternoon, Devin caught a flight from San Diego to Santa Barbara. He had hoped to have time to visit Rachel, but an hour-long flight delay forced him to cancel his plan. He longed to see her.

There was considerable tension in the room when Devin sat down on a makeshift set opposite Wilson van Landingham. They shook hands initially but talked little as both were miked up for the videotaping. The crew—cameraman, gaffer, and producer—must have sensed the awkwardness because none of them said a word. Devin and the man about to interview him had a history.

In the final year of his career, Devin was hit on the head with a ninety-eight-miles-per-hour fastball by a then Saint Louis rookie pitcher with three names who was trying to establish his ownership of the inside portion of the plate. Fortunately, Devin's batting helmet saved him from injury; but angered by what he considered was a deliberate attempt to hit him, Devin dropped his bat and charged the pitcher's mound after Van Landingham. They exchanged several angry punches before players from both sides and the home plate umpire were able to stop it. Both Devin and Van Landingham were ejected from the game. They haven't seen each other since that incident.

"You come with any high hard ones and this interview will be over." Devin stared down Van Landingham as he received a last-minute makeup touch-up. Then suddenly, Devin produced a smile that seemed to break the tension.

Van Landingham returned a nervous smile. "The past is the past, Devin." He rose from his director's chair and offered a handshake.

Devin responded in kind. "Only one subject is out of bounds."

"Let me guess—the general manager's status."

"Correct."

"I think we can live with that," Van Landingham lied.

When asked what was right about the Charros, Devin shone. "Their home attendance of five thousand a night for all but two of their home games represents the biggest turnaround in numbers of any team in the history of minor league baseball." Devin's energy level rose as he pushed on. "Concession sales are up 140 percent over a year ago, and merchandise, particularly Austin Grant's jersey, is flying off the shelf. The Charros have already sold ten thousand of his jerseys."

For a TV rookie, Van Landingham artfully moved the interview along. "You mentioned Austin Grant. How are you going to keep him down on the farm, here in single A ball, when it's clear his skills are practically big-league caliber right now?"

Devin scratched his chin with his thumb and index finger. He knew his answer might get him in trouble with Irving Zeller, but he'd never backed away from the truth.

"I promised GM Haslett she could have him for the entire season, thinking she would need a gate attraction to pull the franchise out of a financial hole caused by too many years in a bad stadium. I don't go back on my word. He's not only become an overnight sensation, but if he ran for mayor right now, we'd also be calling him 'Honorable Austin.'"

The Honeyball story had such potential drama that the producer of the story successfully argued with his bosses to position it in the upcoming edition of the *The Ticket*, advancing it by almost a month.

The reason for the urgency was simply "great fucking television," as the young producer named Evan White had proclaimed by phone to New York. What the boy whiz kid producer had done was secretly pay a county jail deputy a thousand dollars to take still pictures and any video he could of Rachel behind bars or in the main dining area of the jail. The product he received from the deputy was so good boy whiz kid spotted the deputy another hundred for going "above and beyond," as he put it.

What really allowed the Honeyball piece to rise the food chain was a call boy whiz kid got from Miles Rooney requesting that he be interviewed for the story. He promised he had some good dirt on Ms. Honeyball.

The Rooney interview took place at the Riviera home of a friend of Van Landinghams. *The Ticket* crew set up on the owner's pool patio that overlooked the entire city. Palm trees swayed in the background. Rooney needed no prodding from Van Landingham to tie into Rachel Haslett's Honeyball machine.

"The Charros' attendance figures are fraudulent," Rooney said without being prompted. "Fans, young fans mostly, are coming here to see tits and ass, not baseball. They recently staged a 'short shorts night' here that was a like a carnival show. What's next, I wrote in a follow-up column—lap dances for the first ten men who have the winning numbers on their game tickets." He continued, "The Erv has become a nightly frat house party for UCSB students who come here looking for a hookup, not a hook slide into third base. This woman is selling sex, pure and simple. I have to believe a wet T-shirt night is not far off."

Rooney paused his diatribe to take a drink of water. He didn't need to be prompted to continue talking.

"I've researched Rachel Haslett's pro volleyball career and found out her courtside beauty went only skin deep. I have it on good authority that she paid off fellow ABVP players, with brand new Chevy Corvette's from her dad's dealership, to help her with her failed attempt to oust the league commissioner in 2013. Naturally, she would have been the replacement commissioner."

Rooney was on a roll, and no one from *The Ticket* was in a rush to stop him.

"She maintains that Honeyball—my headline writer at least deserves credit for the brand—is not to be perceived as a triumph for feminists everywhere but instead a reflection of the American Dream. Tell that to the twenty-five male employees who were not invited back to the organization this year. And while I have the floor, ask her about her lesbian relationship with another unnamed ABVP player. What's next, a 'bring-your-lesbian-girlfriend night' at the park? Is this what mothers and fathers of young women in this community want their kids exposed to? This woman should be banned from baseball. Hell, Pete Rose is banned from the Hall of Fame for betting on his own team. Rachel Haslett should be banned for betting tits and ass could set attendance records."

All of Rooney's sound bites made air on *The Ticket*'s piece that aired to the largest viewing audience in the show's history.

CHAPTER TWENTY-SEVEN

Rachel's days behind bars—fourteen and counting—were confined to lying on her back on her cot and staring at the drab ceiling in her cell, that and listening to angry inmates shouting profanities at one another and the jail guards. She'd lost inertia, something she'd never experienced in her thirty-five years on the planet. She hadn't showered in three days—against jail protocol—and her hair looked like it had been glued to her scalp. She'd tried reading one of a handful of antiquated pocket books—*The Da Vinci Code* was one—that were made available to inmates by the nonprofit Service League but never got past the first few pages of any of them. She'd even denied a visitation request by her attorney. She figured there was nothing to talk about—a sure sign of depression.

Rachel's malaise was never more evident than during Adrienne Telfair's most recent visit. Not once during the time they'd had together through the glass partition did she ask how the Charros were doing. Her focus was strictly reserved for the NTSB's salvage operation. Consequently, that's all that Adrienne addressed in her brief visit.

"Virginia Westphall called me this morning, Rachel."

Rachel's tired eyes sprung up. "What did she say? Were they able to retrieve the fuselage?"

Adrienne raised her eyebrows. "She didn't discuss details with me other than she said they'd discovered the reason for the crash."

Rachel sat up straight and clinched her fist as if she were about to execute a power salute but didn't.

This was a positive for Adrienne because it was the first sign that Rachel still had a pulse. "She gave me her phone number. She wants to talk to you through the report. I told her you'd likely have to call collect."

Rachel shook her head, an acknowledgement that she understood the jail's strict telephone protocols.

Several hours after Adrienne's visit, Rachel made the collect call to the NTSB's Denver office. Virginia Westphall answered on the second ring and advised the operator she would take the call without even being prompted. She had been advised by Adrienne not to inquire how Rachel was doing or ask anything about why she was serving time in the county jail. Instead, she jumped directly into the details of accident report.

"The people back East who do the wreckage inspection accomplished a great deal in a short period. They flew out here for the inspection that cut their timeline in half. You owe them a debt of gratitude. Maybe you can send them an e-mail when you get out— ah, at your convenience. I mean—"

"It's okay, Ms. Westphall. I'm in jail because I was stupid. That's all you need to know."

Virginia Westphall quickly regained her composure, thinking it was nice of Rachel to excuse her faux pas.

"You'll receive their extensive written report in a couple of days— warning it's at least sixty pages—but I wanted to give you a brief synopsis over the phone because I know how anxious you are to hear the results."

"Yes," Rachel said. She had a death grip on her phone. She fully anticipated that the next few words uttered by Virginia Westphall might be life changing.

"Your father's crash was not pilot error, not health related, and not an accident."

Rachel gasped. It was a good ten seconds before she could speak. "Not an accident?"

The words echoed in Rachel's head. "NOT AN ACCIDENT!"

"Someone made sure your dad's plane would crash."

"Explain." Rachel's voice was shaking.

"I'll try to put it in laymen's terms."

"Please do."

"There was tampering. It's not all that complicated. The control arm that connects the pilot's control wheel to the elevator that allows the aircraft to rotate along its lateral axis, or pitch axis, is a half-inch aluminum rod. Our investigators found that a hacksaw had been used to cut into the rod. The cut was made at such an angle that it couldn't easily be detected during the pilot's preflight check because the incision was nearly invisible. Whoever did it added paint to fill in the gap caused by the cut to further conceal it. All these actions could have been accomplished in less than five minutes. Our investigating team believes the perpetrator left just enough remaining material on the rod so the elevator would work until the aircraft was well established in flight. It was determined that the vibration of the craft eventually caused the rod to break and made the aircraft uncontrollable. It's the conclusion of the investigators that your father's craft went into a high speed, unrecoverable spiral eventually crashing into the ocean."

For Rachel, the image of her father's plane slamming into the water became more vivid than ever. She'd seen it her dreams a hundred times; only now the images were in living color. She could see the perspiration form above his lip and on the top of his forehead as he struggled to find out what was wrong, frantically checking his controls for an answer. She could hear him swearing. *God, could he cut it loose when he was angry or, in this case, scared?* She could hear his booming voice ask God to intervene. After the splash, she could see salt water fill his cabin as his head rested lifeless against a side window. She shook her head vigorously several times in order to bring herself back to reality.

"How do I find out who did it?" Rachel asked, her voice shaky.

"It's assumed but impossible to confirm from the investigator's report that the tampering took place before your father took off from Arcata-Eureka Airport, which is located strangely enough in McKinleyville. The Humboldt County Sheriff's Department probably doesn't have the manpower to conduct an investigation. I researched this. They only have eighty-five people in their department. You'd have to find a private investigator who has extensive knowledge of small single-engine airplanes and the location where it happened."

Rachel apologized for not having anything else to say or ask. She knew her phone time limit was about to expire, so she thanked the woman for her help and the NTSB for expediting their investigation. Upon returning to her cell, she immediately started her review of possible suspects. She quickly discovered that nothing had changed. She reinforced her initial opinion that her dad's accident was clearly the work of someone hired by Jessie, Troy, or Will Greene. She refused to waver on her position.

As if by magic, Rachel suddenly had her spirit back. Within an hour of her phone call with Virginia Westphall, she'd showered, combed out her hair, and put on a clean jail jumpsuit. Anyone who assumed the information that Rachel now possessed about her father's death would bring her closure didn't know her. She was suddenly more motivated than ever to find out who had killed the man that had been her shining light for thirty-five years.

Troy Haslett didn't learn the results of the NTSB's investigation for close to a week. He'd read about it in the *LA Times* when he was rehearsing with Jessie for the *Slo-Go Fit* pilot at a studio in Sherman Oaks. He introduced the subject during a break in the shoot.

"Dad didn't have a heart attack like you thought."

"Oh? Where did you get that tidbit, TMZ?"

Troy went to his dressing quarters and, a few minutes later, returned with a copy of the *Times's* front page. "It's in the national roundup section. Here." He handed her the paper.

Jessie read the entire article. Troy studied her face for some form of expression. Nothing. When she finished reading, she put the paper on her lap and said, "Who would do something like that to Ervin?"

Troy got up off the studio's only sofa and walked to the soda machine located across the main stage. When he returned, he surprised Jessie.

"I'm not trying to bust your chops, but you, as his primary beneficiary for both his life insurance and his estate, have to figure people might link you to his death. If the press ever gets hold of a document or documents showing how much money you pulled in from my dad, your life could become complicated."

Jessie digested Troy's thoughts but didn't say anything right away. She closed her eyes briefly, and her lips tightened.

"If the press does get hold of any such documents, I'll sure as hell know where they came from." She pointed her index finger directly at Troy.

Troy's eyebrows raised. "Why would I do something like that? You're my meal ticket, Jessie. I'm just a bum lying on a beach somewhere smoking dope and living off chicken tenders and Cheetos."

"Your point is well taken, Troy. But you need to stop belittling yourself. I'm trying to reconstruct you into a confident young man."

Troy stared at Jessie without saying anything for an awkward stretch of a few seconds.

"How much do you miss my dad?" He pushed back his long locks—a nervous habit of his. "I've yet to see you cry over him or the mention of his name. You don't seem depressed or lost or brokenhearted. Did you really love him, or did you simply view him as you're ticket to a better life?"

Jessie's piercing eyes locked on Troy. "I miss him terribly, Troy. I don't wear my emotions on my sleeve. Never have." She finished retying her shoelaces and jumped from the sofa to her feet. "It's time to get back to work. We have to finish the pilot today. And I don't want to waste another minute of my life on whodunit or whether I loved your dad. Clear?"

Troy nodded.

They were only halfway through the pilot, but Jessie was demonstrating to both Troy and Halleck Stanley that she was just okay for TV. Stanley worried her high-pitched voice might be grading on the viewer. She had displayed a million-dollar smile when she needed it and, worse, when she didn't. But what male, Halleck Stanley was convinced, wouldn't spend thirty minutes drooling over her body, especially when it was covered in spandex, top and bottom?

It was shortly before 8:00 p.m. when they finished the pilot. Everyone involved in the production was tired after a nearly twelve-hour shoot—three hours alone just for blocking camera shots. Both Troy and Jessie had learned that TV can be a demanding business—prop setups and teardowns, retake after retake, hot studio lights.

Jessie was both pleased and a little surprised at how Troy had come off in the taping. She felt he had a good presence and delivered what scripted dialogue there was with more ease than she'd anticipated. Troy had seldom exhibited such an outgoing personality in the time she'd know him. And he looked great. She had worked tirelessly with him on his upper body, and when she watched the playback of several segments of the video, she saw a buffed guy who would definitely attract female viewers of almost any age. After all, she was nearly forty-five to his thirty-four, but she'd secretly had the hots for Troy from the day they'd first met at Big Erv's sixtieth birthday bash.

They would have dinner and then wait for the results of a focus group's screening in the morning. Jessie wanted time to chill out with Troy, so she asked Halleck if he'd mind if the two of them opted for room service at the Emperor's Palace, where they were staying. He was good with it, saying, "I could use some FaceTime with my Mexican princess."

Jessie laughed. "You rascal you. She's still in the picture?"

"Funny how trips to Puerto Vallarta keep clogging up my schedule," Halleck offered a wide grin.

Jessie laughed. "Like I've said before, just don't involve me in your divorce."

Both budding TV personalities were starved when they got to their room, and immediately Jessie ordered pizza from the hotel's Italian restaurant. She got her favorite, half pepperoni and sausage and a combo for Troy. When Jessie wanted to pig out, which was infrequently because of her compulsion to maintain a tight body, pizza was her calorie monster of choice.

While changing into her hotel-provided bathrobe, Jessie noticed that Troy had brought the section of the *LA Times* that had detailed his dad's plane crash with him to the room. Jessie walked over to where it was resting on the small desk next to the TV and picked it up.

"Why are you carrying this around?" Jessie asked, holding up the paper like it was courtroom evidence.

"It's not every day you learn about your father's death in a newspaper. I just wonder if Rachel knows about it."

"What if she does or doesn't?" There was a hint of anger in Jessie's voice.

Troy plopped on the room's king bed. "I just know she won't let it go. She'll do everything in her power to find out who did it. It's her bulldog nature."

Jessie laughed as she disrobed and invited Troy to join her in the shower. "She's not going to be able to do much with her ass in jail."

"She won't be in jail forever. It will just give her more time to try and figure out the whodunit as you called it."

CHAPTER TWENTY-EIGHT

If Rachel's growing determination for finding her dad's killer could be bottled, it might rival 5-hour Energy drink for shelf space. She had nothing else to do in jail but nurture her appetite for justice. It kept her from going stir crazy. It frustrated her no end that she couldn't make any significant headway with "operation whodunit", as she called it. Making her task all the more formidable was the reality that she had no idea who to turn to run with an investigation.

Trying to conduct business on the only phone on the jail's second floor where she was locked up was virtually impossible. Every time she'd thought of making a call, the line was six or seven women deep. The only sure way of getting to use the phone in reasonable amount of time was to do favor for the guards. That meant slipping into a utility closet with the guard and yanking on his piece until he shot his wad. One inmate in particular, LayVon Perkins, a lean black woman with a fro that could have been mistaken for a pad of steel wool, was so proficient at getting in and out of the closet with results that she never had to wait for the phone. It was automatic.

"LayVon, you may go to your rightful place at the head of the line," the guard who profited most from her time there would say. Making Rachel's task all the more formidable was the reality that she had no idea who to turn to spearhead the investigation.

Add to this is the fact she'd lost any and all jail privileges except meals for a week for being involved in a fight with three other inmates. Rachel was working out on the exercise bicycle in the jail's second floor communal pod trying to burn off some pent-up nervous energy when an inmate who'd earned the nickname Hefty Lefty made her presence felt. She had a three-hundred-pound frame and claimed a history as an amateur boxer who'd fought as a southpaw. Lefty for short, approached Rachel with her fight face powered to turbo. She wanted her turn on the bicycle, and she wanted it yesterday, no matter that Rachel had only been on it for less than five minutes.

From her ponytailed jet-black hair to the scar that accentuated her left cheek and lips that featured tattooed liner, Hefty Lefty didn't appear the type to have had much experience with diplomacy.

"Get your lovely ass off this machine, bitch. Nobody here cares you were once a pro athlete."

Rachel tensed as she continued to pedal. "I just got on this." Rachel was immediately angry with herself for not affecting a more assertive tone. "It's the first time I've used it since I got here."

Rachel had barely finished stating her case when two short Latina inmates sauntered forward from behind Lefty and became attachments to both of her large hips.

"You have exactly ten seconds to get off the bike, little lady." She glanced up at the large clock on the wall next to the guard's station and counted off the seconds.

Rachel realized she was in deep shit, but she'd never backed down from any challenge or any fight in her life.

"Or what?"

She didn't have to wait for an answer. All three women converged on her. Lefty, her arms as big as Idaho, wrapped them around Rachel as she thrust her body against her and yanked her off the bicycle like she was made of Styrofoam packaging, and the Latina duo began pounding their bare fists on her. The one with the red dye streaked throughout her brown hair worked her fists against Rachel's face, while the one with the waistline that could only have been achieved with a discount card to Donut King hammered at Rachel's body.

Three guards, one who'd tripped a siren, arrived at the scene on the run. Each took control of an assailant without much difficulty; the guards where so much stronger than the women inmates. All three ladies were taken down to the cement floor and handcuffed. Rachel remained on the floor, blood flowing from her nose and a nasty bruise already starting to appear under her right eye. The three combatants were given a week in the hole, and even though she was the victim, Rachel was docked her everyday rights—visitations, telephone access, TV, reading material—everything but a three-meal diet primarily made up of baloney and cheese sandwiches.

Later in her cell, Rachel tried her best to wrap her head around the reality that victims have no more rights than their attackers.

Cut off from the outside for a week, Rachel had no way of knowing about a turn of events that would impact her incarceration and allow her to finally push forward in hopes of finding her father's killer.

CHAPTER TWENTY-NINE

Stacy McAuliffe had been a hostess at the five-star El Encanto Restaurant in Santa Barbara for close to ten years. She was a fortyish, moderately attractive brunette, with welcoming hazel eyes and a slim figure, the result of years of working out at the local 24 Hour Fitness just down the block from her workplace. She'd never married, although she'd gotten as far as having once committed to wed a well-to-do financial planner from nearby Montecito. That didn't work out. Turned out, the guy was already married and had two kids—his other family living in Sacramento. "Oh, I figured you be okay with that" was his response when Stacy confronted him while holding a barbecue fork that was pointed at his balls.

The trauma of a love blown apart by a cruel deception had sent Stacy into an immediate and deep depression. As an outgrowth of her depression, Stacy began experiencing panic attacks. She'd never know when or where an attack would strike. She could always identify the attack. Dizziness, sweaty palms, a racing heart, and the fear that death was imminent were her symptoms. Driving her car became difficult, especially over bridges and on four-lane freeways. She would become certain of an impending heart attack that would cause her to crash. Dining out became an ordeal as she became inordinately self-conscious in public. Somehow the attacks never affected her at work, and she was able to keep her job and a degree of her sanity. After enduring these panic attacks for a period of close to five years, she finally sought help. Her general practitioner recommended Dr. Eileen Lindholm, calling her one of the best psychologists on the West Coast.

Stacy saw Dr. Lindholm on a weekly basis for several years. As a result of the doctor's treatment, which included the use of breathing techniques, meditation, and the prescription drug Zoloft, she'd been able to recapture functionality in public and drive her car without the presence of anxiety symptoms.

It was during the last six months of their patient-client relationship that Erin began to notice some unusual behavior by her therapist. On two separate occasions, Erin had run into Dr. Lindholm at the same Starbucks. She felt it was somewhat odd as they lived a good ten miles apart from each other.

Later, the same month Stacy was dining alone at the Chowder House on Stearns' Wharf when Dr. Lindholm entered the restaurant and took a table right next to her. Outside of an obligatory greeting, Dr. Lindholm did not engage her client in conversation. The encounter was so awkward that Stacy left the restaurant without finishing her meal. The next day, she called the doctor and left a voice mail saying that she was discontinuing her sessions indefinitely.

A couple of weeks later, Stacy had parked her car at the beach across La Playa Stadium with the intention of sitting in the quiet of her car and meditating. Several minutes after she'd turned off the ignition, a late model Audi pulled over into the parking space next to her. The driver was Dr. Lindholm. The doctor looked over at Stacy, smiled, and then opened a book and read for the entire time Stacy was parked there. The most recent incident of what Stacy now considered stalking happened at her house located a block from the historic Santa Barbara Mission. The incident made the news.

The headline on page 2 of the local section of the *News-Press* read,

Psychologist Arrested on Stalking Charge

SANTA BARBARA, CALIFORNIA—Respected local psychologist Dr. Eileen Lindholm was arrested early this morning outside the home of an unnamed female who identified herself as a client of the doctor. Police were called to the woman's home around six thirty. The arrest report says the psychologist appeared at the complainant's curtainless bedroom window as she was getting undressed to shower. The complainant reported that Dr. Lindholm was dressed in what looked to be an army camouflage jacket and simply stared at her through the window. The alleged victim said she retreated to her kitchen where she called 911. The doctor, meanwhile, began pounding on the woman's front door, begging to be allowed in the house. When police arrived, she was sitting on the front steps of the house, reading the morning LA Times. She spoke incoherently and was unable to explain her presence there. This is the second time Dr. Lindholm has been questioned by law enforcement agents. Three years ago, a female UCSB student filed a complaint that the doctor had fondled her during a therapy session. Charges were never brought as the young woman dropped out of school and returned to her home in Seattle, Washington. Under California law, stalking of a client by a licensed psychologist is an offense that could lead to the revocation or suspension of a practitioner's license.

Rachel's attorney, Jackson Pennington, jumped on the news like lime on a shot of Captain Morgan. Operating without Rachel's knowledge or consent because of her jailhouse restrictions, Pennington immediately petitioned Judge Fujita for her release on the grounds that Dr. Lindholm would no longer have been available or suitable to counsel her because of her recent arrest. Pennington told the judge he had received a strong indication from DA Thomas Hayes that he intended to prosecute Dr. Lindholm. He presented a letter signed by the district attorney outlining his likely intention of formally prosecuting Dr. Lindholm. That information, plus the fact Rachel would soon be called to testify against Bernard Coffee, who'd insisted on a speedy trial for sexual assault, convinced the judge to lift Rachel's probation hold with the promise she'd return to court to answer to unfulfilled probation mandates at a future date.

Because of the restrictions on her that were still in effect, Rachel had not heard about her good fortune until two jail guards presented themselves in front of her cell.

"You're free to go," the tall, skinny, pale-skinned guard said to her straight-faced and without any emotion. It was almost as if he were opposed to turning her or probably any inmate loose. "Your attorney has clothes for you that you'll find at the exit station on the ground floor."

Rachel was astonished by the news. She smiled wide, shed a tear, and jumped in her small cell like a schoolgirl.

"There is hope!" She said it loud enough for a few inmates who were housed near her cell to clap and shout for her.

"Honeyball is alive and back in the game" came a voice that Rachel recognized as Janella Hopkins, a black private security guard who was doing time for credit card fraud. Janella was the only inmate who'd regularly communicated with Rachel—mostly during meals.

Jackson Pennington was waiting for Rachel in the jail parking lot. When he saw her clear the ominous exit gate, he got out of his car and strode swiftly in her direction. As soon as she recognized him, Rachel broke into a trot. When she reached him, she hugged him for the longest time.

"Thank you, thank you." The words rushed out of her mouth like they were trying to escape a fire. They both jumped in Pennington's Mercedes sports model and headed off in the direction of Rachel's condo. "I don't even know if the Charros are in town. I'm so out of it, Mr. Pennington. Jail is like a time warp. Nothing happens on the inside, while the world outside is doing ninety miles per hour in a sixty-five-mile-per-hour zone."

Pennington smiled at the analogy. Probably in his late fifties, Rachel guessed, he was a short man, with sandy-colored hair and a fast-receding hairline. Rachel viewed his comb-over as Hall-of-Fame-caliber.

The man knew how to dress. His suit and tie was top-of-the-line Italian design. *If times in the law business got tough, he could easily double as a Nordstrom manikin*, Rachel thought.

"I think your team is home to San Jose tonight. I read the other day whether they'd lost something like four in a row, and some media types were questioning whether their bubble had burst. I know they're one or two games behind Rancho Cucamonga."

Rachel searched for information on her iPhone that would substantiate what Pennington was telling her. She couldn't help thinking how much she'd missed a telephone and the Internet during her jail stay. Being disconnected from society in jail was one thing; not having news of the world at your fingertips with a smart phone was a real bummer. She would readily admit she'd felt ostracized.

"Thanks for the update. I totally lost my connection to the organization. I hope I can find some good karma for a change and the team will come roaring back to the top of the standings."

As Jackson Pennington pulled his Mercedes onto Cabrillo Boulevard, the sun was beginning to set on the West Beach Marina. Rachel remarked about the beauty of Santa Barbara and confessed to missing gorgeous scenes like the one before them. After a period of silence, Rachel asked Pennington if he had any idea how she might find out who tampered with the engine on her dad's plane.

"I'm determined to make someone pay for his death."

"You certain of the prognosis?"

"Confirmed."

"Let me ask around. I know a lot of attorneys who've been involved in air crash cases. I'll make some calls for you."

Rachel reached with her left hand and placed in on Pennington's shoulder. "That's the greatest news I could imagine."

CHAPTER THIRTY

Back in the Charros' saddle after a three-day hold for her eye bruise to clear, Rachel entered her ballpark office high on life again. She'd actually skipped like a child during a portion of her walk to the park. She entered her office to a robust welcome from her Honeyball staff. There were balloons and streamers all in the Charros' black and blue colors. Staff members stopped by to welcome her back three or four at a time. Rachel was overwhelmed. To one group, she said, "You really like me. Or is it because I sign your checks?" When Adrienne Telfair poked her head into Rachel's office, it was a welcome-back with good news.

Rachel smiled and got up from her desk to give her a hug. "I will take any great news you have, Adrienne."

"I just read on Minor League Baseball's Web site that we're in first place in attendance per stadium capacity in all the minor leagues. That fact is going on our Honeyball billboards tomorrow."

"You got my okay, Adrienne. Got to push the brand at all times."

For the next couple of hours, Rachel put together an extensive "to do" list and sat with her finance chief to review revenues versus operating expenses. Rachel was pleased to learn the team's income was 110 percent up from last year through the same amount of games. Beer sales were through the roof. Rachel laughed when she floated the notion to herself that UCSB and its fun loving students were making her look like a baseball genius, if not the perfect role model for their sons and daughters.

Several hours before game time, Rachel paid a visit to Dom Benedetti. When she entered the players' locker room, she was overwhelmed by the booming sounds of Bruno Mars's "Grenade" playing on the $50,000 stereo system she'd installed two weeks into the season.

One of the players, Stuart Weisnstadt, a gangly left-handed relief pitcher who was the Nuke Deluche of the squad, walked up to Rachel with a huge grin. "Should have been here yesterday, ma'am. I had everybody rocking to AC/DC."

"Sorry I missed that." Rachel smiled. "Sorta."

When she got to Benedetti's office, she found him engrossed in the paperback edition of *Fifty Shades of Grey*. Obviously embarrassed by the quizzical look on Rachel's face, he quickly jammed the book into a desktop file holder and stood up to greet her. "Found it one of the players' lockers." His reply carried too little conviction.

Rachel smiled. "Hey, there are no rules against reading material, Dom." She wanted to know how things were going and what the reason was for the team's recent four-game slide.

"Focus. Attention to detail. We've got a bunch of good young players who started reading and hearing how good they were, and they got sloppy, especially on defense. They'll get back on track. I promise."

Rachel asked if there were any concerns.

Dom was quick to respond. "Two words—Austin Grant."

Rachel raised her eyebrows. "It can't be related to baseball. My god, he's off to the best start of practically any other minor league player."

"It's his social life I'm worried about, Rachel."

"Uh oh."

"Yeah, uh oh! I hear from one of my coaches that he's hanging out a lot with—what's her name, our fitness trainer."

"Lydia?"

"That's the one."

"That's directly against my policy, Dom. I'll speak to both of them and put a stop to any kind of budding relationship." Rachel stood up to leave. "Any other worries?"

"I'm worried about our guy at first base, Brandon Rollins. He's struggling big time. He's batting .179 through forty games. Can't hit a curve ball to save his behind."

Rachel pushed back her hair and pretended to place it in a ponytail before letting it reset on her shoulders.

"He's the only holdover from last year."

Dom looked for a wastebasket in hopes of tossing out his expired wad of bubble gum. He eventually wrapped it in a tissue and placed in on his desk for disposal at another time.

"He got a million to sign out of Auburn University two years ago. From what I know, everyone in the organization, all the way up to Devin Baxter, thought he was a can't-miss prospect. I don't know if he can survive failing another year at class A. He hit twenty-eight home runs his senior year at Auburn, but since he became a pro, he's hit only five."

"That's so sad, Dom. Is there any hope for him?"

Dom was slow to answer. "Not if he keeps striking out twice a game."

Rachel slipped into thought for a second. "Maybe I could get Devin Braxton to come here for a couple of days and work with him."

"You know Devin, that well? He's a very busy guy."

"Anything for my players," she said, only wishing that she could add what she was thinking. *And anything for Rachel as well.*

Rachel put off for another day confronting both Austin Grant and Lydia Gregory about any kind of relationship between them. Grant was too much of a franchise superstar to reprimand on the word of a coach, who just might be jealous of the chick-magnet Grant had become in his short stay in Santa Barbara.

Rachel put in a phone call to Officer Deke Slayton, SBPD. Deke had been on the Rancheros squad for three years as a catcher. But after failing to get a promotion to double A ball—his lowly .202 batting average sealed his fate—he chose to retire. Instead of returning to his hometown of Pontiac, Illinois, a small farm town a hundred miles south of Chicago, he stayed in Santa Barbara and signed up for the police academy. He finished his training first in class and was given a job on the force after graduation. Rachel had run in to him at two Charros' games this season. He was a handsome blond-haired, thick-muscled guy who had a baby face that belied his competitive toughness as an athlete. Rachel had always liked him as a fan when she'd attended Rancheros' games with her dad. If he'd ever asked her for a date, she would have seriously considered it. She liked his look and admired what she'd heard about his work ethic.

CHAPTER THIRTY-ONE

They decided on coffee at the Peets on Upper State Street close to where Deke shared an apartment with another cop. They exchanged hugs before sitting down to matching pumpkin spiced lattes. At her request, Rachel got Deke's story on why he'd decided to quit baseball, and at his request, she tap-danced around detailing her recent jail experiences.

When Deke asked what he could do for Rachel, she said, "I may have a personnel issue."

Deke sipped his drink and then offered a knowing smile. "Is it Austin Grant?"

"Yep."

"Not surprising, Austin's making quite a name for himself on and off the field."

Rachel briefly checked an incoming text on her phone and then said, "Details, please."

"He's been hanging out at Quinn's Gentlemen's Club on numerous occasions."

"Where's that?"

"It's in a strip mall on the Mesa. Not all that far from your new ballpark, which I must tell you is a real work of art. Your dad's legacy will eventually include the park along with his car dealerships."

Rachel curled her hair with her index finger. "He's twenty-one. Technically, he's allowed to do whatever he wants. Any of his teammates go there with him? Half of our roster is under twenty-one is why I ask."

"From what I've heard from the officers who've answered the calls to Quinns, it's his homies from Southern California. They're the same four or five guys every time. Most of the time they're wearing Pierce Community College leather jackets."

"He specifically has been warned on two occasions that I know of to refrain from boisterous behavior. I personally responded to a complaint this week by the bar manager that he was be overly aggressive with one of the club's scantily clad cocktail waitresses. He supposedly inappropriately grabbed a black girl who had, how do you say . . ." Deke cupped his hands and placed them next to his chest.

"Big tits." Rachel smiled. "You can say that in my presence."

"But you're a lady."

"Thank you for the compliment, Deke, but there are no ladies in the baseball business. Just women who work their asses off." Rachel thanked Deke for his time and asked that if he hears any more about her boy wonder that he give her a call.

Deke got a little red in his already rosy cheeks and asked, "Can I give you a call on a social matter?"

Rachel dropped her chin and smiled. "Sure." She immediately hated herself for saying that. She knew she was on a track with Devin that could lead to something special. *Time to stop being the flirt,* she admonished herself.

It didn't take long for Rachel to get Deke's call. Late the next night after the Charros, despite three solo home runs from Austin Grant, had dropped a 5-4 decision to San Jose in the only home day game on the schedule that featured a one-o-clock start time. The rare start time, which cut attendance in half, was done to accommodate San Jose, which was coming off a twelve-game road trip with a day game of their own the following day. Shortly before midnight, Rachel got the call she wasn't hoping for from Officer Slayton.

"Sorry to bother you this late," Officer Slayton began.

"Not a problem. I have a difficult time coming down from a close loss. Even wine hasn't done the trick after today's loss."

"I don't have good news, Rachel."

"Austin?"

"I'm afraid so. And the charge is serious."

"Oh god."

"I got the call on this one, shortly after nine o'clock. Actually, two of your people were involved. Austin Grant and a female named Lydia Gregory. She identified herself as a fitness trainer for the Charros."

"What happened?"

"According to witnesses, they got into a verbal altercation outside the Surfside nightclub which is located adjacent to the Funk Zone. Apparently they'd both been drinking somewhere else before they got to the Surfside. At some point, Grant grabbed her breasts and shoved her. She retaliated by pushing him back. That led to a skirmish of sorts that ended with Grant punching her in the face and knocking her out cold. A patron exiting the club called 911. Grant had gone back into the club and was doing tequila shots at the bar when I arrived."

"Shit!"

"Your guy is in some serious trouble, Rachel."

"What happened with Lydia?"

"We radioed for an EMT. They took her to cottage hospital. You should be able to check on here there. She was conscious when they loaded her on the gurney. She was able to tell me that she worked for the Charros and asked that we not press charges. I told her that wouldn't be possible."

Rachel went silent for a few seconds while her phone signaled an incoming call. "Oh god, here come the news hounds—my least favorite reporter from the *News-Press*. I have to take this call, Deke. Thanks so much for the heads up."

"You're welcome. Maybe the next time I call, it will be for a different purpose."

"Maybe."

CHAPTER THIRTY-TWO

Jackson Pennington seldom answered calls to his direct line. He had a secretary for that, but Lana San Felipe was off on a family emergency—translated, her sixteen-year-old son was again suspended from school for bullying a fellow student.

"Hello, Rachel! Great to hear from you." Pennington leaned back in his expensive leather desk chair and put his feet on his desk. "To what do I owe the pleasure?"

Rachel laughed. "I haven't been a pleasure to many people lately."

"That doesn't hold water with the person on this end."

"Thank you. You're such a sweetheart." She told him about the situation with Austin Grant and asked if she'd put herself in any kind of compromising legal position by suspending him indefinitely.

"I read where Mr. Grant had gotten himself in some serious trouble."

"I could see it coming from day one," Rachel said. "The guy is good-looking enough to get any woman he wants. And he wanted any woman he could get as soon as he hit town. I've never told anyone this, but he actually came to my house one night after a game, in which he'd hit a pair of home runs and stood at my door, and asked me point-blank if I would have sex with him. 'Your loss' was his response to my emphatic no."

"That's confidence. It's too bad because you hate to lose your best player and fan favorite. But to answer your question, I'm certain every player has a personal conduct clause in his contract with the big league club. Just by being arrested, Mr. Grant, has more than likely abused the intention of that clause."

"I've already received a truckload of grief from the Friars' owner about the suspension. He called me first thing this morning. He was so condescending with me on the phone. 'We believe in "due process" in this organization' was how he justified his objection to my move. I told him what I thought he believed in. Your $2 million investment is up to his ass in starving coyotes for beating up a woman, and you're getting nothing for the money but bad publicity."

Pennington jumped in. "Your suspending him was the right move, Rachel. I'm wondering how you arrived at that decision."

"It was easy, Jackson. How would it look to women everywhere if a baseball organization that prided itself on an all-female staff allow a player arrested on a sexual assault charge be allowed to continue to occupy a roster spot in the name of 'due process'? Ray Rice taught us a lesson about due process."

"Your point is well taken."

"Thank you. I respect your opinion."

"What about your employee—the fitness trainer?"

Rachel sighed. "I have to let her go. I haven't told her yet. She's still pretty shaken up. The hospital isn't allowing any visitors other than family. I really liked the work she was doing. It's almost a bigger loss than the player. Every employee that I hired signed an agreement that contained a 'no fraternization clause.' I'm just disappointed that I didn't get to her soon enough to direct her out of harm's way. I blame it on my being in jail."

"Don't be too hard on yourself, Rach." Pennington asked if Rachel could hold the line as he had another call. "I have some news I want to share with you."

Rachel waited on hold for several minutes, enduring more of Kenny G's melodic tones than she'd bargained for.

Pennington came back on the line with a new energy in his voice. "I think I've found the guy to investigate your dad's death."

"Really. That was fast."

"He's a longtime friend of your dad's. They were golfing buddies for years. You may remember him. Jim Hankins is his name."

Rachel paused for a moment. "No, not offhand. What does a golfing buddy know about criminal investigation?"

"Hold your horses, girl. Let me finish."

"Sorry."

"He's a former Santa Barbara County deputy sheriff—an IT guy. He's credited with cracking the biggest student loan scam in Santa Barbara County. The culprit preyed on UCSB students. In the five years before he retired, he also was a pilot on the sheriff department's air patrol. He meets all requirements. He's a techie who flies. He lives in Arcata which is convenient."

"Doesn't ring a bell, but I'd like to meet up with him as soon as possible."

"He told me he could fly down here the end of the week."

"Book him. You're a prince, Mr. Pennington."

CHAPTER THIRTY-THREE

Shortly after 2:00 p.m., Rachel held a news conference in the ballpark lounge. She felt fortunate that today was an off day for the Charros so that once she got through her news conference, she could chill out the rest of the day and evening. Austin's arrest was big news enough that *Sports Illustrated* sent its lead baseball writer, Jason Nadel. The *LA Times* dispatched columnist Gino Asbury. Arthur Spelling, perhaps the most cantankerous sports columnist on the West Coast, represented the *San Diego Union*. TV crews from both LA and San Diego were also on hand, plus all the local "hacks," as Dom Benedetti so endearingly labeled the Santa Barbara newspaper and TV guys who regularly covered the team.

Rachel stepped to a microphone-filled podium. She could present herself as "beach girl regal" when she chose. This was one of those times. She wore tan slacks, a black polo shirt, and a dark blue blazer with the Charros' logo pin on the lapel. Her hair was uncharacteristically wet; it added sizzle to her look. She spewed confidence with every movement and looked like the celebrity that she'd become.

"I'll make this brief." She did not have notes, instead choosing to make eye contact throughout. "I have suspended Austin Grant indefinitely and released team fitness director Lydia Gregory for their participation last night in an unfortunate altercation at a local bar. Austin Grant was jailed and booked on a charge of sexual assault by Santa Barbara Police. His arraignment will likely take place tomorrow. He's currently out on $10,000 bail posted by a family member. Lydia Gregory is resting comfortably at Cottage Hospital. She sustained a concussion and a fractured jaw." Rachel paused. She fought back tears. "Forgive me for making this brief, but that is all I'm prepared to say at this time. I will not be taking questions." She turned and disappeared into the kitchen area.

Rachel breezed through the kitchen to an exit that led directly to her office, her sanctuary. Her personal cell phone that she'd left on her desktop was ringing. She immediately recognized the tone as the one she'd downloaded for Devin Braxton's calls. *Anyone with a special ringtone must be special*, she found herself thinking.

"Hey, you. It's good to hear from you."

"I'm glad, but you may not want to hear what I have to say."

Rachel inhaled. She hadn't expected any negativity from Devin. "Explain."

"The man in charge here in San Diego is barking at me to get my ass to Santa Barbara and 'straighten you out,' his words."

Rachel was taken aback by Devin's message. "Don't waste your time, Devin."

"I'm coming, all right, but I need you to know that I fully, 100 percent, support the action you've taken."

Rachel let out an audible sigh. "Boy, I thought you'd jumped ship there for a minute."

"You know how I feel about you, you should by now anyway."

"I know, Devin, but this has been a stressful day, and I was beginning to prepare myself for even more shit when you said I might not want to hear what you had to say."

"Sorry, I was referring to what Zeller commissioned me to do, which I won't do. I'm vehemently opposed to allowing Austin to continue playing while the legal process, which could take all season, plays out. There's a reason today's athletes don't understand the meaning of accountability. It's because some fat cat owner, with an ego to match his wallet, will always be there to play the 'due process' card. But it does provide me with the opportunity to hop on a plane and romance you with dinner and—"

"Oh, I like the 'and' part. I could really use some of that. See you when?"

"I get into Santa Barbara at seven."

"I'll pick you up."

"And then . . ."

"Maybe we should just skip dinner."

"What I'm hungry for has nothing to do with food."

"Good."

After a fifteen-minute drive from the airport to Rachel's condo, which featured a significant amount of hand-holding, the two reached a compromise on food and ordered a pizza for delivery.

"Despite all that's been happening in my life, I've honestly been trying to keep tabs on the Friars. You guys got out of the gate fast, but what's your losing streak at now?"

Devin's eyebrows rose and sank. "Eleven. Our starting pitching has been a tremendous disappointment. And we don't have much pop in the lineup. I think old man Zeller was considering bringing Austin Grant strait to the majors—and soon."

"Is he that good? I see what he's done for us, but is he ready for that big of a jump?"

"No. Only one in a million are. It's what happens when an owner doesn't know anything more about baseball other than the fact that the ball is round."

Once home, Rachel, who'd changed to shorts, sandals, and a T-shirt after the news conference, poured Devin a second glass of red, sat down close to him on the couch, and put her arm around him.

"What would you say to me becoming a commuting lover? Every other weekend, I'd fly down to San Diego to be with you."

Devin straightened. "I'd love it, but don't you have your hands full here?"

"Adrienne proved she could take the reins during the time I was in jail. A weekend here and there isn't going to take the ship off course."

"I'm all for it, Rachel—all in." He raised his wine glass in the form of a toast to Rachel's good idea.

Rachel leaned into Devin and kissed him warmly, then passionately. Eventually, they retired to Rachel's bed and another round of what both later agreed was we-can-never-top-this-sex.

In the morning, Devin awoke to a text from his daughter, Chloe.

"I have a boyfriend, Daddy. His name is Eric. He plays baseball at school."

Learning the great news from Chloe and lying in bed next to a lovely woman whose athletic bare leg was extended from under the bed sheets was about as good as it gets in Devin's mind. And that was far better than what it would get in the eight business hours that lay ahead.

CHAPTER THIRTY-FOUR

Devin's first order of business on the new day was to schedule his own afternoon news conference about Rachel's putting Austin Grant on the shelf. He was expected to present the Friars' stance on the suspension. He chose to hold the event at the Four Seasons Biltmore instead of the ballpark. The reason for that would become clear with his message. The same media members that covered Rachel's news conference the day before, plus two more San Diego TV crews and at least three radio reporters from that city, showed up at the swank hotel.

The fact the San Diego contingent had increased substantially offered a hint that this would not be your run-of-the-mill news event. Arthur Spelling, who actually lit up a cigar in the Rose Room where the news conference was to be held, had floated the notion that the Friars were about to call Austin Grant up to the big club in spite of his legal issue.

"Zeller will do anything for a W. He's such an unconscionable asshole, he spouted to colleagues."

"Tell us how you really feel, Arthur," Channel 30's sports manikin said, hoping to dispel Spelling's seemingly ridiculous statement.

The idle chatter that the media members were engaged in subsided the instant Devin Baxter entered the room. He was dressed in an expensive brown pinstriped suit with a blue oxford shirt and a striped tie that matched both colors. He looked as if he were ready for a *GQ* photo shoot. He exuded charisma that had extended well beyond his playing days. The fact he wasn't wearing his "go to" camel-colored Friars blazer was a tip-off to some in the media that something out of the ordinary was about to take place.

Devin chugged on a bottle of water before beginning. "Thank you all for coming. I will make this short and sweet. Friars' owner Irving Zeller has directed me to facilitate the call up of Austin Grant to the Friars' twenty-five-man roster effective immediately."

The buzz in the room was immediate. Arthur Spelling rose to his feet. "I told you, assholes."

A reporter from the same San Diego newspaper shouted out, "Put out your fucking cigar, Spelling!"

"Fuck you."

Devin waited patiently for the commotion to die.

"I am not a lawyer, and I don't know the protocol for reassigning a player to a major league roster who is on suspension and charged with the sexual assault of a woman. The simple fact is I'm not the guy to do that. I've told Rachel Haslett that contrary to my boss, I fully support her decision to indefinitely suspend the young man. At this point, you might be thinking Devin Braxton's opposition to his boss's directive is akin to professional suicide." He took another sip of water, more for effect than from thirst.

"So be it." He paused in the hope of keeping his composure, but his quivering lower lip gave him away. "I'm announcing my resignation effective today, ending a twenty-three-year run as both a player and a member of the front office of the San Diego Friars. I love most everyone in this organization, but I no longer choose to associate myself with an owner that puts the almighty dollar ahead of the legal process. It's been a pleasure working with all of you. Thank you for coming." Devin exited the room to a stunned silence.

Rachel was more shocked than anyone over Devin's announcement. He'd not discussed his decision with her the night before. She'd learned about it in a phone call from the most impacted source, Friars' owner Irving Zeller. His tone could best be described as combat ready.

"You have made a federal case out of a transaction you are legally bound to comply with under the agreement the Friars have with your franchise," he ranted. "Your directive to suspend Austin Grant makes it nearly impossible for me to develop the young man's talents at any level. The key word there is *nearly* because I will now stop at nothing to add him to the Friars' big league roster effective immediately. He has been charged with a crime. Not convicted of a crime. You can kiss his ass good-bye from your club for now and forever. Good luck getting rid of those Austin Grant jerseys that have made you a ton of cash. And just so you know this owner doesn't play games with insubordinate franchisees, I will begin the systematic draining of your talent pool by moving your best players to our double and triple A franchises. I plan to leave you with a bare cupboard. As you may know, I'm not legally compelled to support your twenty-five-man roster. You may have to play center field yourself, darlin'. Maybe you can recruit some of your Honeyball ladies to fill the roster holes. Have I made myself clear, Ms. Haslett?"

Rachel laughed. "Sounds like I'm going to have to lawyer up."

"Good idea because in the lawsuit I'm going to bring against you, I'm going to further punish you by proving you have a romantic tie to my former general manager that influenced his decision to retire from my organization, causing disarray in my front office and impacting the Friars' chances of playing championship caliber baseball."

Zeller was almost out of breath. Almost.

"In other words, Ms. Haslett, by fucking my GM, you just fucked yourself." He hung up.

CHAPTER THIRTY-FIVE

Rachel had to switch gears quickly. She had to push Irving Zeller's vitriol and the state of the Charros out of her mind for the time being in order to prepare for a meeting with Jim Hankins. He'd called her first thing in the morning and said he would be available to meet with her sooner than he'd planned. He'd told her he'd be flying into Santa Barbara Municipal Airport as soon as the maintenance check on his plane was completed—late afternoon he estimated. He asked if she could meet him in the business lounge at the newly reconstructed airport.

Rachel was surprised at the symptoms of anxiety that had suddenly gripped her as she guided her silver Jeep Cherokee north on Highway 101 toward Goleta and eventually the airport. Her palms had become clammy on the steering wheel; her stomach was full of butterflies. It was how she used to get before a volleyball match. She even took a moment to passively wonder if she was doing the right thing by trying to find her father's killer without the support of law enforcement. She worried she'd become too obsessed with the idea and had lost touch with what should be her priority, her Charros.

As she steered the Jeep into the airport's short-term parking area, Rachel took a deep breath and exhaled slowly while mentally scolding herself for even thinking about wimping out on her pledge to find the person responsible for Big Erv's death. It was the only way she would ever find closure. It was a clear case of scoreboard. That's how she'd lived her life, and there was no reason to change it now. She went by the scoreboard.

Jim Hankins was using his laptop when Rachel entered the airport's small inexpensively decorated business center. He was the only person in the room, thus the easy ID. She was surprised that she did recognize him. His sandy hair was thinner and his waistline larger than the last time she'd remembered seeing him, but he was clearly the same guy who used to pick up her dad—never entering the house—to play golf practically every Saturday.

As he got up to shake her hand, Rachel noticed a slight trembling of his left arm. She figured correctly that he was in the early stages of Parkinson's.

"You've grown up to be such a beautiful woman, Rachel. It's been how long since I last saw you?"

"Probably twenty years." Rachel hung onto his outstretched hand while she spoke.

"I'm so glad your attorney—"

"Jackson Pennington."

"Yes, Jason."

Rachel didn't want to correct him.

"I'm so happy he reached out to me to conduct an investigation. Next to you, nobody on the planet wants to identify your dad's murderer more than me. I loved your dad. He was a great man. Intense as a winter storm but with a sense of humor that brightened so many people's lives."

"This job comes at the right time for me. Three months ago, I lost my wife to a ten-year battle with Alzheimer's. It's the ugliest disease on the planet earth. For ten years I lived by myself in a house we shared. The woman I married and loved was living inside that house, but there was no one home in her mind."

Jim took his index finger and wiped at a tear that was trickling down his face.

"I need to be busy so I'll stop constantly thinking about her. And a man can only play so much lousy golf. So let's get this party started."

Rachel took a seat next to where Jim had parked his laptop. "Where do we begin?"

"With my compensation, Rachel."

"Of course."

"There won't be any. This is a freebie. I'm repeating myself, but I want the perpetrator in the worst way. I may not be as spry as I was when I retired from the sheriff's department fifteen years ago, but you won't find a more dogged investigator at any age. I will find this person."

Rachel reached from the chair she was sitting in and placed her hand on Jim's hand. "You're so kind, but I'm prepared to pay you well."

Jim, who had a kind face with sparkling blue eyes and a dimple on his chin, was adamant. "No, this is on me."

Rachel raised the palm of her hand like she did when she was in school and wanted the teacher's attention. "Then you have to stay at my place when you're here working on the case. I have an extra bedroom upstairs. It's presently my workout space, but I can move everything there to the garage. Oh, and I can get you a car from my dad's dealership here in town. Would a Chevy Blazer work for you?"

Jim smiled, and his face grew even nicer. "That's kind of you. All of it works for me."

Finance and logistics out of the way, Rachel moved the discussion to whodunit as she said with a smile. She mentioned the same three names that she'd originally considered as prime suspects: Troy, Jessie, and Will Greene. Jim said he knew each of them.

"Where should I start?"

Rachel closed her eyes in thought. "I would suggest Jessie Santiago. She certainly benefited the most financially from my dad's death." Rachel spoke of Jessie's getting her dad's life insurance payout and almost all his estate. "Which, I've decided, I'm going to contest."

Jim slapped his right hand on his knee. "Jessie Santiago is where I'll begin. I'll keep you informed of my progress at every turn."

Jim got to his feet to again shake Rachel's hand. For the first time since they'd started talking, Jim exhibited a quizzical look on his face. "I'm surprised you named your brother, Troy."

"He's had an intense degree of anger toward my dad ever since he was a little boy. When Dad handed me the reins of the baseball team over Troy, he became distant and angry at me and seemingly everything and everyone."

"Investigating Troy will be painful, Rachel."

"For both of us."

CHAPTER THIRTY-SIX

The road was not the Charros' friend as they dropped each game in a four-game set with Visalia and followed that up by losing three out of four to Rancho Cucamonga. The losses dropped them six games behind Rancho Cucamonga in the standings at the halfway mark of the season. The absence of Austin Grant's big bat had proved to be the difference. With Austin, the Charros had averaged five runs a game, without him, just 2.5 runs.

Dom Benedetti had hoped Brandon Rollins would see Austin's departure as the perfect opportunity to evolve into the club's power guy, but it just seemed to put even more pressure on him. He'd gone into a 0-for-26 slump and hadn't hit the ball out of the infield but twice. The loss of Grant and the likelihood that Irving Zeller was about to raid his roster had taken some of the bounce out of Benedetti's step.

"I don't know if my guys can give you what you deserve," he'd said to Rachel before getting on the bus to Visalia.

Halfway through the series with Visalia, the Charros got even more bad news. The guy who'd replaced Grant in center field, Joaquin Davalos, was busted by an inspector from minor league baseball for chewing tobacco during a game. Davalos was suspended for two weeks. Benedetti was doubly frustrated by the penalty, as he wasn't aware of anyone in the league ever getting caught with a chew. Most managers and front office personnel had been under the impression the rule sounded good, a distinct PR move, when it was adopted by minor league baseball but was so loosely enforced it had become a joke.

Because Rachel had planned to skip the Visalia series—she would later admit she was hanging close by in case Jim Hankins got any leads and catch up with the team when they traveled to Rancho Cucamonga, she was subjected to the wrath of Edith Finnegan, matriarch of the team's longest-standing host family. Edith, who was in her eighties and had just hooked up with husband number 3—husband number 2, drunk off his ass from nipping on his flask of Maker's 46 whiskey, had crashed his golf cart into a large palm tree on the sixteenth hole at La Cumbre Country Club and died from severe head injuries—came storming into Rachel's office with a tale about catching Charros' second baseman, Robby Wine, making out with her seventeen-year-old granddaughter in the bedroom she'd assigned him on the backside of her seven-thousand-square-foot ranch home.

"He was rubbing his hand on her ass too," Edith said, the veins in her neck pushing at her skin and her coral-colored permanent refusing to allow her hair to move, even though she was speaking fast and gesturing with both arms. "I don't want him in my house ever again." She slammed her fist on Rachel's desk.

"I'll have a talk with Robby, Ms. Finnegan. And I'll find another family to take him in."

"Better let some of the testosterone out of his tires, or you'll have the same problem wherever he goes."

Rachel stood up and shook Edith's hand, an indicator that the discussion had just ended. "One question, Ms. Finnegan. What was your granddaughter doing in Robby's room in the first place?"

"Well, Ms. Rachel, are you suddenly defending your player's actions?"

"No, just curious."

"He asked her to help him set up . . . I think she called it a Twitch account."

"Twitter."

"That's it. Like he's four years older and couldn't figure it out by himself?"

Edith Finnegan huffed and puffed her way out of Rachel's office sounding like the little chugger fun train at the Santa Barbara Zoo.

No sooner had the Charros limped back home from Rancho Cucamonga than Irving Zeller, who somehow managed to bring up Austin Grant to the Friars, even though he was placed on his own recognizance by a superior court judge in Santa Barbara, blew up the roster as promised. He promoted slick-fielding shortstop Omar Escobar, catcher Hector Fuentes, and three relief pitchers, including closer Josh Hamlin, to Double A Des Moines. He flat out released Brandon Rollins, even though he had to eat his original signing bonus.

While everyone in the league and the media that covered them expected the Charros to go into the tank as the result of the multiple transactions, Rachel and her Honeyball leadership team (marketing, player personnel, and merchandizing) appeared undaunted on the surface, especially the boss.

"We can't do anything about who plays for us, but we can offer the same ballpark atmosphere as before." Rachel paced the lounge where she'd gathered her staff and talked as she walked. "I've booked four girls from the pro volleyball tour to play a pregame exhibition next home stand. We'll truck in sand and make it like the real deal. We'll call it 'bikini beach night' at the ball yard. Adrienne, make sure we canvas Isla Vista with thousands of flyers. We'll target every guy in that community with a testosterone level above dead." She couldn't restrain a wide smile. "I've also signed the Guerrero Sisters, just off their 'I've Got Music' triumph, to perform their Tex-Mex music prior to the August 1 game with San Jose. We're going to maintain our unbelievable attendance numbers in spite of our wins and losses. And I've got a lot more where those ideas came from."

Rachel was disappointed that Devin couldn't spend more of his suddenly acquired free time in Santa Barbara. But he'd taken a few weeks to visit his daughter and reconnect with her in person, something he was never able to do during the baseball season. And he was hoping to convince his wife to go to court and request a lesser monthly child support payment plan. He was also taking the time to consider an offer by Fox to provide some studio commentary for their *Baseball This Week* show. Rachel understood. A career in broadcasting had often crept into their conversations. He frequently had brought up the subject of life after the front office. She figured it was just a sign that he didn't like his boss.

With a single phone call, Jim Hankins managed to take Rachel's mind off both the Charros and Devin Braxton. He was calling from LA, where he'd booked a flight to Santa Barbara.

"I've been doing a background check on Jessie Santiago, and I want to present you the details in person. Turns out, your dad wasn't her first sugar daddy."

"Why does that not surprise me, Jim?"

"This guy had twice the money your dad had. 'Had' is the operative word. I'll tell you all about it when I get to Santa Barbara."

"Please consider spending the night at my house."

"I'll take you up on that, Rachel."

Four hours after his phone call, Jim Hankins was seated in Rachel's living room. Bags under his reddened eyes made him look tired. Rachel noticed his left arm was shaking more than when she'd first met with him. She worried the investigation had perhaps stressed him too much. He put his glasses on and referred to notes he'd taken on his iPad to tell Rachel what he'd learned.

"His name was Herman Riddick. He owned over three hundred Riddick Tire stores throughout the country. *Get Riddick for the Road* was his ages-old marketing slogan. I even remember hearing that on radio commercials." Hankins went on to describe how he'd left Jessie Santiago, who was in her early forties to his sixty when they met, his entire fortune. "He was worth a hundred million at his death. He had two kids. They got zipped."

"Has a familiar ring to it."

"His kids were shocked, even though they'd been estranged from him ever since he divorced their mother almost a decade ago."

"Happy family."

"Jessie hasn't received anything yet. His estate has been tied up in court for years. The kids contested it. No surprise there. Lawyers getting rich is the end result."

"How did he die?" Rachel asked.

"Supposedly, he was working out on his home treadmill and got his foot caught on the edge of the moving track. It threw him completely off the treadmill, and when he landed off the back of the machine, his head banged against a metal stand that supported several sets of dumbbells. The impact resulted in a giant gash to the back of his neck. He was knocked unconscious and essentially bled to death alone in his state-of-the-art home gym."

Rachel got out of the love seat that was situated opposite her couch where Hankins was seated. "Coffee, Jim?"

"Sure. I'm running a little low on energy."

Rachel fixed them each a black coffee on her Keurig. "Who's your source for all this information?"

"I wondered when you were going to ask. Trust me, I'm not making this up."

"I do trust you."

"He's the former general manager of his Reddick's Glendale store. I contacted him by way of a Google search. Google is amazing." Hankins smiled for the first time. "Everybody's footprint is out there in space if you just look hard enough."

Rachel extended to Hankins his cup of coffee and sat back down in her chair. She curled her hair with her index finger.

"How did they meet?"

"Same as with your dad. She was assigned as his trainer at a fitness club in Sherman Oaks near where he lived. He was big into weight training. He could bench-press 275 pounds—not bad for a guy his age. Jessie's training regimen emphasized cardio. She weaned him off free weights and assigned the treadmill to be his new friend. Apparently, they became an item just a few months after they'd met. She had the same MO that she'd had with your dad. He showered her with gifts, mostly jewelry, and took her on extensive vacations at some of the world's great garden spots. He was in the process of buying her a gym facility of her own. The ex-GM told me he thought Jessie really loved his boss."

"The girl knows how to work it," Rachel said with a smirk. "So his death appears to have been an accident?"

"Yes. But I want to be 100 percent certain. I've got someone—a friend of mine, a former LA County sheriff's deputy—who promised to dig through police records that would provide an account of what happened."

Rachel let out a sigh. "If it checks out as an accident, we're still at square one."

"I'm not finished. I was able to hack her online banking account, and I did find something interesting."

"What, that she's a philanthropist and gives to the poor and hungry?"

"No. I checked her credit card statement for the month your dad died. A week after his death, she bought gas at an ARCO station in Eureka."

Rachel's eyebrows rose. "Maybe Jessie and Will Greene are in it together."

"It's worth my time to go snooping in Will's backyard."

"I'm all for it," Rachel said, extending Jim Hankins a high five.

CHAPTER THIRTY-SEVEN

Losing a four-game series at home to the Bakersfield Blaze pushed Charros' skipper Dom Benedetti to the brink and the Charros into third place, nine games behind Rancho Cucamonga.

"I'm losing my fucking hair!" he'd shouted at Rachel in their most recent meeting prior to another home series, this time against the Stockton Ports. It was the first time he'd raised his voice in her company. "The only way we can hit one out of the park now is if I pick up a used rocket launcher at the Army Navy store. Our relief pitchers should be investigated for arson they fuel so many fires by failing to miss our opponents bats."

Rachel felt sick to her stomach for her manager, a nice guy who, until two weeks ago, was enjoying the opportunity of a lifetime managing a team loaded with talent and revered by the home fans. As she sat next to him at his clubhouse desk, she could see lines in his face that weren't there at the start of the season. He'd had the world by the balls one moment—leading the league in the standings and impressing everyone in baseball with his managerial skills—translated Austin Grant's big bat. Rachel understood better than anyone the depths to which the Charros and their manager had sunk was her fault. *Play the "due process" card and everything would have been fine*, Rachel chastised herself internally.

"I'm going to find you some free agents, Dom. I'm not going to hang you out to dry. Take the next couple of hours before the first pitch and make me a list of positions that you need filled, and I'll go after replacements with a vengeance."

Benedetti rolled his eyes that were lodged below his bushy eyebrows and produced a grunt that reeked of sarcasm. "Where are you going to find replacement players? I don't think Sports Authority is running any specials on amateur second basemen or lefty relievers."

"Just leave that up to me. You'll see." Rachel placed her hand on Benedetti's shoulder before exiting his office. She could feel the daggers he must have been concealing.

Rachel retreated to her office and immediately searched her iPhone for the contact information Devin had given her for the female pitcher who'd lobbied for a tryout with the Friars in spring training. She found it. *JACQUI DAVENPORT: PARENTS: 520-734-5501.* This was an idea whose time had come.

She reached Randal Davenport on the first try. He was an insurance salesman for State Farm who worked out of his home 50 percent of the time. He had a friendly baritone voice and appeared genuinely excited that someone from a professional baseball team was calling about his daughter.

Rachel quickly learned that Jacqui had made the rotation as a freshman on Arizona State's team—a club that was projected early on to win the PAC 12 title but hadn't lived up to its potential and likely wouldn't make it past the conference tournament. According to her dad, she'd already appeared in seven games as a middle reliever and had posted a 2.79 ERA in twelve innings. Randal Davenport was so proud of his daughter Rachel swore she could hear the buttons on his shirt pop as he spoke.

"She's walked two and struck out six," he added. "Her slider is major league level nasty." Randall paused for a second. "Of course, I could be slightly overzealous in my thinking. But it's my daughter."

"How would you feel about her dropping out of ASU and joining the Charros for the summer?"

"She'd jump at the chance. And her parents would fully endorse it."

"Just so you know, by signing with me she'd become the first female ever to pitch in professional baseball. There was a woman. I think her name was Justine something who pitched batting practice for Cleveland in spring training, but no female has ever pitched in a live game at any professional level. It's bound to capture a lot of media attention. Do you think she could handle it?"

"She's already had plenty of local media coverage pitching for the Sun Devils. It wouldn't be a problem. She's a very mature young lady."

Rachel said she would fly her into to Santa Barbara within the next seven days and give her a one-day tryout. "The expense is on me. I'll put you and your wife and Jacqui up at the Four Season's Biltmore."

Rachel didn't want Dom Benedetti to know she was trying out a female, so she kept Jacqui under wraps, which wasn't an easy task. Jacqui had learned how to party at ASU, and as soon as she landed in Santa Barbara, she began inquiring about Isla Vista social activities.

"You're here on a mission, Jacqui" were Rachel's words of advice. "I want you focused on baseball." Jacqui smiled her killer smile and said she understood and that she was just trying to be funny.

Rachel had reserved the baseball diamond at San Marcos High School for an hour and offered the catcher for a semi-pro team in town fifty bucks to work behind the plate. She wanted to see Jacqui pitch against someone of class A-league caliber, so she called on Deke Slayton to see if he would take a few swings against her. That was an easy decision for Deke. Anything Rachel was all good in his mind. Rachel went a step further and purchased a Jugs speed gun online. She wanted an accurate accounting of Jacqui's velocity.

Much to Rachel's surprise and Deke's shock, the girl had stuff. She threw him a predetermined forty pitches, and he hit just seven on the sweet spot. And it wasn't as if a couple of years away from baseball had made Deke rusty at the plate. He'd taken four days of batting practice against several pitchers on the UCSB Gauchos staff prior to his assignment with Jacqui. He hit only one pitch, a hanging curve, over the fence at the three-hundred-eighty-foot mark. He got nothing but air every time she threw her slider.

After consulting with Deke and agreeing to drinks "someday," Rachel decided on the spot she was going to make baseball history. She took all the Davenports to Lucky's, a trendy restaurant in Montecito, and told them, "I'll pay her $800 a month for the remainder of the season, and she can stay at my place when the Charros are in town."

After handshakes all around, Rachel asked Jacqui to report to the team in four days. She advised all the Davenports that, on her arrival in town, the first order of business would be a news conference to introduce Jacqui.

"We can't wait," said a proud Randall Davenport.

Dom Benedetti could have.

Just prior to the series-ending game with Stockton, Rachel called Dom into her office and broke the news about Jacqui. His response caught Rachel off guard. His body language was that of someone who had been defeated. His shoulders were slumped, and his eyes were downcast.

"I don't expect you to be thrilled by her signing, Dom, but I have to keep butts in the seats somehow. Realistically, we no longer have a shot at winning the pennant. We both know that, but it doesn't mean I'm conceding setting a minor league baseball attendance record."

Dom took the news without a response.

"I can't tell you how sorry I am that we're no longer competitive. It certainly wasn't your fault."

Dom got up from his chair and exited the office in silence. It was what he did afterward that shocked Rachel.

Ten minutes later, Cindy Blevins, the clubhouse girl, rushed into Rachel's office barely able to break her sprint in time to avoid plowing into her CEO's desk. Her pale cheeks were pink, and her sandy hair was soaking wet from having just showered. If she'd shaken her head, she would have irrigated every plant in Rachel's office, and there were many. She took a deep breath before speaking.

"Mr. Benedetti just went bonkers in his office. The noise was horrifying. He must have destroyed everything in there."

Rachel didn't wait for any more of Cindy's description. She headed directly toward the player's locker room. She felt her heart pound against her chest as she opened the door. There was no sign of Dom Benedetti anywhere. Rachel relaxed briefly while she surveyed the damage. He had taken a baseball bat to his laptop, overturned his desk, punched a hole in the wall next to the door, and yanked a fifty-inch flat screen TV, which Rachel had recently bought for him, from its wall mount, splintering the screen in a thousand pieces. On the floor next to several framed photos of himself with Charros' players was a handwritten note on the back of a Charros' souvenir program that read, "I FUCKING QUIT!"

Fearing Friars' boss Irving Zeller might further stick it to her by doing something crazy like resurrecting Jenks Houghton's career and sending him to take over for Dom Benedetti, Rachel got proactive. She again asked for Deke Slayton's help. She understood it was a risky move as it was obvious to her he had a crush on her. Over coffee at a Starbucks on Lower State Street, Rachel asked Deke to take over as the Charros' interim manager and also fill the void left by the departure of catcher Hector Fuentes on the twenty-five-man roster.

Deke had chosen a muscle T-shirt for the occasion, and he had muscles to market. Ever since he'd joined the police force, he'd taken to weight lifting. He'd added a good twenty pounds of muscle since his playing days. Jeans and flip-flops rounded out his attire. He'd dramatically improved his tan since the last time she'd seen him.

"Could you get a leave from the PD?" Rachel asked. "It would only be until the end of August."

Deke fidgeted with his sunglasses that he'd parked on small table they were occupying. "Whew. That's a tough one. I've only been on the force a little over two years, Rachel. I don't qualify for any kind of leave. It would really require the chief granting me the time as a favor to you."

Rachel smiled and played with her hair. "It would be a great PR story for the department, don't you think?"

"The only PR Chief Addison is interested in is bagging another bad guy. All I can do is ask. You know I'd love to help you out of the mess that asshole Grant created." Deke reached out for a handshake and gripped Rachel's hand for far too long for her liking.

"Let me know as soon as possible." Rachel awkwardly pulled her hand away and stood to leave.

"Instead, how about I keep my cop job and do some snooping around on the side to see if I can dig up anything on your dad's plane crash? I read about it some time ago in the paper, but I was reluctant to offer my services because I know you already have someone on the job."

Rachel squinted. "How do you know that?"

"I'm a cop."

Rachel slid her eyes into space as if she were looking for an answer. "You're more valuable to me as a player-manager, Deke. But I do appreciate your wanting to help."

Deke nodded, as if he understood, and said, "I'll give you my answer as soon as I meet with the chief."

CHAPTER THIRTY-EIGHT

An introductory session with her new psychologist and a court appearance in Bernard Coffee's pretrial hearing prevented Rachel from devoting any significant time to rebuilding her roster beyond acquiring Jacqui Davenport. Keeping close tabs on Jim Hankins's investigation added to her already full plate.

Her day consisted of an early morning meeting with the psychologist followed by an eleven-o-clock court date. Dr. Thomas Marmar was a short ivory-skinned man with a splotchy salt-and-pepper mustache. He had a noticeable right eyelid tick that flashed repeatedly and appeared to be totally beyond his control. In contrast, he had a quiet demeanor. When he spoke, it sounded like his words were traveling on a velvet blanket.

Unlike with Dr. Lindholm, Rachel was resigned to the fact that she would have to take the sessions with Dr. Marmar more seriously than in the past. She'd brought her personal notebook to the session as evidence of a new attitude. She quickly found herself to be much more at ease with him as they sat face-to-face in his sterile-appearing office. The only picture on the wall was one with him posing with Dr. Ruth Westheimer, the celebrated sex therapist. "My brush with the famous," Dr. Marmar explained.

Everything in Dr. Marmar's office had its place. His desk was completely free of clutter. A Clayton Kershaw bobble head was the only article on his desk other than a telephone. A true blue Dodger fan, Rachel theorized.

Only a minute or two following their initial greetings, Rachel got a shock that she'd hadn't imagined coming.

"I've reviewed your case history thoroughly . . . May I call you Rachel?"

"Certainly."

Dr. Marmar stroked his mustache several times. "I really don't understand how you were remanded to seek anger management counseling. It's a waste of the state's money. In both episodes where you were arrested for aggravated assault, you did what any red-blooded woman or man would do. You reacted with instinctively. You didn't provoke either incident. You shouldn't have been punished for your accuracy, both with your fist and your beer mug. I was fortunate to have obtained Dr. Lindholm's notes—it took a court order—on your three sessions together, and nowhere do they suggest that you're capable of becoming a societal risk as Lindholm was want to believe."

Rachel's eyes widened. "I've always heard you should get a second opinion on everything, and this is a good example."

Dr. Marmar got out of his rich leather chair, walked to the room's only window, and pulled the shade halfway down. The heat on Rachel's face generated by the incoming sunlight was reduced in half for which she was quietly thankful.

"To pursue further therapy is, in my mind, a waste of everyone's time. I'll record this as a fourth visit and waive the remaining six visits that are required by your court order."

Rachel wore a look of surprise. She had a habit of biting her lower lip when she was excited. "You can do that?"

"Not exactly," the doctor said with a sly smile. "But I can make up bogus session notes and stamp the papers as if we'd actually had the sessions. I've done it before, and I'll probably do it again. You have no reason to see me again."

Rachel was so overcome by Dr. Marmar's actions that she leaped to her feet, gave him a giant hug, and kissed him on his cheek. "You're a saint, Doctor."

Bernard Manuel Coffee's pretrial hearing before Judge Helen Wakefield in superior courtroom B on a charge of sexual assault was in sharp contrast to Rachel's low-key visit with her psychologist. County assistant district attorney Hailey Strathford was first to present her evidence. She immediately called Rachel to the witness stand.

Rachel was dressed very businesslike in a gray pantsuit, a black oxford shirt, and medium heels. It was the only true business attire she owned. Rachel was more than surprised to find reporters from both the *News-Press* and the *Independent* in the courtroom. She cringed at the sight of Miles Rooney sitting in the media section of the courtroom. The notion of Rooney possibly frying her again in one of his columns unsettled her stomach. Exhibiting her sternest possible face, lips, and cheeks on lockdown, she caught Rooney's glance and returned fire with eyes that could have launched missiles. He returned fire with a full-on smirk.

The assistant DA was a tall dark-haired woman who had a slender face that was half concealed by a modest bob haircut that was combed forward. Her heavy dark highbrows and the hint of a mustache gave her a masculine look that wasn't becoming but probably enhanced her persona as an intimidator. Her track record in felony cases in her three years on the job was impressive. She had not lost one of her nineteen cases.

Ms. Strathford's first order of business was to fire up an overhead projector. After a computer glitch caused a delay of a few minutes or more, an image of Rachel's bare left buttock flashed on the screen that was located to the left of the witness stand so Judge Wakefield could have a better view. A red arrow was used to highlight her injury. The image clearly showed a six-inch-long scratch on her buttock.

Ms. Strathford asked, "Can you explain the scratch mark we're seeing here, Ms. Haslett?"

Rachel produced a slightly nervous smile. "That was taken by one of the police officers shortly after he'd arrived at my condo. The scratch was from Mr. Coffee's fingernail. It happened when he pulled my panties off." Rachel looked down at her chest. "It actually bled for a few minutes."

Ms. Strathford turned away from Rachel and, with a blank face, addressed the judge. "That is all the evidence I'm prepared to enter at this time, Your Honor."

Judge Wakefield sat up straight in her chair and tried her best to conceal an expression of surprise. After studying a paper that was before her, the judge instructed Bernard Coffee's attorney to proceed with his arguments.

Coffee's attorney asked Rachel to remain on the witness stand. Elgin Bashford was a tall black man in his late thirties, with close-cropped hair, deep-set eyes, and intense expression that made him appear to be ready for combat with a junkyard dog. After pausing to loosen his tie, he immediately went on the attack—Rachel's credibility was his target.

"Ms. Haslett, can you please state what you were wearing on the two occasions my client came to your door"

Rachel wore a puzzled look. "What I wear most of the time—shorts, a T-shirt, and sandals. All made by Chicos. I have a modeling contract with them."

"Just answer my question, Ms. Haslett. I don't need any qualifying statements."

Rachel nodded. "Actually, the first time he visited unannounced, I had on running gear—shorts, bathing suit top, and running shoes. I changed into jeans before I let him in my house."

Bernard Coffee smiled and winked at Rachel from his place at the defense table. Rachel caught his glance and, for a brief moment, thought she might hurl him.

"Was this not your attire most times, even away from your home?"

"I'm known for my casual attire. Am I not allowed to wear those clothes?"

Mr. Bashford quickly turned and faced Judge Wakefield. His eyes reflected anger. "Your Honor, is it too much to ask that the witness not revert to unsolicited commentary or questions with every answer?"

Judge Wakefield took off her glasses and produced a stern look at Rachel. "Please refrain from excess verbiage, Ms. Haslett. Simply answer the questions."

Bashford flashed a satisfied grin. "Ms. Haslett, on the night in question, did you not purposely direct my client's attention to your abundant and exposed physical attributes by telling him that you wished the Charros played more day games because you were yet to get a tan from the moon? And did you not seductively run your hand down your bare leg to help accentuate your dilemma?"

Rachel's face tightened. She bit down on her lower lip. "I did no such thing."

Bashford, who was impeccably dressed in what appeared to be a suit of European design, approached the witness stand from his desk chair in the center of the courtroom. His eyes locked on to Rachel's. "Did you not invite my client to join you in an adult beverage prior to his alleged act of aggression?"

Rachel gasped and shook her head. "I did nothing of the kind. The guy had previously propositioned me with—"

"Your Honor, the witness continues to add commentary."

The judge made a notation on a legal pad. "Ms. Haslett, I don't want to warn you again about answering the question. Is that understood?"

In a surprise move, Mr. Bashford suddenly excused Rachel from the stand and called her next-door neighbor forward. He got her neighbor, a feeble-looking man in his eighties, to state that Rachel frequently had men staying overnight in her condo.

"I'd call it a steady stream of men visitors," Herbert Holland testified.

The old man's fabricated claim wasn't convincing enough for Judge Wakefield. After Bashford had finished with Holland on the witness stand, she set a July 10 trial date and increased Coffee's bail by another $5,000. That pushed his total bail to $25,000.

"I consider you a flight risk, Mr. Coffee," the judge said.

Coffee dropped his head in the direction of his chest and then raised it back. He then raised his eyes toward the ceiling and mouthed the words "I will get you." That sent a chill down Rachel's spine.

CHAPTER THIRTY-NINE

Jessie Santiago woke up at 6:30 a.m.—early for her—on a Sunday, leaving Troy to another hour of sleep before they hit the hotel fitness center. They'd been out late the night before at *Andale* on Santa Monica Boulevard in LA attending a coming-out party for Halleck Stanley and his Mexican cutie Mia Hinojosa. In less than two months, he'd ditched his wife of ten years and left her with their three kids.

Wearing only a Hyatt Century Plaza issued bathrobe—she'd upgraded her living conditions since recording the *Slo-Go Fit* pilot— Jessie finger dressed her sex-messed hair in the hallway mirror and then made a cup of coffee. She wandered from the kitchen and plopped onto her hotel suite sofa and powered on her iPad. Once it booted up, she immediately Googled *Variety*. She'd been given a heads up by Langly-Hoffman's marketing director to expect an online review of the first week of *Slo-Go Fit*. A good review in the "bible of entertainment" would ensure a healthy start to her show and more than likely a long and prosperous shelf life. The pending review had been on her mind ever since the first show had aired.

The commotion from the suite's main room awakened Troy. It was Jessie, swearing at the top of her lungs. He quickly hopped out of bed, made sure he had his balance—three hours of margaritas can leave even the best drinker unsteady—and rushed to the main room only to find Jessie with her head in her hands, her elbows resting on her open laptop.

"Shit! Shit! Shit!" It was all she said. She repeated the cycle several more times.

Troy rushed to her side and sat down on the couch. He put his arm around her and asked, "What is it? Tell me!"

Jessie started crying. After a few seconds, she pointed to the screen on her iPad. She'd enlarged the font so Troy had no trouble reading the story.

"Read this piece of shit!"

New TV Fitness Show Has Weighty Issues
Variety *Columnist Bill Ellerby*

Something called Slo-Go Fit debuted this week. It's distributed in syndication by Langly-Hoffman, which hasn't had a hit show since Dubbya first took office. This show had to have been created by someone with a vendetta against the fitness industry. Webster's defines **lame** *as* **not strong, good, or effective.** **Lame** *is the perfect word to describe this thirty-minute waste of time that gives new meaning to the word* **vacuous.** *The show is cohosted by two television unknowns, Jessie Santiago and Troy Haslett—only Torres is licensed to teach the slo-mo method. The premise of the show is how to lift weights slowly and lose weight at the same time, exercising only twice a week. That's like asking Jim Carey not to show any emotion while doing a scene where he meets the girl of his dreams, only to have her run off with Danny DeVito. The male host (Haslett) is more wooden in his presentation than a* *fence post. While they're both good to look at, the cohosts have the combined charisma of a banana slug. Torres appears to believe she has TV charm based on her obsessive frozen smile that she manages to sustain even while talking. But it's a plastic charm—no doubt manufactured by some overpaid Hollywood talent coach. Here in La La Land, those kinds of personalities are a dime a dozen. Her cohost, who is billed as fitness TV's hottest newcomer, looks and acts like he's been teamed with his mother. For the record, they're eleven years apart in age. How on earth will two people who have no on-camera chemistry pull off a five-days-a-week syndicated show which the sole purpose is to lift a weight slowly and grunt like you're topping Mt. Everest. My advice to Jessie and her manikin of a partner is to take a deep breath and deep six the idea that anyone can get ripped by slowly lifting weights for twenty minutes twice a week. It's the show's sponsor, Weight Stoppers, that's getting ripped off.*

Jessie closed her laptop as soon as Troy finished reading the story. She wiped her tears with the back of her hand.

"We're fucked, Troy."

Troy got up and walked to the coffee maker and made himself a cup.

"It's just one asshole's opinion, Jessie. We've only aired five shows."

Jessie coughed up a laugh. "We'll be lucky to do five more. That asshole you speak of happens to be one of the most influential critics in the whole damn TV industry."

Troy showed no emotion to Jessie's impending doom reaction to the variety story. Instead, he pulled out his iPhone from his bathrobe pocket and conducted a lengthy search for the California League's home page. He studied it for a moment and then said, *"Yes!* The Charros lost their fifth in a row 9-2 to High Desert. Keep those losses coming, baby."

Jessie grabbed a pillow from the couch, jumped to her feet, and smacked Troy in the face with it. She thrust her weight forward and held the pillow against his face until he gasped for air and pushed it away.

"Were you trying to kill me?"

"I feel like it." Jessie's green eyes took on a red hue. "We're hanging to our jobs by our fingernails, and the only thing that gets your attention is your sister's team losing another game. What in the hell is wrong with you? Are you so obsessed with getting even with her that nothing else matters?"

Troy's silence angered Jessie even more.

"Say something. Or are you staging another 'silent Troy moment' that I've heard so much about?"

Troy walked over to the kitchen table and sat down with his coffee. He stared out the window at the traffic twelve stories below. He watched as couples jogged on the quiet boulevard. He might have appeared to be processing what Jessie had told him, but he wasn't. He was simply asking himself why anyone would want to live in LA.

"You need to hear me, Troy." Jessie took a couple of minutes to power her computer back up. "I've got more fucking good news to share with you." The sarcasm in her voice was strong. "I received a LifeLock alert first thing this morning."

Troy's expression finally changed. He flashed a quizzical look at Jessie.

"It's an online company that I pay to protect myself from identity theft. Well, they informed me by e-mail that my online bank account had been compromised."

"How so?" Troy sat up at attention, his body language doing a complete 360.

"I spoke with LifeLock's customer service person after I received the e-mail alert. He told me someone had accessed my checking account and my credit card statements. They couldn't tell me who did it, just what they did." Jessie moved into the kitchen and put away some dishes from the washer before resuming her explanation. "I'm guessing it's someone working for your sister. I'm thinking that it has to do with either your dad's will or his death."

Troy's eyes suddenly locked on Jessie. "Didn't I tell you a month ago she might come at you hard over the will?"

Jessie moved to the kitchen table and sat down next to Troy. "You seem to think it's the will, but I think—call it a woman's intuition—she's having someone look into his death. Just a hunch."

Troy's face dropped.

"What do you think?"

Troy didn't answer.

"Hello, I asked you a question?"

Still no answer.

Jessie put her face up in Troy's and, with her index finger, poked him in the chest. "Is this your 'no talk issue' coming to the surface again?"

Without responding, he got up from his chair, changed out of his bathrobe, and exited the suite, wearing jogging shorts, an old Rancheros T-shirt, and Nike running shoes. He didn't say a word as he closed the door behind him. He never returned.

CHAPTER FORTY

By the time Jacqui Davenport arrived on the scene, the Charros had righted the ship ever so slightly under the guidance of Deke Slayton—he'd agreed to take a graveyard shift upon his return to the police force from his Charros' sabbatical. A series split with Bakersfield and four road victories over Inland Empire helped the Charros cut into Rancho Cucamonga's lead by two games. They trailed by five games with forty-six games to go. Chad Isner, a lightning-quick second baseman, who Rachel had plucked from Hancock College's roster, had joined the Charros two weeks ago and had made a major impact hitting .397, driving in twelve runs, and stealing half dozen bases. Chad was a lean white-skinned mustachioed dynamo on and off the field. His motor ran constantly. And like Austin Grant before him, he ran after women like he ran the bases—full throttle.

Lonnie Wilhelm, a long-legged richly tanned daughter of TireCo president Winston Wilhelm, worked as Charros' account sales assistant and became Isner's first hook-up. After only his fourth game in a Charros uniform, he was caught by an alert security guard having sex with a just-turned-nineteen-year-old Lonnie in the backseat of an orange-colored Zipcar in the stadium parking lot. Upon learning about the incident, Rachel blamed herself for failing to caution both of them about office sex. She'd had to tap dance around a one-week suspension for Lonnie because of her dad, but she packaged it with a five-game suspension for Chad Isner as well. In both cases, fraternizing with the opposite sex was the stated reason.

Adrienne Telfair continued to exhibit her marketing genius. Through the down weeks after Irving Zeller had raided the Charros' roster, she'd managed to keep attracting sellout crowds with nightly promotions like a pregame karaoke competition, an MLB 15 video game contest between two UCSB students that was shown live on the ballpark scoreboard, a fast-texting competition between two Santa Barbara City College female students that was also shown on the scoreboard, and a dueling DJs' event between the best DJs from the four area high schools.

None of this, however, prepared either Rachel or Adrienne for Jacqui Davenport's first appearance in the charcoal and blue. She was selected to start her first game as a pro on a Saturday night at home against Stockton. It was made clear by Deke Slayton to Rachel, Adrienne, and everyone in the organization that she would only pitch an inning or two. It was Adrienne Telfair's idea. She figured if fans knew in advance when Jacqui would be pitching, they'd be more likely to attend to witness the historic moment as opposed to not knowing what night she would get the call from the bullpen.

The event attracted media from all over the country. All three network news operations, plus a reporter from the *PBS News Hour*, had requested media credentials. ESPN was hosting *Baseball Tonite* live from a location just outside the entrance to the ballpark.

At a scheduled news conference that afternoon in the swank ballpark dining quarters, Rachel had introduced Jacqui.

"She stands on the precipice of an epic accomplishment in women's sports" is how Rachel began. "She has yet to flinch from all the attention that has come her way in the last few days, and I don't expect her to tonight."

Dressed comfortably and mildly stylish in a Charros polo shirt and designer jeans and wearing a black beanie that had been given to her by young women from a tribe in Nigeria that she had learned about in a black history class at ASU, Jacqui showed no signs of nervousness.

"Hello, world" were her first words as she took a chapter out of Tiger Woods's PGA debut book. Her sparkling eyes, a smile so big it changed zip codes midmouth, and her infectious personality allowed Jacqui to "capture the love," as she was want to say it, of the assembled media. "I just hope your expectations aren't too high," she told reporters. "I'm just a girl with a pretty fair slider and a lot of faith in myself."

Jacqui didn't disappoint. A standing-room-only crowd of close to seven thousand fans—Adrienne had ordered temporary bleachers installed next to each team's bullpen and begged the city's fire chief to look the other way with his safety enforcement codes—cheered her every pitch. After giving up a lead-off single to Stockton's center fielder, Jacqui settled down and struck out the next three hitters. Each time the third strike was a slider that danced from one side of the plate to the other and down.

After her third strikeout, Melanie Sandberg told her radio audience, "That girl's got a better slider than White Castle."

Satisfied he'd seen enough of his new recruit and not wanting to spoil the party by allowing her to get lit up by going another inning or two, Deke Slayton told Jacqui she was done for the evening and ordered her to hop out of the dugout and tip her cap to the crowd.

On cue, the PA announcer shouted, "Ladies and gentlemen, please share this moment of history with all your Facebook friends!"

Jacqui followed her manager's instructions and added a little flair by actually taking a bow. What followed was a fireworks display that could be seen and heard all over town. Inspired by the pyrotechnics and doubtless a couple of twenty-ounce beers, a young white male in his late teens wearing a "Honeyball Rocks" T-shirt jumped out of the stands and raced onto the field and reprised Morgana, the Kissing Bandit, by planting his lips on Jacqui's cheek before she could retreat to the dugout. After the game, Jacqui told the reporters that the guy had offered to marry her as soon as tomorrow.

The Charros won the game, 4-1, thanks to Deke Slayton's three-run homer, his second since becoming the club's skipper. It was a real plus for the younger players to see Deke produce on the field. They were in shock at the departure of Dom Benedetti and the stripping of the roster. Their collective confidence as a team had been swept away like an ocean breeze pushing away coastal fog.

Despite Deke's heroics, the postgame media attention belonged solely to Jacqui and Rachel.

"I was a little juiced up," Jacqui told reporters. "That's why I couldn't get the ball down to their lead-off hitter."

A reporter for NBC News asked her to put her experience in perspective.

"It was certainly better than my senior prom."

Laughter spilled out throughout the media room that had been set up in the dinning lounge because of the size of the media contingent.

Rachel was asked for her impressions of the historic evening. She stepped to the podium like a proud mother who'd just given birth.

"I'm so happy for Jacqui. What a great kid! More important, she's going to strengthen our bullpen, which is something we need if we're going to get back in the race for the California League pennant."

Even Rachel couldn't believe she was again using the word *pennant*. She celebrated the win and Jacqui's history making successful debut by inviting every last Honeyball lady to a postgame beer, wine, and pizza party at Arnoldi's Café, an old brick structure located at Olive Street, not far from the old Laguna Park, where the Rancheros used to play. She went to the extent of hiring a Dixieland band that played "Take Me Out to the Ballgame" as employees got off the chartered bus to enter the small venue.

Moments after she'd stepped to a microphone and welcomed everyone, Rachel felt the vibration of her phone in her back pocket. Since it was just one vibration, she naturally figured it for a text. The moment she finished her greeting, she checked her iPhone—her habit for always being responsive. What the message contained rocked her world.

"Stop looking into Erv Haslett's death or die."

Rachel felt her legs wobble. Only once in her life had she experienced her strong athletic legs weaken. It was during her match for her first beach tour volleyball championship. The tension was such that the physical exertion from a three-set match made her legs feel like they were made out of rubber. This feeling, however, wasn't from fatigue. It was different. From her sessions with Dr. Lindholm, she recognized it as anxiety. She suddenly felt like she existed in a vacuum. There was music and laughter all about her, but in her suddenly altered world, there was just silence and the text message. The words *or die* had a paralyzing effect on her psyche.

Rachel pulled Adrienne aside and told her about the text and asked her to make up a reason for her sudden departure. She called for a taxi and slipped out of the party unnoticed. On the way home, the words from the text played over and over in her mind. *Who would send such a message?* she wondered.

Her first impulse was to call Deke Slayton and ask for his advice on what to do. Surely he'd been involved in cases where death threats were made. She decided against that idea, not wanting to give Deke the slightest opportunity to move on her romantically. Jim Hankins was the obvious choice, but it was nearly eleven o'clock, and he would, no doubt, be asleep. After several minutes, during which she opened a bottle of Patron and chugged on it, Rachel gave in to her anxiety and called Hankins.

"Hello" came out a consonant and a vowel at a time on his end.

"Jim, I'm sorry to wake you up, but I just received a text that threatened me with my life if I continue investigating my dad's death."

There was a long pause at Hankins's end. "What were the exact words?"

Rachel knew the words by heart. She spit them out with distain in her voice.

"You need to report it to the police. They can track the text to the phone where it originated. With my law enforcement contacts in Santa Barbara, I can get that information." Hankins paused midsentence. Rachel figured it was a memory lapse. Finally, he continued, "This way, you'll have two of us looking to find the source of the text."

Rachel paused. She could feel Hankins's energy begin to fade. "I have a fragile relationship with law enforcement in this town. I'm a little leery of going to the police, even to dispute a parking ticket."

Hankins started coughing and didn't stop for a good thirty seconds. Rachel recognized it as a harsh smoker's cough. "All that cigarette smoking is catching up with me. I just hope I find the guy who killed your dad before I die."

"I won't let you," Rachel said.

"Please, Rachel, it's late. Let me process this in the morning when my head is clear."

Rachel took a deep breath. "First thing?"

"Seven o'clock sharp."

Rachel waited up the whole night.

CHAPTER FORTY-ONE

Rachel's phone rang at 6:50 a.m. She made a quick mental note to thank Jim Hankins for being über prompt. To her surprise, however, the name that appeared on her phone's screen was that of Jessie Santiago. She was immediately annoyed for a number of reasons— Hankins would be calling soon, and she didn't want to miss it, and she had as much desire to speak with Jessie as she would the Night Stalker. Still, she surprised herself by sliding the bar to accept the call.

Jessie's speech was rushed, and she sounded short of breath. "I'm sorry to bother you so early, Rachel. Have you seen or talked with your brother in the last day or so?"

Rachel noted the time on her kitchen clock: 6:52 a.m. She had a great excuse for making the call quick. "I'm expecting an important call in a few minutes, Jessie. Can I get back to you?"

Jessie's voice went up a notch. "It's important. We have a shoot this morning here in LA, and he's, like, disappeared. He walked out on me two days ago after giving me the silent treatment. Is that what he does? I know he's had issues about talking."

Try as she might, Rachel couldn't conceal a laugh. "I haven't seen or heard from my brother since he told me you got all of Dad's insurance money."

The phone went dead on Jessie's end.

Rachel smiled and put her phone to sleep. At precisely seven o'clock, Jim Hankins reawakened it. "Hi, Rachel. Sorry I couldn't spend more time with you last night. When you get to be my age, you need a consistent good night's sleep."

"I should have waited until morning, I apologize."

Hankins was victimized by another coughing spell. "Damn, the first cigarette of the day always does this to me."

"You don't want me to get on you for smoking, do you? Because I will."

"No, I'm a lost cause. Listen, do you have a phone number read out on the text?"

In anticipation of the question, Rachel had written the number down on a piece of paper: 415-867-7200.

"That's a San Francisco area code. I'll check it out and get back to you by noon."

Much to her own surprise, Rachel passed on her morning ritual, a five-mile run along the Cabrillo Avenue sidewalk that ran adjacent to both West and East Beaches. Despite being a year removed from the beach volleyball tour, she'd continued to condition her body like she was still competing. She'd often wondered if it wasn't her subconscious way of holding out hope for a comeback. Instead, she busied herself by visiting on her computer a YouTube link that had been sent to her by an unsolicited prospect via the Charros' Facebook fan page. His name was Erik Bloomquist. He was a sophomore outfielder at Woodbridge College in Cedar Rapids, Iowa. He'd compiled a season and half of his highlights, both hitting and fielding, and edited it into a five-minute *sizzle* video. Despite his small frame—he'd listed his height as five feet nine inches—he showed good power. Rachel counted eight home runs on the video. Defensively, he exhibited good range in the outfield. He included one expert that was taken from ESPN's Sports Center, where he'd raced hard after a deep fly ball to leftfield and snagged the ball just before crashing through a flimsy outfield fence in a game at Iowa Central. Somehow he hung onto the ball for the final out of the inning.

He'd explained in his e-mail how college wasn't for him. He had no idea what he would major in. He said his only interest in life was baseball and that he'd promised himself he'd find a career in the game somewhere, somehow, someplace. In his e-mail, he said he'd read about the Friars' raiding the Charros' roster in the *Sporting News* and figured she would be in need of some good free agents. In his most recent e-mail, he offered to travel to Santa Barbara on his own dime in order to try out for a roster spot.

Rachel liked his self-confidence and telephoned to invite him to come to Santa Barbara at his earliest convenience. She told him she would pick up the tab for his transportation. Even though she'd already extended Erik the invitation, she forwarded the link to his video to Deke Slayton, asking him to let her know what he thought of his talent.

Keeping everyone in the loop was important to Rachel, even though she was beginning to get a creepy feeling about Slayton. In the last week, he'd sent her a dozen texts—all with the same theme, getting together for drinks after a game. She didn't know how much longer she could stall on an answer. He was doing a great job with the team, and if he kept hitting like he'd been the last couple of weeks, the Friars might have a renewed interest in him long term. Rachel knew he'd give the police work up in an instant if he believed there was a chance he could advance in their organization.

Shortly before noon, Rachel heard back from Jim Hankins. His tone was that of frustration. "The phone number was assigned to a Tanya Espinosa who lives in Daly City, just outside of San Francisco."

Rachel said, "What would this Tanya know about me and any investigation into Dad's murder?"

"She knows nothing, and I believe her. I was fortunate to be able to get hold of her. A very nice young lady at Verizon broke with company rules and gave me Tanya's new cell number. I told the Verizon woman I was her sick grandfather and wanted desperately to speak with her before I died."

"You're more of a con artist, Jim, than most con artists."

"Years of experience, Rachel."

"So how does her phone call me?"

"I'm getting to that. Hold your horses."

"Okay, okay."

"Her phone was stolen. She got up from her table to buy a newspaper at a Starbucks, and when she returned, the phone was gone. She questioned people who were sitting near her, but no one recalled seeing anyone snatch her phone. By the way, this happened the same day you received the text."

"So we're nowhere?" The tone of Rachel's voice was suddenly subdued.

"Yes and no. It just means more work for me. I need to find out which one of our suspects was in Daily City on yesterday's date. But that will take me some time."

"I can try to find out if my brother were there."

"Anything you can do to help is appreciated. I'll get back to you when I have something more."

As soon as she hung up with Jim Hankins, Rachel tried her brother's cell. He hadn't answered her calls in eight months, so she wasn't overly optimistic about him picking up now. The call went straight to voice mail. Rather than leave a message, she chose to text him.

"Jessie's looking for you. Call me."

Much to Rachel's surprise, Troy called her several minutes after she'd sent the text. Even more surprising, he asked Rachel how she was doing. "Okay" is all she offered.

"Jessie was frantically searching for you yesterday morning. Said you had a shoot, and she didn't know where you were."

Troy laughed. In their lifetimes, Rachel hadn't known him to laugh often. "No shoot, no show. We've been cancelled, and the guy from Langly-Hoffman—"

"What's Langly-Hoffman?"

"The production company that bought our fitness show. Anyway, he was fired. This all happened this morning."

"Sorry about that, brother. I read somewhere that you'd signed a two-year agreement. Apparently, it wasn't an iron-clad contract."

"Not when your show sucks as bad as ours."

Rachel wanted to ask about his recent whereabouts but wasn't sure what approach to take. If she asked him if he'd been to San Francisco lately, he'd surely be suspicious that she was interrogating him. She took a stab at another angle.

"By the way, I'm recruiting a free agent college player who is flying into San Francisco tomorrow. I plan to drive him to Santa Barbara the next morning—tough connecting between Cedar Rapids, Iowa, and Santa Barbara. Do you know any good restaurants in Frisco where I can take him? I haven't been there in so long I wouldn't have a clue."

Troy paused for a moment. Rachel could envision his brain churning. "I was just—"

"Just there?"

"No," he said, lending new meaning to the word *terse*. "I gotta go."

Like that, he was gone, leaving Rachel to tear her hair out wondering what he was about to tell her before he'd realized he was being baited.

CHAPTER FORTY-TWO

The next two weeks found the Charros' continuing to come back from the dead. What made their mini-turnaround even more special was the news Rachel received from one of the Friars' girls who Devin had recruited to help with the Charros' home opener. She reported that Austin Grant was not only in a 0-for-24 slump with the big club but was also going to miss at least two games to return to Santa Barbara for his pretrial hearing.

The Charros had put together an impressive eight-game winning streak and had narrowed Rancho Cucamonga's lead to three games. Jacqui Davenport continued to be a story. She'd appeared in five games over that span, and her ERA was still sitting on zero. Deke Slayton was using her as a spot reliever, most times facing only lefthanders. He used her when he absolutely needed an out, and she had produced. Her performance had made her an instant fan favorite, and she'd earned the respect of her fellow teammates, many of whom were skeptical about her skills and considered her addition to the roster to be a publicity stunt.

The girls in merchandizing reported that Davenport jerseys were selling at the same pace as Austin Grant's at the height of his popularity. Melanie Sandberg was probably the most responsible for helping to generate a mild Jacqui Davenport hysteria. In her postgame program following the Charros' 5-4 victory over High Desert, a game in which Jacqui got the save by striking out the only hitter she faced, Melanie said, "The bitch can pitch. So long everybody from The Erv, I'm Melanie, and you're not."

Adrienne Telfair jumped feet first on this, ordering a thousand *The Bitch Can Pitch* T-shirts with Jacqui's mug on the back. All of them were sold the next night.

Jacqui's fame was spreading like a mountain bush fire. *People* called and wanted to run a story about her; the *Today Show* interviewed her via satellite; and on an off day, *The View* flew her to New York and allotted fifteen minutes of studio time to her guest appearance. Jacqui killed it each time.

Whoopi Goldberg asked her about her life as an overnight celebrity. Jacqui's answer was a hit. "I wanted to go to the beach one afternoon. We aren't required to report to the ballpark until three o'clock. So I took a taxi to Nordstrom and bought this really cute day-glow orange bikini that made me look like one of those traffic safety cones. I wanted to work on my tan," she said. All *The View* ladies and the entire audience rocked with laughter. "Well, I finally get to the beach," she continued, "and as soon as I put my towel out, a guy selling ice cream from a push cart rushes over and asks for my autograph. Before I knew it, there must have been seventy-five people, most of them males, who were attending a volleyball camp that had surrounded me. Someone—a tourist, I was told—from across the busy Cabrillo Boulevard thought there was a fight going on and called the police. Next thing I know, three uniformed cops are up to their ankles in sand and are calling for my fans to disperse or face arrest. 'This is an unlawful assembly!' one of the policemen kept shouting. I was so embarrassed I left and went back to my motel room where I'd just moved to after staying at my boss's house."

Jim Hankins, on the other hand, was not on a hot streak. He flew from Eureka to Santa Barbara to bring Rachel up to date on his investigation in person. He'd warned her in advance. "I don't have squat. Either I'm too old for this shit, or this is just a tough investigation to get a grip on."

They met shortly after noon in the coffee shop of the Sandpiper golf course where Jim was booked to play eighteen holes in the afternoon. Rachel was already at a table when Hankins arrived. She immediately became concerned about his health as she spotted him entering the coffee shop. He looked pale and had bags under his eyes. He walked with a slight limp she hadn't noticed before, and his hand was shaking more than ever. Rachel couldn't help wondering if a man in his apparent condition should be piloting an airplane.

"Hello, Rachel," he said, taking a seat at the table.

Rachel's forehead furrowed. "Are you all right, Jim? You look tired."

"I am, but I promised you I'd find out who did in your dad, and I'm sticking to my promise."

"Not at the expense of your health, Jim. If you're going to play golf, you need to have something to eat. I've already looked at the menu, and there is a delicious sounding tri-tip steak sandwich that looks like something to die for."

Jim nodded that he could go for that. "What do I care about my health? I can't just sit around all day and watch *Keeping Up with the Kardashians*, can I? I'm playing a round of golf this afternoon with a friend I've known since grade school. That will refresh me, I'm sure."

Rachel took a long sip of her coffee. She quietly wondered how Hankins played golf with his shaky hand. "What have you learned that's new?"

Hankins dropped his eyes and spoke softly. "Jessie Santiago's credit card purchase in Eureka didn't provide any hot leads. I learned from a mechanic at Haslett Motors who used to be my mechanic when he had his own shop in Arcata that Jessie had come to visit Will Greene. Apparently, it was all about him taking over as the company CEO and overseeing all the Haslett Motors' properties."

"Well, my dad's death certainly worked out well for both Jessie and Will Greene."

"All I've been able to dig up on Greene is the fact your dad flew into Eureka to discuss his involvement in marijuana trafficking. I got a lead on a disgruntled former employee of Greene who told me all about how Greene was the top distributor of weed in Humboldt County. This guy—can't remember his name top of my head—had called your dad and apparently ratted on Greene. I actually got hold of him by going through your dad's phone records. There was just one phone number with a 707 area code listed outside of the dealership's number."

Rachel got out of her seat and paced the length of the coffee shop once and then returned. "If I know my dad, he must have been considering firing Will Greene. He wouldn't have gone to the extent of flying there to meet with him if he just planned to scold him. If that was the case, Greene certainly had a motive for taking my dad out."

Hankins nodded. "It's a valid premise, Rachel. But I don't have any way of proving it. Your dad stayed the night at my house and never mentioned Will Greene's name. I had the impression his visit was simply business as usual. I went so far as to check with the night attendant at the airport in McKinleyville to see if he'd observed anything or anyone unusual the night before your dad took off from there in the morning. The attendant said no but did offer me access to the airport's security camera. I checked the video from sunup to sundown on that date. The only image that showed was a guy who transported the airport's fuel truck and filled your dad's plane. He left as soon as he was finished."

Rachel shook her head and then dropped it to her chest and back up. "I have to tell you this is depressing, Jim."

"For me too." Hankins motioned to a waiter that he'd like another round of coffee. "It just could be that we're barking up the wrong tree."

"How so?"

"The damaged rod that caused your dad to crash could have been cut here in Santa Barbara. It might have taken more than one flight for it to finally snap."

Rachel's attention was diverted to the TV over the bar. Women's beach volleyball was showing on ESPN. "That used to be me," she said, pointing to the TV.

"Maybe we should switch our focus to my brother and see if he's clean."

Hankins pulled a cigarette out of his jacket pocket. He knew he couldn't smoke indoors, so Rachel assumed it was his way of saying, "I need a smoke break."

After a short timeout, Hankins returned to the coffee shop. "I've got to find out if he was the one who took Tanya Whatshername's phone. Hankins paused momentarily for a thought. "I'd love to have a look at your brother's computer, assuming he has one."

"I'm pretty sure he does. He's spent most of his adult life in Starbucks, what else would he be doing?"

"I could find out if he rented a car to drive to San Francisco, where he stayed, where he ate, where—"

"In reality, we can't be sure he even knew I'd commissioned an investigation."

Hankins sat up straight and waved at short, rotund man who'd entered the coffee shop, arriving at the same moment as the tri-tip sandwich. Rachel figured the man was his playing partner for the day.

"The only way he could know is if Jessie Santiago discovered I'd hacked into her online banking account. Together, they could have put two and two together."

Jim introduced his friend and hurriedly disposed of his sandwich and a bottled Stella with a slight belch and a big thank-you to Rachel.

"Have a great round," Rachel said as Hankins and his friend headed off to the pro shop. "Always play it like it's your last, Jim. That was my volleyball mantra."

Those words would come back to her again and again.

CHAPTER FORTY-THREE

The afternoon prior to a home series opener against Modesto proved an opportune time for Rachel to survey the Charros' books, something she liked to do every month. It was a pleasant experience. Attendance over last season was up was now up 125 percent, while concessions and merchandise exceeded 150 percent jump; staggering numbers for a first year GM if she did say so herself.

After finishing her financial survey, Rachel spent some time prepping her appearance for the game. She changed her lipstick from fire engine red to a chili red and for one of the few times she could remember put her hair up in a bun.

As she was about to go out the door for her nightly walk to the ballpark, her house phone rang—a rarity for her in the age of the smart phone. The caller identified herself as a Bank of America customer service representative.

"This is Rachel Haslett."

"Your Bank of America debit card has been reported found, Ms. Haslett."

Rachel raised her eyes to the ceiling in dismay. "I didn't know I'd lost it."

"The manager of the coffee shop at the Sand—"

"Sandpiper?"

"Yes, that's it. He phoned it in to us. He said you'd left it on a table. If you don't mind, I have just a couple of security checks. Your mother's maiden name?"

"Jennings."

"Your best friend in high school?"

"Sandra Fisher."

"Thank you, Ms. Haslett. If you wish to retrieve your card, your contact at the coffee shop is Alyn Satterfield, he's the manager, 805-936-5500."

"Thank you so much," Rachel said and hung up with a sense of urgency. A debit card in the most trustworthy person's hands was unsettling. She called the Sandpiper immediately. She was transferred to Alyn Satterfield who confirmed he had her credit card in safekeeping. He wanted to know when Rachel planned to pick it up.

"Now."

Satterfield's tone suddenly changed. "Was it you who was sitting with an older gentleman this morning? He had an arm that trembled."

"Yes, Jim Hankins."

There was a long pause on Satterfield's end. "A friend?"

"Yes. Why?"

Satterfield let go of a lengthy sigh. "I regret to inform you, Ms. Haslett, that he passed away on the golf course shortly after 3:00 p.m. The EMTs that responded to his playing partners 911 call said he died of a heart attack. He had just finished putting on the twelfth hole."

Rachel gasped. "Oh no! This is awful!"

Satterfield remained silent in order to give Rachel time to recover from the shock. After close to a minute, he said, "I do have his scorecard through twelve holes if you think that would be of any value to loved ones. He was well known by the staff here at Sandpiper. He was having a great round, just four over par to the point where he—"

"Honestly, sir, I think you're being entirely too insensitive."

"My apologies, ma'am. I just thought—"

"You didn't think. That's the problem."

"Sorry. Do you have contacts for next of kin? Was he married?"

Rachel answered with a quiver in her voice. "Widowed. That's all I know about his personal life. He was working for me as a consultant. He's a former sheriff's deputy, so I'll try and find someone there who might know about family. Where is his body?"

"County morgue."

"Please hang onto my debit card, Mr. Satterfield. Mr. Hankins's death becomes a priority for me."

Rachel was successful in that a Sergeant Thompson who worked in the county jail knew of a brother of Hankins who lived in Ventura. Rachel was able to locate him by phone. He was grief stricken but promised to take care of all the details of his burial. Rachel had a quiet thought that this gave new meaning to the expression "dead end."

CHAPTER FORTY-FOUR

In the worst way, Rachel needed her some Devin Baxter. He'd bonded with his daughter longer than he expected—close to a month. He'd returned to the San Diego in order to place his $2 million home up for sale. He was to start his job as a Fox studio analyst out of their LA studios in two weeks. Rachel had been in frequent phone contact with him, but in the aftermath of Jim Hankins's death, that was no longer satisfactory. She needed a pick-me-up that only Devin could provide. She called him in the morning and invited him to stay with her for an indefinite period.

"I thought you'd never ask" was Devin's response. "I need another week here to wrap up the San Diego part of my life, and then I'm all yours." If only he'd known that Rachel had something in addition to romance on her mind.

To her way of thinking, Jim Hankins's death left Rachel with no alternative other than to pursue her dad's killer herself. She had decided to confront her three primary suspects face-to-face and ask them point-blank if they had committed his murder. It was a tall order for someone without investigative experience.

Will Greene was first on her list. She'd decided to confront him in person without notifying him in advance. She was a firm believer in the element of surprise.

The drive north on 101 from Santa Barbara to Eureka had taken almost twelve hours. Rachel had factored in time to enjoy Redwood National Park. She'd lived all her life in California but had never been further north than San Francisco. She marveled at the mammoth Redwoods and drove her Chevy Silverado truck through the base of the Chandelier Tree in Leggett and the Shrine Tree near Myers Flay. Mother Nature blew her away. She felt small and insignificant in exploring the Avenue of the Giants.

She arrived in Eureka at six o'clock in the evening. The evening fog had blanketed what appeared to her to be a rather unremarkable city. She would spend the night at the Eureka Inn and be rested for her meet-up with Will in the morning. She didn't sleep well as she lay awake going over the various scenarios she was anticipating. She passed on dinner so as not to upset her stomach. When she played competitive volleyball, she never ate less than twelve hours before a match.

Next morning at exactly nine o'clock, she drove to the Haslett Motors dealership on Broadway and parked on the street where she could see employees entering the building. From the outside, the showroom looked bright and classy, just as her dad would have wanted. Will Greene, dressed in a dark suit and a color-coordinated tie, entered the building at 9:15 a.m. He was also wearing black wing tip shoes.

Rachel had carefully considered her look for the occasion. She had on designer jeans, an oxford shirt, and a buckskin-like blazer. She strove to look Humboldt County centric. She entered the luxurious showroom with the intent of acting like she owned the place, even though in reality it now belonged to Jessie. *How hard was that to wrap her head around,* she'd asked herself? She found Will Greene having coffee with a fellow employee in what looked like a break room. His eyes grew wide when he recognized Rachel.

"Good heavens, what are you doing in these parts, Rachel? What a pleasant surprise." Will motioned with his eyes for his employee to leave.

"It may not be so pleasant, Mr. Greene."

"Please call me Will." It was Will being a salesman.

Rachel's steely eyes locked onto Will's baby blues. "I'm here to ask you if you killed my dad." It was Rachel's way of starting at match point and working backward.

Will nervously looked about his showroom floor as if to see if any of his staff had heard Rachel. Satisfied that no one had, he took Rachel gently by the elbow and escorted her into his office. He offered her a chair opposite his desk.

"Wow, you go right for the jugular, don't you?"

Rachel's first order of business was to get out of her chair and advance to where she could get a close-up look at the photo of Will and her dad that appeared to have been taken at some golf event.

"When times were good?"

"Yes. What on earth makes you think I might have killed your dad? For god's sakes, I worshipped him. He gave me the best job in the world. I have to tell you I resent being asked the question."

Rachel spoke in robot-like tones. "For one, we think his airplane was compromised here while it was parked overnight."

"Says who?"

"The NTSB."

"The plane was made to crash."

"I'm sorry to disappoint you, Rachel, but I know nothing about that."

Rachel continued in a methodic fashion. "Is it true he traveled here with the intention of firing you because of your involvement with marijuana distribution in the county?"

"Yes."

"Then you would stand to retain your little domain here if he were suddenly out of the picture?"

Beads of perspiration appeared above Will Greene's lip. "Yes, but—"

"But nothing. Aren't you now the CEO for all of my dad's dealerships at an incredible raise in salary?" Rachel was just guessing at that fact.

"Yes, but—"

"You're on notice as being a suspect."

"Who are you to be telling me that?"

"The very person who could see you burn in hell. I will be in touch." Rachel grabbed her purse and headed for Will's office door. At the door, she stopped. "I would consider hooking up with a lawyer if I were you, Mr. Greene."

Will shook his head and picked up his phone.

As she guided her truck south out of Eureka, Rachel had a good feeling that she'd scared the hell out of Will Greene. Even if he was innocent, she reasoned he would at least be uncomfortable until she identified the killer.

Next on Rachel's list was Jessie Santiago. Even if nothing came out of confronting her, she'd still have the satisfaction of letting her know she, and a team of attorneys, were contesting her dad's will. But then she'd had plenty of experience with legal challenges to her inheritances, so it might not come as earth-shaking news to her.

Rachel realized she didn't have much with which to rattle Jessie's cage other than her inheritance. If nothing else, she wanted to scare the hell out of her. She found Jessie's home address simply by Googling her name.

The 101 South was heavily congested for a weekend day. Rachel chastised herself for not knowing weekends were the worst traffic time on that section freeway. As she sat behind the wheel in the bumper-to-bumper traffic, she was uncertain what was making her anxious, the traffic or the face-to-face with Jessie. She decided on both. When she arrived at Jessie's Montecito bungalow, she parked her truck by the front gate to her tiny yard. Once through the gate, she took a deep breath and rang the doorbell.

Jessie was so slow to respond that Rachel figured she wasn't home. Just as she turned to leave, the door opened just enough for Jessie to reveal her face.

"Rachel," she said, her eyes wide from surprise. Rachel could tell that Jessie was wearing a man's long sleeve dress shirt and little else. "Excuse me just a moment." The door closed shut.

Rachel could hear a male's voice in conversation with Jessie. It was beginning to appear to Rachel that she had interrupted something. If the voice didn't belong to her brother, Rachel suspected, he would be interested in knowing about. Already she had the upper hand on Jessie.

When Jessie returned to the front door, she apologized for the delay and welcomed Rachel in. Jessie was now wearing jeans and a *Slo-Go Fit* T-shirt and still no shoes. "What can I do for you, Rachel?"

"I'm not here to talk about your abbreviated showbiz career, if that's what you're thinking."

"I don't know what I'm thinking. This is so not like you just to show up at my door and with an attitude no less."

"It's so not like me to have anything to do with you. But time changes everything."

"If you're looking for Troy, I haven't seen him since I called you last."

That confirmed it. The inconspicuous male voice must have been a new lover. Or at any rate, a lover that Troy probably knew nothing about. *Leverage that*, Rachel told herself.

"I hope I didn't interrupt anything, Jessie." Rachel looked in the direction of the back of the living space and flashed a smirk that only another female would understand the intent behind it.

"Just a handyman doing work in the bathroom," Jessie lied. "Would you care for a glass of wine? I've got a great chardonnay from a winery in Paso Robles."

"I could do that." Rachel tried to be as unthreatening as possible as to not scare Jessie off and have her toss her out of her house.

When Jessie returned with the wine, she sat next to Rachel on her living room couch that was cramped for space by all the exercise equipment that occupied her living quarters.

"What is the nature of your unexpected visit?" Jessie had emphasized the word *unexpected*.

"I came to ask you if you had anything to do with the death of my father."

Jessie didn't blink. "No," Jessie sighed and quickly fashioned a look of curiosity. "Troy warned me you'd be coming hard after whomever you figured caused Erv's plane to go down. He was right. But you're barking up the wrong tree with me."

"You knew that plane backward and forward. You flew it more than my dad."

"What do you mean by that?"

"That you would know where the control arm rod was located."

Jessie set her wine glass on her coffee table. Her forehead furrowed. "The what?"

"The control arm rod was cut and was ready to snap at any time. Just the right amount of turbulence and wham! So happened he was over the ocean when it did."

"I wouldn't have any idea where this whatyamacallit rod was located. I just know how to fly the sucker. I have no idea what makes airplanes fly. I always felt like it would scare me to know anything about the mechanics of flying."

"You could have hired someone who did know where it was located. Have them disguised as a mechanic doing routine maintenance. Bingo!"

The bulldog in Rachel would not let up. "How do you explain your recent visit with Will Greene? Were you two in on a plot together? After all, Dad's death has turned out to be a win-win for both of you."

"How do you know I visited Will Greene? Christ, are you following me? I could have you arrested for stalking." Jessie stood up. It was her way of saying this little chat was about to be over.

Thanks for stopping by and have a good life, bitch.

"Got your credit card information."

Jessie put her hands on her hips. Her head was braced. "You are stalking me."

Rachel stood and glared directly into Jessie's eyes. "I'm investigating you, that's all. Investigating and stalking are two different animals."

"Your time is up," Jessie said, motioning her hand toward the front door.

Rachel moved in that direction. "Does my brother know about your handyman?"

Jessie slammed the door, nearly catching Rachel's arm as she exited. After a second or two, Rachel rang the doorbell.

Jessie reluctantly opened the door. "Forget something?"

"Yes," Rachel said. "I forgot to tell you I'm contesting my dad's will."

Jessie didn't blink. "I've been there and done that."

On her drive back to her condo, Rachel felt nauseous and stopped to gas up her truck in hopes of acquiring relief for her jittery stomach. Judging by her physical discomfort, Rachel came to the immediate conclusion that she needed to take a time out before exploring her dad's death with Troy. There was too much back history to make it a pleasant experience. It had to be done—of that she was sure—but just not now.

CHAPTER FORTY-FIVE

Devin Baxter drove to Santa Barbara from San Diego. His recently purchased Lexus LS sedan, grabbed the road the way the TV commercial had promised. The matador red exterior was an attention getter, even at seventy-five miles per hour. Several times on his long journey, females in passing cars waved and shouted at him. One woman, who appeared to Devin to be in her early twenties, pulled up her top and flashed her impressive tits at him.

His first view of the ocean came as he cruised through Ventura. He had all the windows down and was enjoying breathing in the fresh ocean air. He was a Texas kid through and through, but there was nothing as invigorating as the smell of the ocean. He was almost relaxed enough to let his car drive itself. He entertained himself, not by flipping on his radio and playing CDs but by musing about how his life had turned upside down, and he was still standing. He couldn't wait to spend time with Rachel, uninterrupted by the demands of an obsessively demanding owner.

For the first time in his life, he felt free to do exactly as he wanted. He'd been careful with his money throughout his career and as a baseball executive. He was confident he had savings to last him years. If something was to come out of his new TV gig, that would make life even better. He'd managed to convince his ex to reduce child payments by 40 percent. He viewed her concession as an example of the respect that the two had maintained for each other despite their split. Devin had been pleased to learn that Jackie Lynn had a new man, a Longview dentist who treated Chloe like she were his own daughter.

This day, his mind was filled with thoughts of Rachel. It had been almost seven weeks since he'd last seen her. He promised himself it would never again be that long in between contact. He had lain awake more nights than he could count trying to recall the feel of her body next to his. He marveled at how he could feel Rachel's physical strength by touch and, at the same time, find pleasure in her softness. Sex wasn't all that attracted him to Rachel. She was a strong, independent woman who was passionate about all of life's offerings. Like him, she'd been a competitor most of her life. He liked having someone at his side that recognized he was a competitor too who appreciated the inherent value of that characteristic in everyday life. She made him proud to be in her presence. He believed she felt the same way.

Years ago after divorcing Jackie Lynn, he'd made himself a promise to take any new relationship slow. Before Rachel, there was a brief fling with a black San Diego attorney that he thought had possibilities until he found out she was married with two kids. He had to be sure this time. He was already pretty sure about Rachel.

Divorce was the single most difficult thing he'd ever had to deal with. The pain was still with him all through his recent visit with Chloe. He never wanted to experience a split again. He was pretty sure the same line of thinking grounded Rachel. He was sure one thing. He'd find out about it in the days and hopefully weeks ahead as the man in Rachel Haslett's life.

Rachel greeted Devin in her ballpark office. He had started his drive up the coast a little after noon. But stops for gas, a snack, and a bouquet of flowers slowed his travel progress to where he knew Rachel would already be at the ballpark. It was just a couple of hours before game time with mighty Rancho Cucamonga when he peeked his head into Rachel's office.

"Is there a lovely lady in here?" he asked. Rachel jumped up from her desk, accepted the flowers by kissing them, and then laid them across her desk. She stepped toward Devin and melted into his big arms. They hugged and kissed for several minutes.

Rachel's smile was as wide as the Pacific.

"Your timing is impeccable, Mr. Baxter. Jacqui gets her first start tonight. Everybody in the entire organization is holding his or her collective breaths that she does well. She's not pitched more than two innings at any one time. Our relief corps has been really overworked of late, so it's important that she gives us at least five innings. The bad thing is she's up against Rancho Cucamonga's best pitcher. He's got a league leading 2.14 ERA."

"I'm excited to be here," Devin said, his eyes dancing. "Not to take anything away from Jacqui, but she's got second billing in my mind."

With Rachel taking the lead, they headed for the Charros' locker room. She wanted to introduce him to Deke Slayton.

"Reintroduce," Devin said. "Don't forget I'm the bad guy who didn't move him up the Charros later, and he subsequently quit baseball. He may not be all that excited to catch up with me."

Rachel took Devin by the arm as they continued walking. There was no longer any effort on Rachel's part to conceal the fact they were an item. Rachel was wearing jeans and her Charros jacket. The fog had moved in over the ballpark late afternoon. She used her cell to call her merchandise director and ordered an extra-large for Devin. "It could get nippy by the end of the night."

As they approached Deke Slayton's office, Rachel made a conscious effort to have her arm through Devin's. Her motive was strictly selfish, she would admit. She wanted Slayton to see that there was something going on between the two of them. It served Rachel much better that way rather than having an awkward sit-down with Deke to explain that she didn't want him to consider her dating material.

Deke was stone-faced, except for the movement of his eyes that bounced back and forth between Devin and Rachel. He stood up from his desk and extended his hand to Devin. He had the look of someone who badly needed an explanation.

Rachel was first to speak. "I understand you two know each other."

Deke put forth a nervous smile. "You could say that. Devin is why I'm a cop."

Devin's eyes dropped for a second. "I have to own that, Deke. I hear you're doing a great job here. And if you keep hitting the way you are, you might want to put the cop thing on hold."

"So what brings you here, Devin? I heard you resigned over the Austin Grant issue."

Devin smiled and turned to look at Rachel. He placed his hand on her shoulder. "She's what brings me here."

Deke's face dropped. It was as if someone had deflated all his tires, and it was miles to the nearest TireCo store.

Devin examined Deke's photos that covered all four walls. He pointed to a picture of himself giving Deke a batting tip—a spring training event. "Sorry I couldn't get you over the class A hump, Deke. I really thought you'd be the Friars' starting catcher one day."

Deke wore an aggravated look. His eyes closed, and his lips became tight. "I'd just as soon not talk about those days if you guys don't mind." He grabbed a lineup card off his desk. "I have to submit my lineup if you folks don't mind."

Rachel gave Devin a let's-get-out-of-here look.

"Good luck tonight," Devin said, taking Rachel by her elbow and escorting her out of the manager's office.

"The guy still hasn't forgiven me, Rachel."

"Or me."

"What do you mean?"

"He's been trying to hook up socially with me for a month now. I've managed to keep him at arm's length. I don't think he liked seeing the two of us together."

"He'll have to get over that."

"Yes, he will."

Before Jacqui Davenport made her first pitch, Rachel made a pitch of her own that would have a major impact on the California League pennant. Twenty minutes before game time, she hustled Devin Baxter into her office.

"Something I want to run by you" is how she framed it as she stood in front of a large portrait of Big Erv. She offered to pour him a glass of wine—she kept bottles of a local merlot on hand at all times for important guests of the club.

"Prying me with alcohol so early in the evening?" Devin asked.

"You may need the whole bottle when I'm through with you."

Devin laughed. "I like the sound of that."

Rachel poured him an ample portion of Crooked Bend's finest. She set the bottle on her desk when she finished pouring and then put her hands on the lapels of Devin's sports coat.

Rachel closed her eyes and said, "Ready, set, go."

Devin squinted. He had no clue what was coming.

"What would you think of coming out of retirement and playing first base for the Charros for the remainder of the season?"

Devin's mouth opened, but no words came out. He stepped away from Rachel like a staggered boxer.

"I'd love to help your team in any way possible, Rachel, but I haven't swung a bat in anger in almost eight years."

"I'll have Deke put you through fielding drills and batting practice for a week before we launch."

"We're five games behind Rancho Cucamonga, with twenty-five games to go. We're playing on guts alone right now. We have no pop in our lineup—haven't had any since Austin Grant. We need a home run hitter, Devin. You're still in great shape, and you would have the added benefit of being able to sleep with the general manager."

Devin was still too shocked to make a qualified response. "Wow!" He motioned for another pour of her merlot.

"This is not a stunt to attract attendance. I want to win the pennant, and you can help me do that. When I came up with this idea, I quickly nixed it, thinking that playing class A ball would tarnish your legacy. But then I told myself, 'I know this man. He won't be worried about his legacy because he's comfortable with who he is. No one can take all those major league home runs away from him.'"

Devin stepped toward Rachel and put his arm around her.

"Is this a good sign, Devin? To ensure this won't be perceived as a publicity stunt, I won't make any announcement. The media will have to figure it out on their own. When they hear the PA announcer say 'Now batting number 35'—your old number—'Devin Baxter,' then, and only then, will they know. We'll work you out in secret." Rachel took a deep breath and, like a schoolgirl, crossed her fingers. "What do you say, Mr. Braxton?"

Devin flashed his perfect teeth with a smile that barely had boundaries. He hugged Rachel and said, "I'm in."

Rachel shouted so loud Adrienne Telfair burst into her office to see if everything were okay.

"Devin's going to play first base for us and hit cleanup." Rachel put her finger to her lips. "You can't tell anyone, Adrienne. We're flying below the radar as far as publicity is concerned. I know you'd love to run with this, but I don't want it perceived as a stunt. Heaven knows we've been accused of that enough this season."

Rachel opened the door to her small office fridge and pulled out a bottle of Dom Pérignon champagne. She handed it to Devin to pop the cork.

"I hope this doesn't look like I expected this to be a done deal before I asked you, Devin."

Devin laughed. "Of course, it does. But it was a *good* done deal."

Before taking a long sip of champagne, Rachel cautioned Devin that she wouldn't always be there to hold his hand during his comeback.

"I've been left to find my dad's killer myself. I'm as determined to be just as successful in that endeavor as I am with the Charros. I hope you understand."

"Thanks, but I'm a big boy, Rachel. When do I start?"

"I'll have to speak with Deke about his availability, but I'd like to get you started ASAP."

Devin took Rachel's hand in his. "Just to confirm, my contract will state that I get to sleep with the boss, correct?"

Rachel put on a sly grin. "You don't need a contract for that, ever."

Jacqui Davenport's first extended start was superb. Combining an eighty-mile-per-hour fastball, batting practice speed, and her wicked slider, she pitched five scoreless innings, allowed just four hits, and struck out the league's leading hitter, Kevin Madison, three times—all with breaking balls.

Jacqui's performance produced even more radio gems from Melanie Sandberg. "She's got better stuff than a Bob's Big Boy," about her third inning single, her first as a professional," Melanie said. "Explain that to your grandkids, Arturo Jimmenz. You just gave up the first hit by a girl in professional baseball. *Lo siento, muchacho.*"

Unfortunately, the Charros were held scoreless and lost to Rancho Cucamonga, 2-0. The loss dropped the Charros to six games out of first and in a tie with San Jose for second place. The need for Devin Baxter's big bat had become even greater than it had been twenty-four hours earlier.

CHAPTER FORTY-SIX

Troy Haslett hadn't spoken to Jessie Santiago since he'd walked out of their hotel suite following the devastating *Variety* review of *Slo-Go Fit*. He was convinced the failure of the TV show was his fault, and he'd never dealt well with failure despite having had a lifetime of experience at it. Several weeks after the show's cancellation, Jessie Santiago reached out to him by phone to say she'd found a new sex partner and to tell him she was certain he was the next suspect on Rachel's list of who killed Ervin Haslett.

"I hope you've got an ironclad alibi because she will try very hard to mine the truth out of you—just a warning. You might consider leaving town for a while."

Troy was more concerned about Jessie's rejection of him. "I guess I'm no longer of any use to you. I must have been a prop, huh, Jessie?"

"You're smarter than I give you credit for, Troy. I will say you're good in bed. Nobody can take that away from you."

Troy scoffed at her statement. As for his sister's investigation, he wasn't too worried. His knew his bases were covered. He just didn't know how he would handle "big sister" possibly pointing an accusing finger at him. It produced the same feelings he'd experienced when they were kids. He'd always had to explain anything he was perceived to have done wrong to Rachel rather than his parents. She was his judge and jury. He would never forget how she'd accused him of soaping the family swimming pool when he was twelve. His sister was convinced he'd done it and went to her parents with her conclusion. Turned out it was a neighbor who'd done it because he had a crush on Rachel and wanted her attention. Her accusation still resides deep in Troy's psyche.

Troy didn't have long to wait for Rachel to track him down. She'd parked her truck outside of his apartment around 10:00 a.m. and waited for him to appear. She had to wait an hour for that to happen.

When Troy finally surfaced, Rachel intercepted him as he made his way, laptop in his backpack, in the direction she assumed of the nearest Starbucks. Troy stopped to engage his sister and then thought better of it and began walking away.

Immediately Rachel fell in step with him. "Hello, little brother."

Troy hated being called that, and Rachel knew it. "What a surprise," Troy said, his tone dripping with sarcasm. He kept a half step in front of her and responded without looking at her. "I understand you might be informally charging me with Dad's murder."

Rachel pulled alongside her brother and grabbed his shoulder to get him to stop and look her in the eye. "I'll decide that, Troy."

"Just like you decided if we should have ice cream rather than cake for dessert. Just like you decided we should watch *Friends* instead of *NYPD Blue*. Just like you decided a family campout at Refugio Beach would be more fun than a tour of the animal history museum." Perspiration formed on Troy's forehead. He felt Rachel's eyes were trying to zoom into his soul.

Troy spit out his alibi, his face turning red in the process. "In case you're wondering I was in LA the day before Dad's plane went down. I was scoring a shitload of grass from a dealer in Compton. You probably wonder how I get money to survive. Now you know.

Big Mo is his name. He's the man in all of South Central LA." Troy stopped walking and pointed his finger at his sister's chest. "I'm a dealer, not a murderer." Troy started walking again.

Rachel found it easy to move and keep pace with her non-athletic brother. "Sorry, but that doesn't get you off the hook. You could easily have hired somebody to sever the control arm rod and not get your hands dirty."

"Why would I want Dad dead?"

"A couple of reasons come to mind."

"And they are?"

"You and Jessie could split his estate. Apparently, she beat you to the punch. But your hate for Dad started with the pony carousel incident, and it never ended. If anyone on the planet had a reason to get even with Dad, it was you."

Rachel's claim hit a nerve. Troy stopped in his tracks. "That's a lame reason, Rachel. He was my only source of income. Why would I want to off him?"

Rachel chose this very moment to gamble with her investigation. "What would you say if I asked you if I could have your computer for twenty-four hours?"

"And look for what?"

"I know you use it mostly for porn. But there might be something there that could prove your innocence or guilt. Think about it. If you don't want me to go to the police with my theories, then let me hire an IT specialist to inspect your laptop."

Troy's eyes drooped, and his head suddenly sank in the direction of his chest. "You just never give up, do you, Rachel? Here," he said, freeing his backpack from around his shoulder and digging out his laptop. "Knock yourself out, sis. Just fucking leave me alone for the rest of my life."

Rachel accepted the computer and said, "You probably won't believe me, but I hope I don't find anything that would incriminate you, Troy. I don't hate like you do."

Rachel hired an IT guy from the service provider that had hooked up the Charros' ballpark Internet network. He reported finding a history of porn that was representative of an addict.

"He must have jerked off every day," the guy told Rachel. He also said someone with access to the computer had downloaded blueprints of a Cessna Skyhawk, the same kind of plane owned by his dad. Rachel would later confront him about the findings.

"I was researching aviation history for a technical writing class at UCSB extension" is how Troy justified it.

The IT guy concluded nothing could be proved by what he'd found on Troy's computer, especially since Rachel had indicated that when Troy turned twenty-one, his dad made an unsuccessful attempt to get him interested in aviation.

Rachel had made detailed notes of all her findings from Will, Jessie, and Troy. After reviewing them all, she was disappointed that in the end, nothing appeared to point to any of the three being involved in Big Erv's death. She'd reached a dead end and realized that replacing Jim Hankins with another private investigator would be an exercise in futility and a waste of money. She was so despondent over her failure to identify her father's murderer that it took Devin Baxter a week to coax her out of her funk.

CHAPTER FORTY-SEVEN

Not even Troy could put his finger on why, after fifteen years of self-imposed indifference, his mother suddenly decided to seek him out. She'd called his cell one morning, naturally waking him, as his life was usually programmed to begin each day at noon. Troy was surprised to learn she'd at least kept up with his life just enough to have his phone number. He was certain she didn't get it from Rachel. Katherine Richardson asked him to visit her at her Santa Ynez home. She promised to text him directions and hung up. The next day he borrowed a car, a brand new Corvette, from Haslett Motors and showed up at his mother's ranch-style home located on the outskirts of the small town of Santa Ynez, not far from Michael Jackson's Neverland.

As Troy pulled into the driveway, two German shepherds that appeared to have free run of the front yard barked at him like the watchdogs they were expected to be. Katherine responded to the commotion by rushing out the front door.

"Oh, Troy, they won't harm you!" she shouted. "Buster, Sade, stop your barking," she commanded, and they did.

Troy got out the Corvette tentatively, the dogs only a few feet away from where he was standing. "I figured they'd treat me like a wishbone," he said with a nervous laugh. "One dog to a leg."

"Not to worry. Please come in, Troy," his mother said, motioning toward the front door.

There was no hug or handshake. She appeared to have aged poorly. Troy remembered her as sexy and athletic-looking. She reminded him of his grandmother now. Her face bore the wrinkles of a cigarette smoker, and she'd put on a considerable amount of weight, at least thirty pounds. Katherine offered Troy a glass of lemonade while she fixed her own vodka on the rocks.

"It's a little early in the day for vodka, but it isn't every day that I get to spend time with my wayward son."

Troy's expression indicated he was mildly agitated by her comment. They talked about small things: allergies they shared in common, cigarette smoking that neither could shake, and Troy's failed TV show.

"That was your father's lover you were teamed up with, I found out."

Troy nodded. "Mine too."

Katherine's eyes widened. "She was a little young for him, didn't you think?"

"And too old for me."

Katherine backed off the subject like it had suddenly become diseased. Just then, a young boy, probably twelve was Troy's guess, bounced into the living room.

"Where are my scissors?" the boy asked Katherine without acknowledging Troy.

Katherine chose not to introduce the boy to his stepbrother. "I'll get them for you in a moment, son. Run along to your room now."

Troy had a puzzled look on his face.

"He's my son, Peter. He's a special-needs kid," Katherine said, wiping at a tear. "I'll spare you and me the details."

Troy then got a brief update on his mother's life. She'd married Harlon Richards only six months after divorcing Troy's dad. She'd met him online, and early on, everything clicked. Harlon grew avocados and was extremely successful in the stock market.

"What about after 'early on'?"

"That's for another time, son."

Like Rachel, Troy had gone through a stretch where he'd felt directly responsible for his parents' divorce. He understood that he had caused them both a great deal of pain and agony, perhaps too much for any couple to withstand.

Katherine offered her son some rich Belgian chocolate and asked him how his life was going.

"Shitty" was Troy's answer.

"I doubt it's worse than mine, Troy."

Troy cocked his head as if he were waiting for details.

"Two years after we were married, Harlon had an affair."

"Men do that," Troy said stoically.

"With a man," Katherine said, reaching for a Kleenex. "It's why I drink vodka, son. I've been a boozehound for over a decade. I'm not proud of it, but it helps me with my depression, which at times is so severe it's almost crippling. I've been in treatment for years, but it just allows me to stay at status quo."

Troy reached and touched his mom on her arm. "I'm sorry to hear that. Can I do anything to help? Not that I'm qualified to be a healer with all the trouble I've had keeping a balanced existence."

Katherine shook her head to her son's offer. She changed the subject by finally asking about Rachel. "I hear she's running Ervin's baseball team."

"She is."

"I've seen her on the news a couple of times."

"I saw her just the other day. She actually confronted me about Dad's death. She wanted to know if I had anything to do with it.

"Oh no," Katherine said, putting her fingers to her lips and wearing a sad face.

Troy got to his feet and paced his mother's spacious living room. "His crash was not an accident as you must have heard by now. Rachel wanted to know if I had done something to the engine of his plane to cause it to go down."

Katherine shook her head and dropped her chin before offering a knowing grin. "Little brother tattling on big sister. Some things never change."

Troy suddenly felt the sting of his mother's chastising comment. But that was just Katherine's warm-up act. What she went on to tell Troy over the next ten minutes sent him into a state of near shock. Only the very best weed a man could buy helped him successfully guide his Corvette back home to come face-to-face with the biggest dilemma of his lifetime.

CHAPTER FORTY-EIGHT

Rachel had managed to secure the baseball diamond at Santa Barbara High School for Devin's "spring training." She'd booked it from 9:00 a.m. until 10:00 a.m. No summer school students would use the facility until mid-afternoon. Devin, Deke Slayton, and a borrowed catcher from an area semi-pro team attended. All of them wore basic gray sweat pants and tops. Rachel watched from her truck that was parked nearby and had a good line of site to the diamond.

Devin and Deke spoke very little to each other in preparation for batting practice. It was clear from his body language that Deke lacked even a hint of vitality for what he called the experiment. He would have preferred spending his off time working on his novel about a corrupt fictional California police force. The Charros had a night game set with High Desert that made for a potential thirteen-hour day for Deke. There was no overtime pay in class A ball.

Deke took the mound as the designated pitcher. He had briefly gone over signs with his rented catcher and waved his glove forward to indicate he was finally reading to start serving up pitches to Devin.

As he dug in at the plate, Devin experienced butterflies for the first time since he'd retired from the Friars. Those were quickly converted to anger when Deke's first pitch buzzed Devin's chin and sent him into urgent bailout mode. Devin glared out at Deke as he stepped back in the batter's box.

Deke smiled and hollered. "I owed you one!"

Devin acknowledged his comment with a nod. "Point well taken, Deke. It always helps a hitter establish a rhythm when he has to duck to save his face."

Rachel was so upset by what she'd witness that she jumped out of her truck and ran to the pitcher's mound where she gave Deke a stern lecture about being a team player. "Do that again," she said, "and you'll be a cop again by the end of the day."

Deke nodded.

The session proved to be successful as Devin, after fouling off the first three pitches thrown to him and whiffing on the next two, hit nothing but frozen ropes to left and center field. Out of forty pitches, he crushed five over the outfield fences, which, of course, were set up distance wise for high school kids. He later told Rachel he was happy with the session and was further along on the first day than he expected to be.

Once he was through hitting, Devin fielded ground balls at first base. He could tell he'd lost a step in fielding his position but was still pretty satisfied that he didn't embarrass himself with the glove. He and Deke followed the same routine for a couple more days until Devin, working ahead of schedule, declared he was ready to go despite tweaking his hamstring during his final workout.

After conferring with assistant team trainer Marci Williams, who'd treated Devin's hamstring, Deke Slayton added his okay, and Devin was inserted into the lineup in Visalia as the Charros opened a four-game set there before returning home to face Stockton and Bakersfield. Rachel was all for it as Devin's comeback would be a lot further from the limelight returning to baseball in the small town of Visalia, which didn't have a big media following.

In the four games with Visalia, Devin struck out five times but hit two home runs, one that sailed 430 feet do dead center field, and drove in six as the Charros won three out of four and cut Rancho Cucamonga's lead to four games with seventeen to play. The California League had abandoned its playoff system two years ago. It used to be that six teams, including the winners of the first and second half of the season would qualify for the playoffs. Competition from major league baseball's postseason schedule forced the league to go old school and declare the team with the best record for the season the winner of the pennant.

When the Charros and Devin Baxter returned to The Erv, the media began circling like blackbirds on road kill. The first night, ESPN again did their baseball show live from the ballpark, and Devin spent a good two hours before the game doing interviews with all the San Diego TV stations, Fox Sports One and CNN. Most of the reporting heralded Devin for risking his legacy and praising Rachel for another bold move. The only negative pushback was provided by a reliable source, Miles Rooney, the *News-Press* columnist who'd given birth to the concept of Honeyball.

Honeyball Throws a High Hard One at Tradition
Miles Rooney

Chief Honeyball matron Rachel Haslett has bent, squeezed, and stomped on California League tradition in her resolute hunger for a shot at the championship by hiring a boatload of free agents—the latest being former major leaguer Devin Baxter. Once her roster was raided by San Diego

Friars' president Irving Zeller in reprisal for her suspension of Austin Grant, Haslett turned to the free agent market, pulling in second baseman Chad Isner from Hancock College; Erik Bloomquist, a left fielder from Woodbridge College in Cedar Rapids, Iowa; Jacqui Davenport from Arizona State University; and Deke Slayton from the Santa Barbara Police Department. Her actions are comparable to a construction company bringing in nonunion metal workers to help existing union metal workers get a project done quicker, thereby earning the company a bonus. Not since the then San Jose Bees in 1984 has the California League allowed any team to bring in free agents. Currently, all teams are obligated to be affiliated with major league clubs. Only after her dad, the late Erv Haslett, threatened to pull his team out of the league two days before the start of the 2005 season because of a bad player draw from the parent club, did the Charros, then known as the Rancheros, obtain the right to hire free agents. They've maintained that right; some will tell you through Haslett's generous annual contributions to the commissioner's office.

Calling on a former major league player of Baxter's status is going too far. It doesn't matter that he's been out of baseball for seven-plus seasons; he was a seven-time National League All Star, so his assignment to the roster gives the Charros a distinct advantage as teams struggle down the stretch to claim the pennant. Baxter and Haslett have enjoyed a great working relationship this season, and there are those who suspect their off-field relationship is even better. Baxter quit as the Friars' general manager after he defied his San Diego boss by supporting Ms. Haslett's suspension of Austin Grant because of an assault charge against a Charros employee. And now he's recruited by the same Ms. Haslett to join her team and put them over the top—winning the pennant. I'd call this a publicity stunt of the highest magnitude if it weren't for the fact that Baxter has, in just four games, shown he still can be a major asset to the team. Bottom line, even if the Charros win the California League crown, the accomplishment will be tainted.

Rachel couldn't remember being more angry with anyone at any time in her life than she was with Miles Rooney over his recent diatribe against her management of the Charros. He'd become a giant thorn in her side that she had to do something about. She began by having Adrienne Telfair pull his credential.

"No more Charros games for Mr. Nice Guy" is how she put it. Her next move was to get even. She assigned Lorena Volques, second in command in corporate sales, to research every column Miles Rooney has written for the *News-Press*, where he has penned something derogatory about women athletes or female sports figures in general. She gave Lorena two weeks to complete the job.

CHAPTER FORTY-NINE

The Charros were forced to open up the temporary bleachers for Devin's first appearance at home. Seventy-five hundred tickets had been sold, a team record.

Charros' fans gave Devin a standing ovation as he stepped into the batter's box for the first time. He was walked on four pitches but was doubled up on a grounder by Deke Slayton. His next time up, Devin didn't disappoint. With runners on first and third, he launched a breaking ball thrown by Visalia's best pitcher, the crafty Lyle North, out of the park for a three-run homer to give the Charros a 3-1 lead through five innings.

"It's Devin to the heavens" is how Melanie Sandberg described his home run. The score stayed that way through eight innings when Jacqui Davenport was called on to pitch the ninth. After she walked the first two hitters she faced, Jacqui then struck out three in a row to preserve the win. For one of the few times since she'd joined the Charros, Jacqui was not the focus of the media's attention. That honor belonged to Devin Baxter.

"I'm just happy I've been able to contribute," he said, his tone suggesting that "I've been here before."

Following the game, Rachel treated Devin to a late night snack at Arnoldi's. The moment they walked in the door, patrons, many of them wearing Charros gear, gave them a standing ovation. Rachel acted like a schoolgirl glancing downward at her shoes and fidgeting with a self-conscious smile. Finally, she waved to everyone and turned to Devin and broke out an I'm-not-worthy bow. Laughter bounced off the walls of the all-brick structure.

Devin wore an ear-to-ear grin the entire time they were in Arnoldi's.

"This is an amazing experience," he said to Rachel. "There is no pressure because there are no expectations. I feel like I'm a kid again in my backyard, swinging at imaginary pitches from imaginary pitchers." He put his arm around Rachel and hugged her tightly.

It was a few minutes after midnight when the two of them set out for Rachel's condo. Devin offered to drive her truck. Rachel sat in the passenger seat and leaned her head against the window. She was the picture of contentment as she looked glowingly at Devin as he expertly, for a stranger, negotiated a complicated surface street route. For the first time in a long time, she felt the happiness of having a man in her life. Until this moment, there had never been a man other than Big Erv whom she'd felt completely comfortable with and whom she respected so much.

As Devin guided her truck along Cabrillo Boulevard, the light of the full moon shone on his face. Rachel was content to just stare at him and give his free hand an affectionate squeeze. As he approached the driveway to the parking lot leading to Rachel's condo, Devin slowed the truck to a crawl and took one hand off the steering wheel and pointed to a Santa Barbara Police black-and-white that was parked across the street. As soon as Devin entered the driveway, the police car's lights came on, and the car was started up.

Devin stopped the truck to get a look at the driver. "Wonder what that was all about," he said, looking at Rachel.

Rachel's eyes rolled back. "I hope it isn't what I think it is."

"Explain."

"Worst-case scenario, it's a cop buddy of Deke's checking out if I'm home alone or have you with me."

"That's a little spooky."

"He's been acting strange ever since you arrived on the scene, Devin."

"A crush."

"I fear that's what it is."

Neither spoke of the incident the rest of the night. Both she and Devin were tired from a long day of being on for the many media requests that had come their way. Rachel was looking forward to snuggling with Devin in front of her fireplace; the evening fog had produced a chill worthy of a three-log fire. Rachel opened the front door and ushered Devin in. Devin stopped short before she could clear the door.

"Who are you?" he said in a threatening tone as he walked in Troy Haslett's direction.

Rachel put her hand on Devin's shoulder that stopped his movement toward what Devin considered to be an intruder.

"It's okay, Devin. It's my brother."

Troy, wearing jeans and a Rancheros sweatshirt, was seated on Rachel's couch. He fashioned the same blank expression that he'd exhibited the day he told Rachel their dad's plane was missing. He looked at the two of them, said nothing, and then turned back to gazing straight ahead out the window.

"What are you doing here, Troy?" Rachel's tone was accusatory. She felt her body tense up at the déjà vu moment before her.

"Mom did it." Troy continued to lock his eyes on the window before him.

"Did what?"

"Had Dad killed."

Convinced this was not a confrontation, Devin took off his sports coat and rested it on a dining room chair and then sat down in the chair.

Rachel slammed her purse on the love seat, her eyes not once leaving the bead they had on Troy's.

"Dammit, Troy! Where do you come up with a statement like that? This is not a joking matter. Is this what you do when you're not getting enough attention? Just like when we were kids?"

Troy finally turned toward Rachel. "It's not a joke. She told me herself in person."

"What do you mean in person?"

"She invited me to her house."

"I told her you suspected me of killing Dad."

Rachel flipped her head back, and her blond locks moved with the motion. "What you're saying is you were impersonating the tattletale that you were as a young boy. How disgusting that you just can't seem to grow up, Troy."

"I kinda wanted to let her know she might be a suspect too."

"Where would you get that idea?"

"You seemed to be investigating everyone that ever knew Dad."

Rachel got Devin's attention and pointed to a kitchen cupboard. "I need a glass of wine," she mouthed.

Troy turned away from Rachel and again stared blankly at the full moon outside the window.

"There was a guy familiar with operators of the private plane section of the airport who was hired to tamper with Dad's Cessna. He did it while the plane was tied down here in Santa Barbara."

"Did she give you a name of this person?"

"No."

"Did you ask?"

"No."

"Did she say why she had Dad killed fifteen years after they divorced and she had more money that she knew what to do with?"

"You'll have to ask her that."

Rachel got up in Troy's face. "You're telling me that it was my mother who threatened to kill me in a text?"

"Like I said, you'll have to ask her."

CHAPTER FIFTY

Rachel thought making love with Devin would help her to eventually fall asleep. After tossing about so much it left her skin feeling raw, she woke him at three in the morning with an apology and a soft hand. Even after an hour of great sex, she still couldn't get to sleep. She continued to play Troy's words over and over in her head. There was no filter for it. In a million years, she wouldn't have suspected her mother of being capable of murder. To add to the confusion, she could easily suspect her brother of making up such a story. He had a history of creating false alarms.

Rachel was still trying to decide what action to take on Troy's revelation when she arrived at her office mid-afternoon. She decided to confront Deke Slayton about the cop car in front of her condo. She found the locker room empty when she went looking for him. Usually he was there an hour before his players. Not this time. On his desk, she found a note.

Rachel,

> *I'm resigning as of this date as both a player and manager of the Charros.*

Yes, the black-and-white outside your condo was my advance scout. He needs some work on his detective skills. I suspected you and Devin Baxter were an item, and now I know. I have been infatuated with you ever since we met. I accepted your invitation to play for and manage the Charros only because I wanted to be close to you. Since that option appears to have gone the way of beepers, I have no desire to try and trick myself into thinking there is a place for me in the game of baseball. Thanks for giving me a second opportunity. FYI, the offer to help find your dad's killer is still there.

Deke

Rachel placed the letter back on her ex-manager's desk. She felt a sense of sadness in that she was losing a respected baseball man from her roster having just gained a respected baseball man in her life. *I'm apparently not allowed too many good things going at once*, she reasoned.

She returned to her office and called Devin on his cell. "You're not going to believe what just happened, Devin."

"Irving Zeller called you and offered you my old job?"

"Not on your life."

"Deke just quit. Left a resignation note on his desk."

"I know what you're going to ask."

"How do you know?"

"I know you. And yes, I'll take over for him."

Rachel giggled like a twelve-year-old. "You're the best, Devin. Have I ever told you that?"

Devin laughed. "Now it's the manager who's sleeping with you. You get around, girl."

"If you were here, I'd smack you, Mr. Manager."

"If you're planning on getting physical with me, I'll allow it."

"Cute, now get your ass over to the ballpark and address your players."

Rachel took the rest of the afternoon off to weigh her dilemma. Her mother was at the center of her thoughts. Should she confront her and report her to authorities or just let the whole thing slide? It was a tough decision because she had already invested so much time and energy into seeking the killer. She would admit to anyone that seeing her mother tried and convicted would be a horrific experience even if they were estranged. This was the woman who'd breastfed her, bought her the cutest clothes of any girl in school, got her the very latest Barbie Dolls, taught her about menstrual cycles, consoled her when her first boyfriend broke up with her, and took her to the beach to surf nearly every day in the summers. Nothing could bring her dad back.

She tried to imagine what action he would want her to take. Carrying all those thoughts, she hopped in her truck and drove thirty miles south on 101 to the town of Summerville and arrived at the Summerville Café, a trendy hangout for Hollywood stars who want some privacy away from work. She took a table on the front porch and ordered black coffee and a croissant. Just as the coffee arrived, her phone signaled an incoming text. It was from Troy.

"Jessie had something to do with it."

The complications were piling up. Rachel suddenly worried that determining what family member or associated member had killed her dad would surely sidetrack her focus on the Charros and their chances of winning the pennant. Secretly she was hoping to be named minor league executive of the year. Despite the Charros' great attendance numbers, winning the pennant was the only way that could happen. After a lengthy mental back and forth, she decided to call Troy.

Troy answered right away. "You got my text?"

"I did. It needs explaining, but you're going to leave that up to Mom, I assume."

"I am."

"How can I reach her by phone?"

"No clue."

Rachel spent the evening removed from the ballpark, researching how to locate her mother by phone. She did not want an unannounced direct confrontation. Her mother had never done well when directly confronted by any family member, especially her ex-husband. The time he caught her having mid-afternoon cocktails with her tennis instructor at one of those trendy cafés on Upper State Street left her close to a mental breakdown. She'd locked herself in their spare bedroom and didn't come out for a week.

It would have been so much easier if Troy had offered to help Rachel, but he was being Troy, trying to make her life as challenging as he could. She decided to cold-call restaurants in the Santa Ynez-Solvang area to see if anyone had her phone number from possible reservations she might have made. No luck.

Devin had some pretty good luck against the Stockton Ports. In his first game as manager, he led them the team to a 1–0 victory. He provided the Charros with their only run, a towering blast over the left field fence.

"I think the guys were a little intimidated by me," Devin told reporters after the game. "It's one thing to have a former major leaguer as a teammate, but when you're responsible to him as a player, it can make you overly anxious. I mean when was the last time the Charros committed four errors in a game?"

Errors or not, the win allowed the Charros to keep pace with Rancho Cucamonga, four games out of first.

They were both awakened out of a dead sleep by a frantic call from Adrienne Telfair. Rachel's clock read 2:30 a.m. She figured it had to be an emergency for Adrienne to contact her at that hour.

"I just got a call from someone on the city desk at the *News-Press* asking for a comment on Deke Slayton's death."

Rachel shot up in bed. "His what?"

Devin stirred, following Rachel's loud response. "Who is it?" he muttered.

Rachel waved her hand at him. "Quiet," she mouthed the word.

"According to the reporter," Adrienne continued, "he was coming out of the Left Bank in Goleta, and someone walked up to him and shot him point-blank with a handgun, first in the chest and then, before Deke hit the ground, directly between his eyes. The cops told the reporter that no one witnessed the shooting. The killer is on the run."

Try as she might, Rachel had difficulty getting her head around Deke's murder. She got out of bed and made coffee. Devin joined her at the kitchen table. Before that, she'd thrown up in the downstairs bathroom.

"So the cops have no clues."

"That's what Adrienne told me."

"Do you have any ideas, Rachel?"

"I fear I do have one," Rachel said, her face expressionless. She then threw back the last of her coffee like she was angry at the drink. "When I asked him to become our player-manager, he offered instead to 'snoop around,' that's how he put it, and see if he could shed any light on who might have killed my dad. I thanked him, but I convinced the Charros needed him more. He never offered his services as an investigator again." Suddenly, Rachel started to cry, her chest heaving as she broke into a full-out emotional meltdown. "It's my fault, Devin. I know it."

Devin got up and put his arm around Rachel. "You can't let it eat you up."

"It already is. How many more people have to die before we know the truth about my dad's death?"

CHAPTER FIFTY-ONE

Adrienne had arranged an eleven-o-clock news conference for Rachel to comment on Deke Slayton's murder. If ever there was something Rachel would rather not do, it was to get in front of the media and salute a dead employee. She dressed for the occasion in black jeans, a black blouse, and black cowboy boots. Her hair was in a bun. She spoke without notes. She'd never admit it, but she looked like she hadn't slept in days.

"Everyone in the Charros' organization is both saddened and angered by the untimely and senseless death of Deke Slayton," she began. "This franchise will always view Deke Slayton as an MVP for coming to the team's rescue at a time when we were in dire need of a spark—not to mention a manager. Deke Slayton accomplished everything I asked of him and more. So much more." Rachel paused to wipe away a tear that was starting to make its way down her face. "Deke loved baseball and in addition to helping turn around our second half fortunes, was having so much success as a hitter that he was beginning to have second thoughts about giving it one more shot at the big leagues. Somewhere along the line, he felt he best served his fellow men as an officer of the law." *Sometimes you just have to lie,* she told herself.

"In order to preserve Deke's legacy, I've commissioned a bronze plaque in his image to be placed over the entrance to the Charros' clubhouse. The inscription will read, *In Honor of Deke Slayton, A Baseball Man*."

Devin was in the mix, mingling with the media after Rachel had finished. It was common knowledge, thanks to one of Miles Rooney's columns that Devin had blocked Deke's road to the big leagues. The media swarmed on him at the conclusion of Rachel's news conference.

"I did what I had to do based on performance. Deke just didn't have the numbers at the plate to move up in the Friars' organization." He quickly changed the subject. "I haven't known Rachel to be despondent over anything, but Deke Slayton's death has rocked her. I expect her to turn Charros leadership responsibilities over to Adrienne Telfair for the remainder of the season. I'll help wherever I can, but my job is to keep our players on point. We're not that far off from seriously challenging for the pennant, and that's my goal as player-manager."

Rachel understood that Santa Barbara Police would be all over Deke Slayton's murder—a cop killer is always public enemy number 1 among those with whom the victim shared the same badge. But she promised herself to work in the shadows of the police after she'd had a dream that Deke's death and her dad's might be related. In her dream, she somehow found out that Deke had been working on the case without telling her. She believed he was trying to win her over by heroically finding and capturing her dad's murderer. She understood it was a dream, but with each passing day, it had become more real to her.

Rachel's first priority was to get her brother to talk—no small task knowing his history. He'd already indicted their mom and Jessie Santiago. Were there more?

Troy Haslett had spent his post *Slo-Go Fit* days doing what he'd done prior to his fifteen minutes of fame: drugs and Starbucks. Never one to back away from a challenge, Rachel stopped by his East Beach apartment only to find it empty. She sought out the property manager for an explanation. She said her name was Miriam—gave no last name—and that she had evicted Troy because he was four months behind on his rent and suspected him of dealing marijuana.

"I couldn't prove it, but people—mostly guys—would stop in for a short while, like fifteen minutes, and then be gone. The smell of that shit lingered long after they'd gone. Your brother was a sweet young man who frequently helped me and other tenants with their groceries, and he took it on his own to water the roses in the front of the facility."

Troy had no real friend that Rachel could turn to for help in finding him, so she decided to stake out his favorite Starbucks on Lower State Street. Before that, she sought to locate some ammunition that might entice Troy into talking—drugs—specifically. She turned to one of her players for advice. She stopped by the ballpark early, about four hours before the final game with Stockton. She targeted Chad Isner, who, she believed, was the most street-smart of any of the Charros. At twenty-three, he was the oldest on the team. She found him in the weight room and was impressed to see him benching what she quickly calculated to be 280 pounds.

"That's awesome," Rachel said.

"Just warming up." Chad flashed his famous shit-eating grin.

Rachel was wearing jeans and a Charros T-shirt, not her usual game-time attire of slacks and a sweater. Even in summer, it could get chilly at night at The Erv. She could sense from Chad's darting eyes that he was undressing her as she spoke, but that was nothing out of the ordinary from him. She'd been told by several of the girls that worked in concessions that Chad got more pussy than all the players combined.

"I need your help, Chad."

"Happy to oblige."

Rachel inhaled before breaking out her question. "Where's the best place in town to buy drugs?" She held out both hands, a gesture that looked like she was imitating a stop sign. "I'm not implying anything. You have to understand that, Chad. It's just that you seem to have a feel for the pulse of young people in this community. I know you're the player who most often goes on our school visits. I know for a fact—don't forget who was our most recent manager—you're a club hound. I can name at least five nightclubs that you visit regularly."

"Really!"

"I don't just buy bats and balls for you, guys. I have an investment to protect. I stay informed. Back to my question."

Chad feigned searching his mind for an answer. "There's a house on Almond Avenue that has a reputation for dealing all kinds of drugs—cocaine, maryjo, meth. But there was a bust there about the time I joined the Charros. It was all over the news. The popo hauled in a half dozen guys."

"I was thinking of a park somewhere. I always suspected the park next to the *News-Press* was where most got their drugs."

Chad shook his head. "The homeless don't do anything but the cheapest of cheap-ass drugs. Mostly meth. That's not a safe place for you, too many crazies hanging out there. A person of your stature and visibility should not be buying drugs anywhere. I tell you what,

I can get one of my homies in Santa Maria to buy for you. You won't be risking anything that way. What is it you want me to get?"

Rachel chuckled briefly. She had a hard time realizing what she was asking. "The best dope your contact can buy. I'll pay him a 25 percent commission, but I need it ASAP."

"Done."

"And we never had this conversation, correct?"

"Just curious who you're buying it for."

"Let's just say I'm independently working to find out who killed Deke Slayton."

Chad did an eye roll. "Wow! Be careful, boss."

"I will."

Rachel didn't tell him she was fighting fire with fire. If she could pry Troy with drugs, she might get him to talk.

The next day, after a Charros' 5-2 win over Stockton that featured a three-run homer by Devin Baxter moved them to within three games of Rancho Cucamonga, Rachel received a text from a phone number with an 805 area code that she didn't recognize.

It read, "Meet at Macy's parking lot. Red Kia. In an hour."

Fortunately for Rachel, the Macy's in the La Cumbre Plaza wasn't doing all that well, so picking out a red Kia wasn't all that difficult. She pulled up next to the car and flashed a thumbs-up to the person in the driver's seat. He was long-haired with pasty-colored skin and a goatee that reminded her of crabgrass. He motioned for Rachel to get in his car. She did. He asked if she'd be okay driving to another location. Rachel agreed. He set off northbound on Highway 101. Five minutes and a couple of changes of direction, and he'd reached his destination. It was called Tucker's Grove. At one time, it was a popular picnic area; but judging by the lack of parked cars and the rundown nature of the grounds, Rachel perceived it to be a good place for a drug transaction.

Chad's contact—he didn't offer a name—reached under his seat and pulled out a small Ralph's shopping bag. "This is some good shit. It's known as purple haze. It produces an intense mental high."

Rachel was clearly uneasy being in the guy's presence. She continuously scoped the park's landscape. For what, she wasn't sure.

"How much?" She was angry with herself for allowing her nerves to thin her voice.

"Just $300 for a quarter of a gram and my commission."

Rachel pulled out four crisp $100 bills from her fanny pack.

"Now can you get me back to my car?"

"Can't," the guy said, shaking his head.

"What?"

"When the deal is done, we're done."

Rachel's eyes sparked. "You're seriously going to leave me here?"

"Can't risk returning to where we hooked up. Not smart. You have your cell phone. Call a cab."

Rachel unlatched her passenger door. "I'm going to tell Chad you're a prick."

"Fuck Chad. He thinks he's so big time, playing professional ball and all. He's still the same little dick who was always too scared to make a sale. Tell him I said thanks for the lead. He didn't tell me you'd be some fucking gorgeous chick."

Rachel was already walking on the path to the park's entrance and may not have heard the guy's evaluation. On the trip to the park, she'd noticed a Shell station about a block away. She called for a taxi to meet her there. She couldn't help feeling like a criminal.

Once she got back to her truck in the Macy's lot, Rachel called Devin and told him she wouldn't be able to attend tonight's series opener with Bakersfield.

"I might be on to something" is all she said to him.

Devin was very understanding as always. "Take all the time you need, love. I've got you covered."

Rachel was taken aback. She paused her conversation a moment. It was the first time the *L* word had crept into one of their conversations.

"Did you just call me *Love?*"

"I did."

"Does that mean what I'm hoping it does, or was it just an expression?"

"You should know by now that I'm in love with you, Rachel."

Rachel put the phone in her lap and clapped her hands and hollered, "That's not for your three-run homer last night! It's because I love you back, and I'm so happy." She said it like a schoolgirl accepting an invitation to the prom—which she never received. She told him she'd see him sometime after the game. When she hung up, she looked at the bag of ganja sitting on the passenger's seat, and she thought, *Maybe I should just go get high without my brother.*

It took her most of the evening to finally locate her brother, and it was strictly a case of blind luck. Just before midnight, she'd stopped for gas at a Chevron station located a couple of blocks from the ballpark. There he was, exiting the station's restroom. He looked like a homeless person: full beard, hair's a mess, clothes in need of a Laundromat. Rachel's heart skipped a beat.

Instead of filling her tank, Rachel approached Troy. When he saw her coming, he tucked his head to his chest. It was a signal he was ashamed of where she'd found him.

"What are you doing in this neighborhood, Troy?"

His eyes searched the ground beneath him. "I had a drug hookup down the block, but the guy never showed."

Rachel placed her hand on her brother's shoulder. He didn't recoil from her touch as he'd done most of his life. "Let me take you home, Troy."

Suffering from a major league case of sad eyes, Troy looked up at his sister and said, "I don't have a home."

Rachel rocked his shoulder slightly. "I meant my home. You look like you haven't eaten in days. Devin Baxter is staying with me, but he's probably in bed by now."

"So that's a thing?"

"It is."

Troy accepted the invite and got into Rachel's truck.

Rachel decided against pumping gas. "We need to talk, Troy. I've got some stuff in the bag you just placed on the floor that will make talking more enjoyable. I'm told it's some really good shit. Only the best for my unpredictable brother."

A slight smile crossed Troy's lips. "You're going to do weed with me? You must really be on a guilt trip."

"Let's try guilt for $200." Rachel laughed at her own humor.

CHAPTER FIFTY-TWO

Devin was asleep when Rachel and her brother arrived at her condo. He'd left a note on the kitchen table: *We got killed tonight, 11–0. Got to sleep it off. Love you.*

Rachel's sentimental side surfaced as she folded the note and put in on her desktop for a future filing. Rachel cringed silently as Troy plopped on her prized couch.

"When's the last time you changed clothes?"

"Two days ago when I got kicked out of my abode."

"Surely you have enough money to pay rent and outfit yourself, Troy?"

"I will when I get paid for my week on *Slo-Go Fit*. Oh, I've got some stocks that Dad gave me years ago, but seriously, big sis, I don't know what they are, where they are, or what I do with them when I find them. I've been trying my damnedest not to slide back to selling drugs. Trust me."

Rachel reached into her purse that she always kept an arm's length away. She pulled a card from her wallet. Here's the guy at Schwab who takes care of my accounts. Give him a call."

"I will."

"What happened with your TV show? I thought you were on your way to fame and fortune."

"Jessie happened to it. She wasn't any good. The word I heard was *phony*. Plus there's no action in a show about slowly lifting weights. It was a dumb-ass concept. I should have researched the production company. They had a track record that had more flameouts than bad charcoal."

Rachel grabbed the brown bag containing her newly purchased weed and told Troy to roll them both a joint. "Isn't that how I'm supposed to say it?"

"You're speaking the language."

"It's called purple something."

"Purple haze?" Troy's eyes opened big. "That is good shit. You rock, sis."

The first half hour, they reminisced about life as a Haslett. Rachel was right about her hunch that Troy would open up with the help of weed. They talked like never before—about family picnics, Disneyland, Christmas in Mexico, friend's weddings, and their first experiences with pot.

"Mom caught me toking out back of the garage," Troy said. "God, she was pissed. Took away my Sony Dishman."

"Discman."

"That's what I said."

"This shit will do that to your brain," Troy said, taking the roach out from between his lips and examining it.

By the time their musings about life as a Haslett started to run out of steam, Rachel was feeling "hella good," as her players would likely describe her condition. Good enough to ask about their mom, now that Troy had broached the subject.

"How is she?"

"Miserable."

"What's new with that?" Rachel took another deep hit on her purple haze.

"I told you she had Dad killed."

Rachel dropped from the couch to the floor and stretched her legs out. "That's all you told me."

Troy pointed at the brown bag on the table. "There's enough for a couple more."

"I'm good. I'm already feeling like taking a swim in my pool."

Troy laughed. "Now you're definitely a captive to it. Just curious, when was the last time you smoked weed?"

"Never, brother. I was a dedicated athlete, remember?"

"A virgin?"

"Yep."

Rachel could count on one hand the number of times she'd seen Troy smile big like he was at the moment.

"I know, Rachel. Mom didn't cut the control arm rod on Dad's plane. She wouldn't know which door to open to get in the damn plane. She hated that Cessna because it had put them in a financial squeeze at the time. Then Dad bought the baseball team to really make her crazy."

Troy took another strong hit and rolled his head onto the arm of the couch and stretched out his legs. "She hired someone to do it. Actually, Jessie hired someone."

Rachel's eyes shot up her forehead. "How did Jessie get into the picture?"

"Mom wanted me to have most of Dad's estate as payback for his shitty parenting. She figured Jessie would get some of the money, but if it was to get half, it was worth the risk. We both know how that worked out."

"Boy, Dad could pick 'em. His ex and his girlfriend conspiring to kill him." Rachel laid her head against the other arm of the couch. She kept reminding herself that she had to stop smoking in order to be able to remember everything Troy had and would tell her.

Troy asked if he could roll a third joint with what was left.

"Feel free." Rachel hadn't witnessed him talk this much in thirty-four years.

"The real motive for Mom's death wish surprised me," Troy continued. "I had no idea. She told me that Dad forced her to abort what would have been a third child—our sibling. She said he didn't want to take a chance on having another boy and refused to learn the gender ahead of time. I guess because of how I turned out. She was devastated by his edict . . . Is that a word?"

Rachel smiled. "It is."

"Good. This shit is so good I thought I was making up stuff."

"But why all these years later does she decide she wants him dead?"

"Well, her kid with her new husband has special needs. He's not a Down's syndrome kid, but it's something in that ballpark. She blames herself for having a kid at forty-four. She knew it was risky, and she and her husband got burned."

"Translated. Dad's fault."

"Yep."

"So her hatred of Dad was rekindled when Peter Richards didn't come out, right?"

"Something like that."

"When's the last time you saw or talked with Jessie?"

"In our hotel suite in LA. When we found out our review. She was starting to get on my nerves. But I do miss the sex. She was firecrackers every time."

Rachel shook her head. "So you took over for Dad?"

"I did. And she said I was better."

Rachel rolled her eyes and chuckled. "What is it with men and their sexual prowess? We have to be the most dysfunctional family since the Louds of Santa Barbara hung out their dirty laundry on national TV in the seventies."

Rachel got up and went to the kitchen for a bottle of water. She hoped it would help with what she would acknowledge as a major purple haze high.

"You know Jessie and Mom could both face murder charges. How do you feel about blowing the whistle on them?"

"The only blow I want is in that bag." Troy pointed to the Ralph's bag.

Rachel had enough of her wits about her to realize her brother was fading fast. He'd rolled off the couch onto the carpet and yawned over and over. She had one last proposition for Troy.

"Is there any way you could find out from Jessie who she hired to tamper with Dad's plane?"

Troy's body flinched. He'd momentarily fallen asleep and then caught himself.

"I'll try her computer." It was the last thing he said before slipping off.

In an attempt to help her with recall of their conversation, Rachel powered up her iPad and made notes. The last word she entered was *abortion*. She wrote it in upper case and clicked on bold type.

While she was doing this, Troy awoke from a dead sleep. His speech was thick. "Who's the chick that does your radio?"

"Melanie . . ."

"Thaz da one. Can you fix me up her? Wid her. She's sooo cute." In an instant, he was back asleep.

When Rachel woke up late the next morning, she felt as though someone had taken a hammer to her head. The veins at her temples throbbed. Her eyes felt like they'd been sandpapered. It took her a few minutes when she came downstairs from her bedroom to discover that Troy was missing, as in gone. *For who knows where?*

Devin was also gone but left a note. "Got to deal with something urgent in Charros' land," it read.

Not to worry. She couldn't help think what a prince of a man he was. She made a point to book the president's room at the Four Seasons Biltmore for his forty-third birthday next week.

CHAPTER FIFTY-THREE

Rachel arrived at her office slightly out of breath. She had showered and dressed as quickly as she could after she'd picked up Devin's note. She was dressed head to foot in Nike gear, and her hair was wet. Devin was seated at her desk, casually dressed in black walking shorts and a black –and-blue just out-of-the-box Charros T-shirt. *He'd look good in a fire retardant suit*, Rachel thought to herself.

"It appears you want to get attorneys involved," he said to whoever was at the other end of the line. "We can do that. Meantime, we're planning on playing on Bakersfield tonight, and if we have to, we'll recruit umpires from the stands. If Bakersfield refuses to play, we'll take that as a victory for the Charros. Wins are hard to come by late in the season. We can certainly use any that come our way on the field or in court." Devin hung up the phone.

Rachel stood in front of her desk with a quizzical look on her face. "What's up? You sounded combative."

Devin shook his head before answering. His lips were tight, his eyes penetrating. "Both Visalia and Cucamonga want me to be suspended until further notice."

"For?"

"Being me. Their general managers have filed a complaint with the California League commissioner reciting a clause in the league's bylaws that restricts any former major league player or executive from competing or working in the league if they've been affiliated with a major league franchise the same year."

Rachel rolled her eyes. "How deep did they have to dig to come up with that?"

"They just want to make sure Honeyball doesn't win the pennant. The way we're coming on as a team, save for last night, has them worried we might win it all."

"Hardball."

"High and inside."

Rachel stepped around her desk and behind where Devin was sitting. She put her arms around his neck and hugged him. "Don't you worry your sweet self about this, Devin. Give me five minutes on the phone, and this threat will be history."

Devin smiled ever so slightly and looked at his watch. "You're on the clock, Ms. Haslett." He exited her office to allow her some privacy.

In four minutes and thirty seconds, Rachel hung up her phone. She texted Devin that she was finished with her phone call.

Devin bounced into her office all smiles. "What happened?"

Rachel stuck her chest out as if to say, *I won that one.* "I spoke with the commissioner himself. The highly regarded—by his family—Mr. Arthur Spelling. I reminded him about my dad's annual contributions to the league's front office—translated, Spelling. I remember my dad telling me that every year he sent a $50,000 check in Spelling's name. I also reminded him that my dad was a meticulous businessman who kept accurate records of every transaction that had his name on it and most that didn't. I told the commissioner he even used to save his ticket stubs when he went to play the ponies at Santa Anita."

"And . . ."

"You will not be suspended."

Devin grinned and gave Rachel a peck on the cheek. "You have scored another big win for Honeyball, honey child."

"Honey child?" Rachel raised her eyebrows.

"That's what we young men in Texas used to call the pretty girls."

"Well, we're not in Texas anymore." Rachel laughed.

"Time to bring the hammer down," Devin said to his assembled team in the Charros' clubhouse prior to the opening game of a four-night set with the Bakersfield Blaze. "We have to forget all about last night's blow out. Stuff like that happens. You just have to let it go and focus on Bakersfield. I want you to make winning each of our last ten games your mantra—each one of you. And that includes me. I expect as much out of myself as I do you."

Devin held up his end of the deal. Each of his three hits was a home run, giving him eleven in his eighteen games as a member of the Charros. He drove in five in an 8-0 win. Jacqui Davenport was called on to pitch the final two innings in relief of Stoney McMurtry, and she went six up, six down to bring her ERA to a remarkable 1.24.

After the game, Rachel reported to the Charros' clubhouse to spread some "Atta boys" among the players. "Charros rock!" she shouted.

The players picked up on it immediately, and it quickly became a Rachel-induced love fest.

Rachel asked Devin to come with her for beers at Rusty's Pizza, but he begged off, citing his need to watch another episode of *House of Cards.*

"You're getting pretty domestic pretty quick, slugger."

"I told you I'm too old for you." He pointed his finger at her as if to remind her of what he'd actually told her when they first started getting serious.

Rachel motioned for Devin to step outside. He was dressed in his uniform top and sliding pants. "Speaking of cards, I'm sending out invites to your birthday party next week at the Biltmore. Is there anyone in particular you want to invite?"

"We didn't discuss any birthday party."

"I know. I wanted to make it a surprise, but the mechanics of pulling it off after a night game and amid everything that's going on in my life were too formidable. I hope you're okay with that."

Devin smiled, looked around to see if anyone was watching. All clear, he planted a big league kiss on Rachel's lips. "You're the best, girl—the best thing that has ever happened to me. Thank you for personally coming to bitch at me in spring training."

"You might still have a job if you hadn't blown off 'due process.'"

"I much prefer the blank checks you give me."

"Touché."

Devin hugged her then held her at arm's length. "I'm having the time of my life, girl. Oh, and I just thought of someone for the party. Chloe will be out of summer school. I'll fly her out here. I can't wait for her to meet you."

"How sweet." Rachel smiled. "I'm looking forward to meeting her."

The next morning Rachel got a call from Troy. "I talked to your guy at Schwab," he said. "He set me straight. I have a ton of money—okay, not a ton but a lot available to me at the snap of my fingers or a couple of clicks on my computer. I have $250,000 at my command. Thanks, sis. I don't have to sleep in a cardboard box anymore."

"Happy to help, Troy."

"I have some good news for you. I sneaked into Jessie's place in Montecito. I did it in the morning when I figured she was training someone somewhere. The credit card trick still works on old locks. I found her laptop and started searching recent e-mails. A friend at city college taught me how to do that maybe ten years ago. It still works today. There are a couple of e-mail exchanges with a Robert Galvan that were dated a week before Dad's death. They were kind of—what's the word I'm looking for—innocuous."

"That means vanilla."

"As in not very revealing. But in the last e-mail between the two of them, Jessie asked, 'Is it a done deal?'

"'Yes, the deal is done,' Galvan responded. I'm guessing, Rachel, that, judging from his previous e-mails, he washed private planes at the airport for a living. Seems like it would give him access to any plane in the yard. His e-mail address is RG54@gmail.com."

Rachel's voice reflected a new energy. "Great work, Troy. You may have just uncovered a cop killer."

"Always glad when I can help law enforcement types," he said with a smirk.

Rachel didn't waste any time calling Deke Slayton's former roommate, a cop himself, Barry Vuccenivich. "I have some information on who might have killed Officer Slayton," she began.

"Who is this?"

"I'm Rachel Haslett. I hired Deke to take over as an emergency manager of my baseball team, the Santa Barbara Charros."

"Sorry, I've got you now. You caught me snooping on you."

"Yes, I did."

"I felt so bad about that. I was just doing my roomie a favor. He was pretty hung up on you. It really burst his bubble when I told him you were with another man. What have you got?"

"E-mails from what I would call a person of interest in both my dad's death and your roommate's. His name is Robert Galvan. I believe he may have been hired to tamper with my dad's plane that crashed in the ocean. The NTSB said it was not an accident. This Galvan guy works washing private planes at the airport. His bank account should tell you everything you need to know."

"Whose e-mails did you intercept?"

Rachel took a degree of pleasure in answering the question. "Her name is Jessie Santiago. She's a local fitness trainer who had a two-year relationship with my dad. I'm almost 100 percent certain she hired Galvan to tamper with my dad's plane. The motive is a story for another time. My brother has copies of those e-mails. I suspect Deke got a little too close in his unofficial investigation of Galvan, and as a result, the scumbag took him out. I want desperately to bring this guy down. In case you need it, I have Galvan's e-mail address I can share with you."

"Thanks so much for the information. I'll take this to my sergeant right away. Deke was a great guy and a very conscientious cop. He could have been the poster boy for good cops everywhere. I honestly thought, based on his performance as both a player and manager, he might have earned one more shot at making the bigs. Is there a memorial?"

"Yes." Rachel paused to compose herself. "We're having it at the ballpark. It's the second one there this season."

"That's not something you want to lead the league in."

CHAPTER FIFTY-FOUR

Things started falling in place for Rachel at warp speed. Lorena Volques had come up big in finding dirt on Miles Rooney's written works. In order, over four years of *News-Press* columns, he'd dissed: Serena Williams, calling her a man; Amy Wilhelm, UCSB's career-leading scorer in basketball, calling her a self-absorbed selfish teammate; LPGA golfer Missy Lopez from Montecito, calling her a lesbian, who should be tested for growth hormones; Olympic team diver Sandy Pomerantz, calling her out for being a choke artist for failing to medal in London; and calling Sissy Merchant, a contender for the U.S. women's soccer team roster, an overrated player who may have once been really good during grade school recess.

Rachel had Lorena put these facts into a flyer that she had distributed throughout the county. The end result was that after doing their due diligence, the editors of the *News-Press* suspended Rooney for a month without pay and promised readers a more professional sports column by promoting Amy Tasker and demoting Rooney to a beat writer for all UCSB sports.

The Charros behind Devin Baxter's monster bat—his home run total had landed on twenty—had pushed to within a game of Rancho Cucamonga with five games to go; Austin Grant was given a trial date in November; Bernard Coffee pleaded no contest to a lesser felony charge of assault; her brother was finally acting like a brother should; and Devin's birthday party was an overwhelming success. Five of his former staff members with the Friars attended, along with the lovely Chloe. She was everything Devin had bragged about: confident around adults, engaging, and pretty as can be. She wasn't self-absorbed Kardashian pretty but sixteen-year-old girl pretty, with precious blue eyes, delicate facial figures like her dad, and an infectious laugh. And Devin had received some great news. The MLB network had pledged to do a story on his return to baseball and the motive behind it. He'd also learned via an e-mail from the president of the Baseball Writers Association that, despite the fact he was no longer working in the Friars' organization, he was on the ballot, along with two others, for executive of the year. The honor, he was told, was based on his stance of upholding the suspension of Austin Grant.

What topped off Rachel's impressive list of good happenings, however, was the lead story in today's *Santa Barbara News-Press*.

Airport Worker Charged in Officer's Murder
Linda Shaffer

SANTA BARBARA—A thirty-year-old Goleta man, Robert Luis Galvan, was arrested early Tuesday morning at his apartment on Holland Avenue and charged with the first-degree murder of Santa Barbara Police Officer Deke Slayton. Slayton, who had just been reassigned to duty after a two-month leave of absence to become a player-manager for the Santa Barbara Charros baseball team, was gunned down August 17 at point-blank range as he was exiting the Left Bank Restaurant in Goleta. Police public information director Hal Overton said a Beretta 92FS handgun, the same model that was used in the Slayton shooting, was found in Galvan's apartment, along with unspent ammunition that matched the two rounds that killed Slayton. After receiving an anonymous tip regarding Galvan's possible involvement in the shooting, police were in the process of carrying out a search warrant when they came upon the suspect just as he was leaving his apartment to go to work as a private plane washer at nearby Santa Barbara Municipal Airport. Galvan may be facing an additional murder charge in the death of Ervin Haslett in April. Police would only say that the two deaths could be related. Galvan will be arraigned tomorrow at the Santa Barbara County Courthouse.

Rachel was on such a roll of positives that she did the unthinkable, all the while knowing it would take a miracle. In an effort to top off what would surely be the one and only season of Honeyball—good marketing calls for fresh ideas every year—she'd contacted Madonna's agent on the feint hope she'd be able to talk the singer into performing before the Charros' last game of the season. It would be a perfect fit. "All the Way" Mae Mordabito from the 1992 movie *A League of Their Own* about the Rockford Peaches of the *All American Girls Professional Baseball League,* playing *The Erv.*

Madonna's agent surprised Rachel by responding by phone. "It sounds like the kind of off-the-wall thing Madonna likes to do. I know she's aware of Honeyball. She even went so far as to say to me that she thought the Honeyball story might make a good film."

Rachel was impressed that the agent—she went only by Sue—knew so much about the Charros' season.

"Our last home game is on September 7. We'd market it as a fan appreciation concert." Rachel couldn't hold the excitement in her voice. "I'm just thrilled that she would even consider performing in Santa Barbara."

"Are you kidding? It's one of her favorite places to visit. She played the Bowl there several years ago." Sue had an incoming call. "Sorry, I've got to take this. I'll be in touch and give you a definite answer in a couple of days. I know she has the date open. It's just a matter of me talking her into it."

"I've already got my fingers crossed. Thanks so much for considering us, Sue."

Rachel couldn't wait to tell Adrienne Telfair about her phone call. She burst into her office, only to find a crying Melanie Sandberg seated across Adrienne. Rachel aborted her excitement of Madonna to address Melanie's distress.

Adrienne brought Rachel up to speed. "Melanie's been given a ten-day cease-and-desist order by the FCC."

"What for?"

"Excessive use of foul and unprofessional language," Melanie said, her voice breaking. "Some ancient listener ratted me out."

Rachel looked at Adrienne. "Don't they have to give you a warning when they're about to blow up your broadcast schedule? Are they going to pay our sponsors for future ads that we wouldn't be able to deliver on?"

Adrienne shook her head. Rachel paced in front of Adrienne's desk. She was deep in thought and hot under the collar.

"Screw it. We're not going to honor their edict. What are they going to do—come here and physically pull the plug that shuts Melanie down?"

Melanie thanked both Adrienne and Rachel for their support in the matter and then went absolutely bonkers when Rachel relayed her conversation with Madonna's agent. "Maybe I can interview her before the game."

Rachel held up her right hand. "Let's not get carried away about this. It's in the pipedream phase, but yes, I would suggest she do an interview with you."

Melanie's demeanor had done a 360. "Too cool," she said as she gave both Rachel and Adrienne a peck on their cheek.

Rachel's euphoria lasted just long enough for her to return home for a quickie nap. She'd long given the ocean air credit for allowing her such quality naps. She had just dozed off on her office futon when her doorbell rang. She scrambled to her feet and threw her favorite oxford shirt over her bra. She'd kept her short shorts on while lying down. The doorbell rang again before she reached the door handle.

"Hold on!" she shouted from mid-living room. When she opened the door, she was shocked to see the drastically altered image of her mother, Katherine Richards.

"May I come in, Rachel?"

Rachel's face was frozen from surprise. Instinctively, she waved her hand for her mother to enter. She appeared nothing like she'd remembered her. She was disheveled. Her hair, which was always perfect, looked windblown, but there was no wind this day. She was without makeup. Her eyes were swollen and droopy, and her customary year-round summer tan had vanished. This was clearly not the woman who had walked out on her family all those years ago. This was a broken woman. Before anything significant was said, she brushed away tears.

Rachel finally diffused the awkwardness by offering her mother a drink. She was thinking soda or iced tea.

"Vodka rocks. Plenty of vodka."

Rachel couldn't remember her mother ever drinking in the daytime. "What brings you here after all the years, Mom?" Rachel had a difficult moment deciding whether to refer to her as Mom.

"Oh, you know. Let's not play games, Rachel. I know you've spoken with Troy about your dad's death. Well, I'm here to make it official. I had him killed."

Whether she wanted to hear the details that she already knew didn't matter. Rachel was going to hear them again from the horse's mouth—after a detour.

"Your baseball team is really doing well. I always knew you'd be successful at whatever you did—quite unlike your brother. I read somewhere you have this new old player hitting the ball like he was a kid."

That observation provided Rachel an opportunity to shock her mother, something she'd always aspired to do even as a little girl. "You're talking about Devin Baxter, correct?"

"Yes. Big black guy."

"He's my first baseman and my new man, my lover."

Katherine's face dropped. "Oh!" She chugged her vodka and motioned for a quick refill. "Is it serious?"

"It's getting there. He's a wonderful guy."

Katherine accepted the fresh vodka and attacked it. "I've often wondered why you've never married."

"Never found the right guy. No one was the equal of Dad." Rachel got up and poured herself an iced tea.

Katherine's eyes rolled, and she shook her head.

"Can we get back to why you're here, Mother?" Rachel quickly realized she hadn't used the word *mother* in so long that it was as if she'd never had one.

Katherine raised her sloppily maintained eyebrows. "Going somewhere? It's only every fifteen years that your mother pays you a visit." Suddenly, her veneer changed dramatically. She began to cry, and that quickly advanced to bawling. "I'm not sorry about your dad's death. I've hated him for so long, but the young police officer that was shot—"

"Officer Slayton."

"Yes. It tears me apart that a young man like that with so much of life ahead of him had to die because I wanted your father dead. You're positive of the connection. I made out Galvan's check, $50,000, to make sure your father's plane went down. Later, he wanted more, another $25,000. I gave it to him." Katherine tried to wipe her tears with a tissue from her purse but failed in her attempt. "Enough about death," she said, inhaling deeply in search of her composure.

"More vodka, Mom?"

"Yes. I want to drink myself silly."

"Well, I'm happy to inform you that you're on target. Are you drinking a lot lately?"

"Only every other hour. Peter won't bring his friends to the house anymore. It's just like that ad on the radio about alcoholism. It's me the boy on the radio is talking about. It's meeeeee!"

"You can sleep it off here. We have a game tonight."

"No. I want to know what you are going to do about me. Are you going to turn me over to the auth-author-authorities? After all, I am a murd—"

Rachel got up and paced her living room end to end several times. "I've thought a lot about this, Mom—agonized over it. If it had just been Dad."

Katherine let out a shriek. "Oh god almighty! You're going to turn me in, aren't you?"

Almost as if on cue, she reached into her purse and pulled out a small handgun. Rachel guessed that it might have been a Derringer. At any rate, she didn't want to be on the other end of a gunshot, no matter how small the weapon. She quickly assessed her mom's alcoholic condition and, with a swift sweep of her right hand, grabbed her handgun away, all the while praying that it would not go off in her chest.

In the process, Rachel bowed her neck and said, "I am going to turn you in. Surely you knew I would before you showed up at my doorstep." She reached for her purse and pulled out her phone. She'd preprogrammed her phone for the police dispatch, knowing that this day would come. "I have a confessed murderer in my presence. I'm at 429 Cabrillo Boulevard, unit 9. Please hurry."

Ten minutes passed. A Santa Barbara cop showed up and knocked on the front door. He had beady eyes and a thin face that looked as if he caught his head in a vice at some time in his youth. As she watched Officer Dewey help her mom to her feet and out the door to a waiting squad car, Rachel broke into tears. She had just witnessed the death of another parent, one who would rot to her death in prison.

Katherine Haslett–Richards, RIP.

CHAPTER FIFTY-FIVE

That evening, right in the middle of the Charros' game with Bakersfield, they won again—they're seventh straight. Rachel was called to come to the police station. The officer who called her told her that her mom was not cooperating with their investigation.

"She won't talk—period," the man who identified himself as Officer Heinrich said. "We need some explanation from you in order to hold her. Otherwise, she could be released in the morning."

What kind of havoc she could unleash if she were released, Rachel wondered. She put in a call to Troy, asking him to come with her and corroborate what she would tell the police.

Katherine Richards was still in the drunk tank when Rachel and Troy arrived at the police station. She hadn't yet been taken to the county jail and wouldn't be unless Rachel and Troy made a strong case for a murder charge.

The siblings were escorted to a small sterile interrogation room that reeked of perspiration. The only articles in the room were four chairs and a table. There was little need for pieces of contemporary art or indoor flowers. Lt. Archie Hayes introduced himself and said that they take a seat. He was a green-eyed monster, a black man about six-foot-four, who had more muscles than a person needed. He wore a tiny mustache and had a nasty scar left of his chin, perhaps an indication that he wasn't always on the right side of the law.

Rachel and Troy each told their story about their mother's confession, and Rachel advised they could probably find the checks she'd written to Robert Galvan in her bank statements.

"That's the guy she . . . well, really, Jessie, hired to tamper with my dad's plane," Troy volunteered.

Lieutenant Hayes's eyebrows shot upward. "Who is this Jessie person, and how does he fit in the picture?"

"She," Rachel said.

Troy was quick to continue. "She was both my dad's and later my girlfriend."

That got the lieutenant's attention. He sat straight up in his chair.

Troy continued on as Rachel pondered the irony of the situation. Here, her mom was the one not speaking, and Troy seemed uncommonly eager to tell his story.

"This gets complicated," Troy said. "Are you recording this?"

The lieutenant nodded.

"My mother was looking out for me, not so much Rachel. A couple of weeks before Dad was killed, my mom actually called him. I don't know how long it had been since they last spoke. Their divorce was bitter. Shitty bitter. Mom apparently asked my dad if he'd written a will. He told her he hadn't and wanted to know what business it was of hers. 'Looking out for our kids,' she supposedly told him. That's where Mom pulled Jessie into her web by having her do the dirty work. She called Jessie—it was the first time they'd ever spoken to each other—and lied to her, saying that Ervin had drawn a will that called for her to be the sole beneficiary of his estate. A day later, 'sniveling like a two-year-old,' that's how Mom described her act, she again called Jessie and begged her to share Dad's estate with me. 'There's plenty for the both of you,' she'd said. She told Jessie that Rachel shouldn't get any of the money because she'd been treated like a princess her whole life by her dad."

Rachel acknowledged the word of her mother's snub by faking an abbreviated bow in her chair.

Troy squinted, as if to say "I'm talking here, sis." "So my mom looked to get her revenge by pulling strings like a puppeteer. A week later, she phoned Jessie again and asked her to assist with Ervin's murder. 'I get what I want, and so do you' is what she told Jessie. Well, she figured correctly that Jessie was the gold-digging tramp that she's turned out to be. Enter Galvan. That's his name, right?"

Rachel, whose eyes were riveted on her brother, nodded.

Troy took a sip of the bottled water that was made available to both of them. "What my mom hadn't figured on was my dad, in response to her asking him about a will, had decided it was time to have Andrew Sutton actually draw one up with Jessie as the sole benefactor minus the Charros and change."

Lieutenant Hayes rolled his neck as if he were having trouble keeping up with the scenario.

"Jessie all but admitted to me to hiring this Galvan guy. Just as my mom had suspected Jessie wanted Dad's money sooner rather than later, so in her mind, getting Jessie to take out her ex-husband was a made-to-order plan that Galvan executed to perfection."

"Better come up with some hard evidence, Mr. Haslett. I can't bring her in on what you've just told me."

"I understand, Officer. I do have copies of three e-mails between Jessie and Galvan. In one, he claimed the deal was done."

"Where is Ms. Santiago now, since you seemed to have known her quite well?"

Troy accepted the lieutenant's offer of bottled water. "She's probably long gone. Both my dad and her sugar daddy before him took her on trips all over the world. She knows her way around the globe. She'll be tough to find."

The lieutenant excused himself and departed the interview, leaving Troy and Rachel staring at each other.

"Are you okay with turning Mom in, Troy?"

Troy displayed a confidence in his demeanor that Rachel wasn't accustomed to hearing or seeing. "I am. She killed our dad. She and I both hated him, but that doesn't mean I'm good with anyone's murder."

Lieutenant Hayes returned to the interview room after a lengthy absence, no doubt to confer with his superior. "You're free to go. I thank you for your trouble. I know this must have been a difficult decision for you both. Your mother will be arraigned in court tomorrow at 1:30 p.m. The charge is first-degree murder of Ervin Haslett."

Following their police interrogation, Rachel and Troy decided on a drink—Troy making it known he'd rather go the purple haze route and Rachel claiming the product was too expensive for her blood. She suggested the Toma Restaurant and Bar near her place. The two of them entered to rousing applause from the bar patrons.

"Another one down!" a beer-bellied guy wearing Charros gear shouted out.

Rachel asked for the score. She'd lost touch with the game during the police probe.

"It's 5-zip, Charros," the man replied. "Baxter had three hits. One was a three-run homer. You're a genius for picking up that guy."

Rachel gave Troy a good-natured elbow to the ribs. He smiled in return. She requested a seat from the bartender, not wanting to smother her brother with her celebrity. It was only the second time she ever remembered sitting down to an adult beverage with Troy.

"Life is better now?"

"Much," he said.

Rachel ordered a top-shelf margarita for both of them. "It's on the house," their waitress announced.

"What would you have done about Mom if I weren't in the picture?"

"Probably let it slide." Troy puckered his lips. "This is good. I can't count on one hand the number of these I've had. I never liked sweet drinks. This is rad."

"Rad?"

"It's a throwback word."

"I'll say."

Rachel twirled her napkin with her pinky finger. "What changed your mind?"

"The cop that got killed. I know he'd been and was again part of our—your—baseball family. Two lives lost was one too many."

Rachel settled her eyes in direct line with Troy's. "Who sent the text threatening me with my life?"

Troy sat up straight. His eyes briefly searched the room as if he were calculating his response. "I did. I was trying to protect Jessie. You were barking up her tree about Dad's death, and I wanted to throw you off her scent. I had no idea at the time that she was involved."

"How did you get the phone you sent the text from?"

"You're not going to believe this," he said with a glint in his eye. "I went on Craigslist and advertised for an adventurer who liked clandestine activity. You won't believe how many responses I got."

"Tell me."

"At least twenty-five. I went with the guy who quoted me $500 to steal anyone's phone. I also gave him the text message I wanted sent and your phone number."

Rachel ordered a second round of margaritas. "I want to throw something out to you. I know you were pissed when I didn't offer you a job with the Charros. I didn't blame you. No matter how this season turns out, the Honeyball campaign will likely go the way of the Capistrano swallows. And I plan to loosen my grip on an all-female staff. It will have served its purpose by the end of the season. We will have proved by then that women, working together as one, can accomplish anything on this planet if given the opportunity. Volleyball taught me this. Two women have to be one to be winners. It dispelled the common notion that women can't collaborate as equals the way men can. However, to continue reinforcing that notion would, I believe, eventually lead to a pushback from the baseball community and society as a whole, as in *enough already with your feminist manifesto.*"

Troy looked at Rachel's margarita, took her straw in his hands, and stirred the drink. "What's in there? I certainly never expected to ever be invited to your party."

"You don't have to answer me now. Just think about it. I could seamlessly plug you into any position?"

Troy sat back in his chair. "What a difference a day makes. Mom's off to prison, and I'm off your shit list. Who would have thought?"

Rachel offered a subdued fist bump.

CHAPTER FIFTY-SIX

Hollywood couldn't have come up with a better script for the Charros' final regular season game. It started early afternoon. Rachel got to her office dressed in her game-time attire of a black blazer, blue oxford shirt, and tan slacks and immediately began preparing for the worst, a loss that would end the Charros' season a game short of tying for first place and forcing a one-game playoff. How to thank her fans if the Charros didn't win was her top priority.

The game marked the completion of a three-game series with the Rancho Cucamonga Quakes. The Charros had won the first two games of the series on great pitching by starters Wade Rollins and Seth Richards—each tossing four hit shutouts—to pull within one game of the Quakes for the league's best record. San Jose, which had closed with a flourish—winners of nine in a row—was perched a game behind the Charros. They'd completed their season with a come-from-behind win over Visalia the night before. Based on social media chatter, Rachel realized every franchise in the league was pulling for the Quakes to knock Santa Barbara and its Honeyball regime into next week.

"Get them the hell out the post season," the owner of the Stockton Ports tweeted.

The general manager of the High Dessert franchise tweeted, "This Honeyball thing has made us the laughing stock of minor league baseball. Go, Quakes!"

Nearly three hours before game time, Rachel left her office for a quick trip down the hallway to have a word with Adrienne Telfair about the fan appreciation postcards she'd had printed. As she approached the door to Adrienne's office, out walked Troy. His attire was identical to hers.

"The Haslett twins," Rachel said with a smile. "And?"

"We're cool." Troy wore the biggest smile Rachel could remember seeing on him.

Rachel gave him a high five. "Be ready if we lose."

"Got it covered, sis."

Rachel could not remember ever seeing her brother in a sports coat, not to mention acting unbelievably pleasant toward her. She quietly wondered if what she was seeing was a mirage. High on Rachel's agenda for tonight's game was prepping for Madonna's appearance. Her first order of business was to ensure that the singer had a private camper for a dressing room. It was parked outside the ballpark opposite the home team's bullpen. She'd hired a local production company that specialized in outdoor concerts to set up the stage and sound booth. The stage was big enough to accommodate a volleyball game. It had to be big to allow for her backup singers and a twelve-piece orchestra. No one was more surprised than Rachel that Madonna had accepted the Charros' invite. And even more incredible, she'd made it clear through her agent that her performance was a freebie, as in no charges for her service.

"Like Rachel Haslett, I believe in women working as one for a common goal, and this is the best example of that in America," she was quoted in recent edition of *People*.

A single-engine Cessna, much like the one flown by Big Erv Haslett, was already circling the skies above the ballpark, carrying a trailing banner that read, "THE BLACK-AND-BLUE SANTA BARBARA CHARROS WELCOME THE TRUE BLUE GIRL, MADONNA." The Material Girl was bringing enough material for five songs.

Adrienne Telfair had gone to the police chief to get a waiver on attendance limitations. He was all in. Temporary seats were brought in—enough to accommodate an additional five thousand ticket holders—double the stadium's normal capacity.

Before Madonna's performance, she'd consented to do a quickie interview with Melanie Sandberg. After the words "I'd like to welcome..." Melanie fell apart. "I'm fucking interviewing Madonna," she said and then immediately froze up. The blank look on Melanie's face signaled that she had officially choked. After nearly a minute of dead air and out of breath, Melanie said, "Just say anything that comes to mind, Madonna, please."

Madonna bailed Melanie out by shouting into the microphone that had been patched into the PA system, "Let's get this party started, and let's hear it for Honeyball!"

Madonna's song list included "La Isla Bonita," "Like a Prayer," "Like a Virgin," "Material Girl," and "True Blue" in honor of the Charros. News helicopters from Los Angeles buzzed the sky overhead and captured live video for their respective six-o-clock news shows. The Drone Dragon that had made its first and only appearance at the ballpark opening night buzzed the fans in the stands augmenting the four-camera setup that brought Madonna's image to the huge scoreboard in center field.

At the conclusion of her rousing performance that had featured patrons dancing in the aisles and participating in a start-to-finish sing-along, Rachel hopped up on stage and presented the megastar with a bouquet of roses and a Charros jersey number 1 with her name above the number. The crowd applauded her for a full five minutes. When she left, it was what you'd expect of a megastar. Her private helicopter landed in center field. She boarded it with a giant wave of her arms and a hand-to-lips kiss.

Her appearance marked the only time in her illustrious career that Madonna had taken the roll of warm-up act. Despite what any critic would label a show-stopping performance, Madonna, her chopper still visible in the fading sunlight over the Pacific, instantly became second fiddle to the game at hand.

The Charros and Quakes did not like each other. During their previous games, there had been a couple of beanball incidents involving both teams that had threatened to break out into brawls. Quakes owner, Rollie Henderson, a San Bernardino homebuilder, was extremely vocal about his dislike for the Charros and their practice of importing free agent talent.

"They've got a guy who hit damn near four hundred major league home runs playing against kids who are just starting to shave," he'd told one LA news station.

Because the Charros' starting pitching rotation had been heavily taxed in the closing days of the season, Jacqui Davenport was designated by manager Devin Baxter to start only her second game of the season.

"She's cool under pressure," the assembled media had quoted Baxter as saying. Most in the media held the opinion that Jacqui was in over her pretty little head.

The crowd still buzzing—and in some cases already buzzed from the offerings of "craft beer night"—over Madonna's appearance, Rancho Cucamonga got to Jacqui early, scoring runs in both the first and second innings on four singles and a walk.

Meantime, the Quakes' Justin Hammer, who came into the game with a 2.02 ERA, best in the entire league, had worked into the fifth inning without giving up a single hit. Charros' fans were getting uncomfortable about Hammer's domination over Charros' hitters. A couple hundred of Charros' regulars started chanting and flashing their middle fingers. "Hammer this! Hammer this! Hammer this!"

Melanie Sandberg offered her own thoughts on the radio. "Charros' hitters have got to be patient against this *motha*," she said, knowing that an FCC crackdown was unlikely because of Rachel's complete lack of fear from their threats to carry out a cease-and-desist edict.

The Charros finally got on the scoreboard, thanks to a frozen rope homer to right field by Devin Baxter. Uncharacteristically, Devin unpacked his "slow" home run trot that he'd displayed only a few times during his major league career. It was designed to shake things up even more. Several Quakes players gave Devin the middle finger as he rounded third base.

"The Quakes are quaking in their boots now folks" was Melanie Sandberg's retort as opposed to report.

With the score locked at 2-1, Quakes in the home half of the seventh inning, a play that would derail the Charros' pennant express, occurred courtesy of Chad Isner. He was on first base, following a leadoff single off Hammer. One a 3-1 count with Devin at the plate, Isner inexplicably broke for second. It was obvious to everyone in the park that he was about to be a dead duck. Toast.

The gamer that he'd proved to be since having joined the Charros midseason, Isner wasn't about to settle for a putout, so he slid into second with his spikes waist high. As Quakes second baseman Manny Trujillo applied the tag, he took both Chad's spiked shoes to his left quad. The force of Isner's momentum left skin-breaking skid marks on Trujillo that resembled railroad tracks. He dropped to his knees in pain, and immediately, the entire Quakes bench emptied with one singular goal: to rip Chad Isner's heart out.

While Trujillo rolled in pain on the infield dirt, Isner stood before him at the ready to take on any advancing Rancho Cucamonga players. Five of them got to him, and then all hell broke loose. The Charros' bench emptied in order to help protect their second baseman, and fists were flying everywhere. Devin was one of the first of the Charros to join the melee. With a haymaker right hand, he knocked a couple of Quakes players to the ground. He proved to be a major league brawler, stating after the fact that he was not about to allow any player of his to take a beating.

It finally took ballpark police to help break up the fighting. One security cop used a nightstick on the Quakes' Hammer who was just standing near the center of activity trying to show support for his teammate but not wanting to injure his pitching arm. After five minutes, peace was restored, but both Chad Isner and Devin had been ejected from the game and would likely face some kind of league action for inciting a near riot.

That left the Charros without their two best hitters and a manager. First base coach Dokie Edwards took over running the club for Devin. He'd elected to stay with Jacqui, who'd completed eight innings giving up just the two early runs until he called for relief help in the ninth. The now punchless Charros went down one, two, three in the bottom of the ninth, and Rancho Cucamonga came up a 2-1 winner and securing the California League pennant. No doubt, most rival owners and executives let out a big sigh of relief.

Rachel's preparation for a loss had been a smart move. She had her director of operations roll out a small portable stage and asked the disappointed fans to hang with her for a few more minutes. The first thing she did was ask all her players come out and line up on either the left or right baseline. She then invited Adrienne Telfair to join her and hand out Apple watches to every player, the two coaches, and manager Devin Baxter.

Adrienne also came with great news that she whispered in Rachel's ear. "Just got a text from the executive director of minor league baseball. We had the best attendance of any team in the minor leagues with a stadium capacity of five thousand. We did it, girl."

Rachel smiled, jumped, and relayed the good news to the fans. Applause was long and loud. Rachel apologized for going off message and returned to the subject—the Charros players.

"You have shown the courage of lions," she said, looking up and down the two lines of players. "Against all odds, and the interference of one Mr. Irving Zeller, you came to within a game of forcing a one-game playoff for the crown. I'm so proud of your effort. Please, never hang you head over what happened here this evening. I know my dad is looking down on us right now, and he's a happy man. You all are responsible for making The Erv a household word in Santa Barbara and a shiny star in the Santa Barbara landscape. I wish you all good luck in your baseball careers. I'd love to have you all back and do it again next year, but I know how baseball works, and I understand you all will want to be looking at Santa Barbara in your rearview mirrors for the sake of advancement to B league ball or beyond."

The seven to eight thousand fans that'd elected to stay for the postgame ceremonies clapped their approval for several minutes.

Next, Rachel pulled off another giant surprise. She announced that she would be leaving the Charros for a new job as commissioner of the ABVP.

"I'll be the first woman to hold the position. I owe it to the players, the fans, and my Honeyball ladies for helping me to make history. My heart has always been with volleyball, so now I must go where my heart tells me. Thank you all for supporting Honeyball and understanding the significance of what we've accomplished this season. I hope you will continue it in the future. Looking to the future, my brother, Troy Haslett, will be taking over as CEO of the franchise, and Adrienne here, will become general manager and chief operating officer."

Adrienne waved off a response, enabling Troy to come up on stage and speak. "I want to thank my sister for this opportunity. I've had a long history with this Santa Barbara franchise, working nearly a decade for my father when the team was called the Rancheros. So I guess you could say I'm already invested here. This is the best thing that's happened in my life, and I promise you, fans, that the Charros will pick up where Honeyball left off next season. See you all next April 13."

Tears rolling over her cheeks, Rachel hugged her brother for one of the few times in her life and then began thanking everyone one for coming when she was interrupted by Devin Baxter who had uploaded his large frame onto the stage and stood next to Rachel. He was dressed in half a uniform—his bloodied pants and a T-shirt.

"Likewise, I'd like to thank you all for your great support of this team and hope you'll do the same in the coming years," he said. "I thoroughly enjoyed my time with the Charros."

Without an invitation from either Rachel or Devin, Jacqui Davenport got up on the stage and stood between the two. She didn't say anything, but she was carrying a small box. Rachel shook her head in disbelief that she would interrupt Devin's speech.

Devin didn't even acknowledge the young pitcher's presence. He continued on. "The reason I say hopeful is that I'm hopeful"—Jacqui pulled a ring out of the box she had carried to the stage—"this ring will encourage Rachel Haslett to say yes to my proposal of marriage." Devin turned to face Rachel, and Jacqui immediately presented her with the ring.

Rachel's eyes were as big as the full moon that had fortuitously appeared in the night sky upon darkness.

"Will you marry me?" Devin asked Rachel.

The crowd went nuts, whooping and hollering for several minutes.

Rachel took the ring out of the box, examined it, and, with a smile that stretched the length of the central coast, allowed Devin to place it on her finger.

"Yes, I will marry you, Devin Baxter."

They hugged and kissed until the stadium lights dimmed.

On cue, the UCSB marching band entered the field from the Charros' dugout, playing the Sammy Cahn song "Love and Marriage."

Still being held in Devin's arms, Rachel was in tears. "I'm not sure I'm not dreaming this."

Still dressed in his baseball pants and a sweaty Charros T-shirt, Devin said, "It's not a dream."

Rachel wiped away her tears as best she could. "To think I have Jenks Whatshisname to thank for all this."

ACKNOWLEDGMENT

Thank you to my wife, Alicia Aguirre, for her encouragement and support of my work.